Holy Smoke It's A GODMAN

Satish Georgy Kashyap

Vitasta
Let Knowledge Spread

Published by
Vitasta Publishing Pvt Ltd
2/15, Ansari Road, Daryaganj,
New Delhi - 110 002
info@vitastapublishing.com

ISBN: 978-93-82711-14-8

Although autobiographical, this is a work of fiction. Resemblance to anyone living or dead, is purely coincidental.

Typeset by Vitasta Publishing Pvt Ltd
Cover Design by Vitasta Publishing Pvt Ltd
Printed by Vikas Computer and Printers

Contents

Acknowledgements

Special thanks to my family – SK Kashyap, Darshna, Sangeeta, Pari, Pranav and friends Manmohan Kashyap and Rishi Bharti who tolerated me...

In the never-ending list of creative individuals who boosted me all the time: OleBrekke, Cathrine Karlsson, Murari Lal, Emmy Nielson, Janik Møller, Narayan, Pawan micromax, Dr Mahende Kumar, Pt Suryabhanu Shastri, Prof Sunil Vashistha, Dr Mogens Hansen, Jane, Aparna Sharma, Sandhya Sharma Raman, Mihir Ranjan Patra, Manju Mehta, Renu Kaul Verma, M D Chhabra, Gullu, Vicks, MC,

Dr Pavneesh Madan, Per Jakobsen, Rakhi Dalal, Kiran Malhotra, Neeraj Gupta, Yashpal Sharma, Dr RK Yadav, Rajiv Bhatia, Dr Sudhir Sharma, Sanjoy Roy, Anoop Michoo, Kirti, Rakesh Mittal, Harish Lohia, Makrand Deshpande, Irfan Khan and Dr Sandeep Gupta. Last but not the least Baba Ram Dev and Amitabh Bachchan.

Letter to US President George W Bush

Dear Sir,

How to start! You don't know me and I don't know you either, but I have enough acquaintance with you through newspapers and television. My name is Redne, Redney Yog. Sir, unknowingly you have played a crucial role in shaping my life and making me a billionaire.

When you were delivering a lecture in the White House, I was 'house-less', surviving on the streets of Copenhagen as a street performer. You were lecturing on 'War Against Terror' and I was making my livelihood out of terror.

Without your unintended help and involuntary support I could not have achieved what I have; and wouldn't have documented all this in the form of a testimony or a chronicle. In short, how much impact your speech can have on people living in different parts of the world, viz., Hamburg, Copenhagen, Kashmir and Kandahar is a story waiting to be told.

Thank you very much, sir.

Regards,

Redney Yog

Copenhagen

I am Redney, Redney Yog, alias 'Yogi' but bluntly speaking, I have nothing to do with yoga or meditation; I live in exile in Denmark. Whenever local folks ask me where I am from, I say, with a mischievous laugh, 'I am an alien, directly from the Moon.'

'Come on, you don't seem European. Are you South American, hybrid, African or Asian?'

'I am none of these, I am only a Homo sapien.'

I declare myself South American or Chilean, sometimes Portuguese and sometimes even Lebanese or Yemeni.

Reasons are quite clear: my stout build, sharp features, long curly hair, brownish-white looks are quite similar to those of the folks of the aforesaid nationalities. In addition, different types of hats, headgear and scarves help me hide my original nationality. Local folks are least bothered about my ancestry. Rather, they are more focused on the quality of beer, weather, sex etc. I am just a foreigner to them.

Moreover, my name Redne Yog is so perfect that sometimes it appears 'Chinese' and sometimes 'Italian' to folks. Once I even pretended that I was a Buddhist. In fact, Redne is not my original birth-name. Why I transformed myself to Redne is a classic example of Darwin's theory of survival of the fittest.

My original name is Yogender; how I became 'Yogi' and then 'Redne' was purely an accident. A blessing in disguise.

On a Saturday night when everyone was boozing and dancing on the streets and I was totally disheartened and anxious, struggling to find a job, an idea flashed into my mind on the most happening street of Copenhagen. I decided to dissect my original name into two parts the way the British dissected India in two unequal parts in 1947.

In a flash, I sliced up my name 'Yogender' into 'Yog' and 'ender'. I reversed 'e-n-d-e-r' and became 'r-e-d-n-e'. 'Redne Yog' seemed smart and attractive.

Immensely delighted with my new invention, I started to deliver an extensive speech full of verses and songs. Soon I found myself surrounded by street performers and pedestrians. Gaining in confidence, I delivered a detailed soliloquy on humanity and existence of the human race. My friends later told me that I was discussing the evolution of humans from monkeys in my monologue that night. This dramatic action was the result of my stressful rebellious inheritance. Or maybe it was the outcome of an overdose of alcohol. If I try to recall what exactly happened on that special night, I can only remember that passers-by were impressed with my speech and the capacity of my vocal cords and gifted me many cans of beer. This new name was potent enough to face the new challenges and humiliations of criminal society. I always used these names with slight variations like Redne, Reddy, Yog, Jog, Yogi, Jogi, Jagga etc. The last name Jagga was flexible enough to adjust to radical immigrant Muslim and religious Sikh communities. To make myself familiar to the immigrant community, I became Mohammad Jagira in one instant and Jagtar Singh in another. Born in a folk theatre family of performing artistes, I had inherited the art of making people laugh and think.

I am divorced from my Danish wife, Linda Christensen, and blessed with a lovely son, Aryan. I have sweet memories and, of course, bitter experiences of Denmark. I made a lot of money, but lost everything else.

Now 34 years old, I was born in a small village in a remote area of India. I struggled to get two square meals in my teen years. Spirituality and religion, inherited from my pseudo-spiritual parents, were never acceptable to me. I searched for an alternative philosophy and the search is still on.

To date, I have managed to survive on my knowledge of human nature, persuasive tongue and basic theatre techniques.

Within three years I have progressed to a position where I can support not only myself but others too. I have the reputation of being jovial and capable of speaking many languages.

Muslim Graveyard
Brondby, a Suburb of Copenhagen, Denmark
Saturday 9 August, 11.30 am

I was not comfortable the day I was summoned by a Muslim imam (clergyman) named 'Chacha' for a nasty job. It turned out to be the most stressful day of my life since I came to Copenhagen and became Redne Yog. First, some people had painted *swastikas* in a Muslim graveyard of Copenhagen, generating a lot of anger in the immigrant Muslim community. Second, a Danish cartoonist, Kurt Westergaard, had made some infamous cartoons of Prophet Mohammad in the leading newspaper *Jylland Posten* which created a lot of anger and tension. Chacha Imam Khatib, the front-line leader of this community, had pledged to take revenge for this insult and humiliation. Imam Khatib is the term used for a person who has memorised the holy *Quran* and is supposed to bring justice to humanity. But I always had doubts about this self-made Chacha Imam. I had been avoiding Chacha for long, as I didn't want to be party to such revengeful people and their scheme of things. Being an integral part of the immigrant community, it was my bounden obligation to criticise the recent events and Kurt Westergaard in particular, although I always like humorists. There was a lot of difficulty avoiding him this time. All the members of my business gang were diehard supporters of Chacha Imam. It was such a tricky situation that I decided to apply my ever-trustworthy tactic of saying: 'Yes sir, Yes sir' and doing nothing.

I was standing alone at the entrance of Brondby graveyard outside Copenhagen when I saw Chacha Imam approaching. All memories of my past flashed before my eyes.

Without wasting a minute, looking into my eyes, he said, 'See, I am like your father. You are our man. I am also god-fearing, but we want to teach these racist Danish assholes a perfect lesson.'

He stopped and stared hard at me, looking straight into my eyes.

Frightened, I just nodded without understanding, and only uttered, 'Yeah'.

'How long can we remain silent? Where is our existence? Can´t we have our own mosque after forty years of hard work and struggle?'

'Of course, sir,' I replied.

'They still call us foreigners. Even our children born and brought up here are foreigners for them. What a stigma! I know you are not a coward. You are a qualified, smart, religious young man. You can plan our revenge.'

'Me?' I said in a low tone.

'Enough is enough. This is an insult. Who the hell is this Kurt Westergaard?'

'Chacha, he is a humorist; I mean cartoonist.' I said promptly.

'That I know, but how dare he slap us like this? Gun down

the bastard Westergaard or blow up the Central Station; millions of dollars will simply flow down into your coffers. God will be a witness to this very holiest action of your life. We have international funding for this project. If you have any inhibitions, spit them out right now. I want no delay. We must not die like cowards.'

It was a long monstrous, monotonous, boring lecture of hatred which had no scientific base or truth. I stopped listening to him, instead I resumed vigorous nodding with, 'Yes sir, Yes sir.'

'Chacha Imam' is my self-proclaimed father and he was convincing me for a deadly inhuman act in the centre of wonderful Copenhagen. He has no blood relation with me, yet he addresses me as his son. The more he uses the word 'son', the more I feel like a bastard in my heart. My mind is repeatedly blasted with warnings and threats not only from 'Norrebro' in Copenhagen but also from far-flung exotic zones like Kandahar and Kashmir. It is the result of my frustration over the last few years since President Bush declared war against terror in Afghanistan in retaliation to the World Trade Centre attack. Although I have always been confident of handling pressure situations calmly, yet somehow today I feel shaky in my legs.

I know this 50-year old for many years, smelling foul, with his long beard like Albert Einstein's, but far removed from science or technology. Always chewing tobacco, his yellowish-red teeth make a mockery of the existence of dentistry for human healthcare. He considers himself a messenger of God and believes he has legitimate right on all immigrants in Copenhagen. When he preaches, he thinks that he is the messiah of the human race and every word of his is a jewel. This ugly genetic chromosomal abbreviation is like an outdated steam engine. His words are venom and have no effect on the second generation immigrants or humans gifted with a little knowledge.

'Chacha' means uncle; a popular name used by his illiterate followers, inhabitants of this metropolitan city, who are unfit in any given civilisation. They might be fit for ancient Mohenjo-Daro or the Harappan era. Integration is a defeat and communication with the government is a crime for them. Instead of communal harmony and love, Chacha is used to preaching hatred.

While standing in front of him, I pretend I am listening, but my rebuttal syndrome is active as usual. This is my childhood gift: when I listen to somebody, I am also preparing for the situation. Everything that Chacha Imam was saying was contradictory.

I am not as literate as hyped by Chacha Imam. I acquired the language skills not because of academics, but because of my passion for theatre and drama. My father was an outdated doctor and uncle a struggling stage performer. Both played a great role in shaping my personality. Accidentally, I was a child artiste fond of music and dance. In St Mary's School, I was not interested in what the teacher was teaching but how he was teaching. I was an imitator, a sort of stand-up comedian. Sometimes I mugged up the whole topic in order to create comedy to amuse my schoolmates and friends. I can copy anybody and speak five languages of different continents.

Chacha was deadly serious, but I was quite amused to observe him and felt like laughing as I could see his yellowish red dirty teeth, and smell pungent tobacco. Somehow, I managed to control my emotions. His speech was loud with a broken rhythm. In totality, a Dracula was singing classical music. For me, he was standup comedy material to imitate. The situation being highly tense, I kept my mouth shut and head nodding.

Secondly, 'god-fearing', as claimed by Chacha Imam was not digestible. I am not god-fearing but a god-loving person. I have had big quarrels with God since my juvenile years. Let me tell you why—hypothetical comparison of two countries, geographically covering almost the same kilometre-area, super-rich Denmark and super-poor Bangladesh, has convinced me that God is not doing justice. The rats of Denmark eat ten times better food than Homo sapiens of Bangladesh. It seems impossible that in the coming hundred years, humans of Bangladesh will get better food than rodents of Scandinavia which are enjoying better social security in their underground sewage system, thanks to wastage of Burger Kings, McDonalds and KFC. On the contrary, this imaginary character 'God' has gifted the poor country Bangladesh with regular floods, droughts and earthquakes in regular intervals of four years without any interruption since I started understanding life. If God exists, then he should look down and differentiate between humans and rodents.

Thirdly, I know I am not brave. Basically, I am a coward. Situations and our acts tend to make us brave. The truth is that I have nothing to lose. When you have nothing to lose, where is the worry? Instead, my work history in crime speaks volumes of my courage and intelligence. Make-believe is my *mantra* and *karma*.

While Chacha Imam was prompting me, I knew for sure he had plans to eliminate me if I refused to follow his instructions.

Finally, Chacha Imam said, 'Ok, Yogi, my son, we are meeting at American Plads at the evening *namaz* to finalise the plan of action. Keep faith in God. You know, we are nothing and can't do anything without His will. Do something big and leave your everlasting prints behind for the coming generations to remember you forever.'

With this ultimatum, Chacha left me all alone in this Brondby graveyard. Later part of his speech was full of warnings and consequences. My trusted associates, with whom I was running my little business, were waiting for me at the central station of Copenhagen. Frustrated and irritated, I walked out of the graveyard and started to proceed towards Brondby train station. After a 15-minute long and annoying wait, I got into the S-train from this satellite town to the central station.

American Plads

Today, the 9th of August, is the most stressful day of my life. I am tightly cornered. 'Guruji Suryaswami' has shut all the openings of my escape. A flurry of calls from Afghanistan have fattened my heap of worries. Still I am not sure whether this 'Afghani Salliulla Bukhari' is a real tout of Guruji Suryaswami or not. Bukhari perhaps has connection with Chacha Imam. All my doubts finally are focused on Guruji Suryaswami. Intuitively, I feel it is Guruji Suryaswami who is sneaking into my private affairs. I can also feel that Chacha is not a big fish, but he can be a lethal irritant. It is high time I did something really drastic.

I was assigned the most dreadful task of my life. This group of immigrants wanted me to lead their group to take revenge on Kurt Westergaard. Why had they chosen me? It was entirely my fault. I was running a small-time business of selling marijuana, in the hippy town of Christiania. Some members of a religious group were also a part of my business group (hash group). A few of them proposed my name for this action. Reason, I think, was that I could not keep my profile low. For them, I was a Punjabi-Muslim Jagga, having a good command over the local Danish language. I was outspoken and always tried to infuse humour even into serious matters. So, I was trapped. For the first time in my life, my ever-amusing talent of making people laugh landed me in deep trouble.

Recent deals in hash had made me richer and it raised the eyebrows of these extremist groups, but I was maintaining cordial relations with local Danes because of my amiable nature. My bad luck! The theatre skills and humour that had endeared me to all finally landed me in trouble! I admit, I can be a good thief but never a terrorist or a killer. My only fault was that in order to have command over my group, I always bragged about murders, knives and pistols. Once I even pretended to kill a man during a hash deal to show my courage and supremacy, but inside I knew that my group members would certainly stop me from shooting. This habit of exaggeration, to show off as extraordinarily courageous, had actually entered into my original character ever since I started acting. This courageous act was, in fact, a part of my earlier experience of theatre and special training in vocal cords. My voice thundered. I could also modulate my voice to be as feminine as possible. Moreover, I had the advantage of being closer to the local Danes because of my hippy looks, smiling face, freaky behaviour and command over their language.

I always keep a German pistol, HK.45 with sound suppressor at a safe place for my safety as well as to show off my guts. But inside I know it requires a lot of courage to shoot a person.

Both the terror acts suggested by Chacha were out of my dreams and imagination. Honestly, I had no problems with the Danes or the Danish government. I was married to a Danish girl. It was impossible for me to think of any harm to the country that had given me everything, including a bunch of good Danish friends who helped me during my days of struggle. My simple funda was to make good money and enjoy life.

I often thought about what might be the root cause of the integration problem of the immigrant Muslims. Children born of immigrants were unfortunately still called foreigners in Denmark. During the years I stayed in Denmark, I painfully realised that immigrants were never properly treated. Rather, they were insulted and humiliated. They always felt the sting of racism. Just learning the Danish language would not help the Muslims solve their problem of integration. The cartoon controversy and European clashes over the headscarf had raised the question of Islamic integration into the western world. It is a cultural rather than political dispute.

Frankly, I always supported the Danish Folk Party led by Pia Kjærsgaard with her own typical moods and whims. Danish Folk Party was against the corrupt methods adopted by the immigrants. In my casual discussions with local Danish friends, I once joked that I would request Her Majesty Pia Kjærsgaard to give me a chance to fight elections on behalf of her party.

Old saying: 'Iron cuts iron'.

As soon as I reached the Central Station of Copenhagen I was received by my most trusted associates Raja and Saleem. I was eager to chalk out a plan with my friends to counter Chacha Imam. After exchanging customary pleasantries and some food I disclosed to them what Chacha had said to me in Brondby graveyard. I told them that Chacha wanted to see me in the evening at American Plads mosque.

I was shocked to see the expressions on Raja and Saleem's faces. They were not smart enough to hide their feelings, though they tried their level best. In a flash, I realised they already knew the plan of action. Somehow, I cracked a joke to Raja's taste. It was best to keep them in a happy mood. But I was losing my entire feel for laughter. Continuous calls from Guruji Suryaswami and Salliulla Bukhari bogged me down and increased my blood pressure. Was Chacha Imam a tout or the mastermind? This was a mystery I wanted to solve.

Evening was approaching and Raja was ready with my Toyota car to drive me to Plads mosque. It was a windy day and a drizzle began when we were about to leave. I wished

Chacha Imam could reschedule the meeting because of the rain but without thinking and counting on my luck, I got into the car with Saleem in the backseat. Raja chose to drive, which made me a little upset as I always trusted the driving skills of Saleem more.

When we were approaching Vesterbrogade, the main highway, I felt I was being followed by some strangers, maybe Arabs or Somalis. At the next red light it was clear who was following me. I regretted my idiotic attitude of over-confidence. When I got out at the graveyard at Brondby, I found a black Somali guy outside. He was the one who had travelled with me till Central Station. It was crystal clear to me that I was trapped.

Raja from Pakistan and Saleem from India, both immigrants, were my trusted associates, but somehow I felt I couldn't trust them today. They were illegal immigrants who had entered Europe through a special visa category called 'Donkey' visa. It had taken them three years to reach Europe from their respective villages in Pakistan and India. They used all the methods of transport created by modern era. They walked 10-km per day; and floated on a boat for two months. They were hidden behind chickens and egg boxes in a transport truck. At temperatures as low as 13°C, they crossed frozen mountains in Kiev in Ukraine, barefoot and sometimes with slippers only, dodging the border police of different countries. Out of a gang of 42 adventurous youth, only 12 could make it to Europe and these two to Denmark. This traumatic journey made them compulsive friends.

Donkey visa means travelling without travel documents like a donkey. You can be put in a drum of Coke or parceled with spare parts of Toyota car or hidden in furniture.

I was bracing for my final 'No' to Chacha Imam even at the cost of my flourishing hash business. If, by some stroke of luck, Chacha spared me this time, I was never going to be a part of their activities.

At the square of American Plads just as we took the right turn, my W800i Sony cellphone started buzzing; it was Guruji Suryaswami. I did not answer. I had been avoiding him the whole week. Hardly a minute later, adding to my tension, it was now Saliulla Bukhari trying me on my cell phone. Out of my tested faith in Saleem so far, I handed over the mobilc to him to handle the situation.

Prayers were nearly over at the American Plads. We parked our car near 'Pizza Hut' at the corner of Vesterbrogade Main Street, there being no other place around the mosque for official parking. Lots of cars were parked zigzag. As I got down, I could see Chacha talking to three shady-looking guys outside the mosque. Walking some distance through the jammed parking, I could easily identify two of them. They were the same Arabs spying on us. I was amazed at their reaching earlier than us. They must have taken a short-cut. When we came a little closer, I could identify two of them: one Mustafa and the other a Turk named Ayan. Third was the same Somali guy who had followed me from the Brondby graveyard. I did not know his name.

My sixth sense started working as I found myself alone amongst them, although I had been working with this group for a long time. I was confused. Inside I did not agree to their kind of spirituality, reason being I didn't fit in with their line of beliefs. I was walking towards them but was completely lost in my own thoughts. As I walked further, Chacha turned his gaze and happened to see me. He walked faster towards me. His accomplices followed him. We stood face to face almost in the middle of the dense parking.

Again he started his lecture full of venom against the local government and the local Danes. It started with the blessings of the Almighty and ended on the same confusing subject. This time it was full of more warnings and consequences if I did not follow his commands. Mustafa and Ayan, both looking as good as wrestlers, resembled the Japanese sumos. They were surely hiding some weapons inside their overcoats.

'Listen with attention. August 18 stands fixed. Who will lead the operation? None but you, Yogi. This will be our first declaration against the Danish government. No smartness, no delay.'

Then looking straight and hard into my eyes he said: 'If you miss now, remember, you will lose everything, maybe your life too.'

Then his face softened. Raising his hands and eyeballs upwards, he remarked, 'Without His will nothing can happen. It is His wish. He is the doer. We are just puppets in His hands. Get up and do something.'

All eyes turned to me. 'Listen, Chacha, I respect you and I understand that this problem is quite genuine, but I can't be a party to it. I may do anything else for your good but no killings, no murders, no mayhem. My conscience doesn't allow me to be part of this plan.'

There was graveyard silence. Nobody uttered a word. All of them gazed at me with their blood-shot eyes. Chacha's gaze slightly turned towards Mustafa; instantly I could see a pistol in his right hand. I was trapped. Instead of prompting their anger, I could easily have manipulated these shawarma and pizza-making guys in my usual comic style. To save myself, I shot Chacha point blank right in the centre of his forehead with my German pistol. I remembered my hatred for Guruji Suryaswami while gunning down Chacha Imam. Before Mustafa could aim at me, I shot him a little above his right knee. Ayan fled the scene like a coward. The Somali guy followed instantly and hid himself behind the cars. Raja stood utterly confused, but Saleem appeared neutral and composed.

At this moment, in my true originality, I shouted at Saleem and Raja, 'Won't you now stop believing in these Arab bastards?' Then I quickly changed my tone and said, 'I have enough money for you. Come out, follow me, idiots.'

We flung ourselves into our car and raced away, not knowing where.

ॐ

Hide and Seek

We were in the car on the Vesterbrogade highway without knowing where to go. Frightened and shocked, I started to doubt Raja's intentions even though he was following my instructions on each and every turn. Immediately, I sensed the gravity of the situation and tried to emotionally blackmail Saleem and Raja.

I opened the conversation while declaring that my game was over and I would be caught any moment. I promised Raja enough money to marry off his three sisters and Saleem to construct his own house, which he desperately wanted. Feeling them tilting in my favour, I relaxed in the back seat of my Toyota. As expected, they wanted only money.

Now with confidence, I directed Raja to drive to Christiania, a popular hippy town. I thought of going to Abdul, one of my friends in Hamburg, Germany. I dropped the idea fearing I would be caught at the border. I also thought of escaping to Malmo, Sweden. Hosts of ideas were crossing my mind.

Some time later, we were speeding on HC Anderson Boulevard, the giant road of Copenhagen when I finally decided and asked Raja to turn back and drive me to Kingosgade Street, where my wife Linda was living with our only son, Aryan. Even though we had separated for the last two years, I loved both of them. On the way, I had yet another call from Guruji Suryaswami. As planned, Saleem answered it. I could hear and understand the same usual threats and warnings to which Saleem was responding on my directions.

When we were about to reach home, we saw a police van outside Linda's apartment. Again bad luck! Here Raja showed a great sense of alertness and turned the car smartly and confidently. No police officer even glanced at us. They were too busy jamming the area with yellow tape and red traffic hurdles. Taking a big U-turn, we were back on HC Anderson Boulevard.

I was again thrown into confusion even though I was behaving quite confidently. I was sweating, my hands shaking even in this harsh cold weather. Without a thought, I said, 'Off to Radisson Blue.'

As soon as we entered the Radisson parking, I asked Salim

to go and book a room in his own name. I covered my neck and half face with a big trendy scarf. I got down from the car. While trying to avoid any known person, I engaged myself in casual talk with foreign taxi drivers.

The murder news had broken out and the taxi drivers were discussing the shootout. Some were saying that it was the result of a gang war between Hells Angels and foreigner gang Black Cobra over hash. Abruptly snatching Raja's mobile phone, I moved to a corner; called up Gurinder in New Delhi and told him everything in short.

'Gurinder, listen carefully, if I am able to reach New Delhi safely then be ready for the final onslaught. Ask your friend Kamini to be ready. Chances are almost nil, but if, somehow, I reach you, I will expose everyone over there; believe me. *Satnam Shree Vahe Guru*. Make arrangements for me'.

I did not check into the hotel, rather I sent a text to Saleem to wait for me in front of Radisson until I was back. I asked Raja to drive me to Christiania.

Christiania is a place in Copenhagen which changed my life forever. It is the most free and democratic town in the world. It is like an unorganised colony in Delhi or Bombay. I always refer to it as mini-India.

We were heading for our rented basement flat called 'kælder'. We used to dump the waste material and sometimes valuable hash (marijuana) in this basement. At times I also used to hide some very important confidential materials there. This flat was at 1.5 km distance from Hotel Radisson Blue.

I went down to the basement and picked up one of my most prestigious bags out of the many worn and torn ones. This dark blue bag was my first carry bag which I had purchased from Paharganj in New Delhi for Rs 120. While Raja was waiting outside, I swiftly collected my passport and other documents. Then I filled my bag with all the cash which I got in euros in my last hash deal.

Patka is a most versatile and multi-purpose commodity. It can be a towel or a bedsheet at the same time. It could be used as handkerchief or blanket too. It might even help you change your physical appearance and identity. Last but not the least, it could also be used as headgear.

After collecting all the stuff I felt myself relax a little. Raja drove me back to Hotel Radisson; Saleem was waiting for us outside the lounge. At once, Saleem handed me the keys to the room and I speedily went to the elevator to find my room number 707. I was happy and relived as my lucky number too was seven.

After locking the room, I took out my Indian passport. I happened to look at the mirror hanging on the back wall. To my utmost surprise, I looked totally different from the photograph in my passport.

I looked like a hippy or a soccer fan eager to see the match between Sweden and Denmark. I was wearing FC Kopenhagen football club scarf round my neck and a funky Danish hat covering my long curly hair. Without a second thought, I took off my hat and scarf immediately. While getting the *patka* out of bag I tied my long hair with the scarf. Then I tied it neatly under the *patka*. Wearing my old-fashioned specs, headgear and the *kurta*, I looked like the same old gentleman who had come to Copenhagen a decade back.

Theatre skills helped me to perfect my looks and mannerisms. Within minutes I looked like a philosopher or preacher ready to participate in an international summit for communal harmony.

It was midnight; I was ready to take a chance to escape. I knew that my end was near but there was no harm trying my luck. Raja and Saleem were sipping coffee in the lounge. Initially, they were shocked but later they understood everything. I asked Raja to arrange my earliest flight to Delhi and asked Saleem to drive me back to Kingosgade Street. There was surprisingly no police in front of Linda's apartment. I realised that even earlier the police had not come for me; the officers may have been doing their normal duty with yellow strips and red barriers.

When I rang the doorbell, it was my son Aryan who responded. He was happy to hear my voice. He opened the main door to the building. I was allowed to meet him but not in these odd hours.

As I reached the apartment on the 4th floor, Linda opened the door, drunk. She greeted me with the same arguments which had resulted in our separation. Luckily, she was holding a bottle of Tuborg beer, which made her a little cool. Aryan tried to diffuse the tension between us.

He whispered some words in Linda's ears in Danish which made her a little calm. I didn't know what that was. Immediately, he led me to his own room.

'You look amazing, Pap', he said.

'Darling just listen', I said. 'I am going far away somewhere; I don't know where exactly. I love you, and, your mom too. I will surely meet you some day. Here is something very useful for you; take it, keep it safe. I am in big trouble and cannot tell you anything at the moment.'

Aryan kissed me on both my cheeks when Linda peeped in and gave me a look similar to when I met her for the first time. While holding Aryan in my arms I waved to her but didn't get any response. I kissed Aryan and got out of his room. I decided to leave Copenhagen forever in the early hours of the morning.

It was Saturday night at Copenhagen. Unpredictably, the rain had stopped. We were driving back to Radisson, the best place for me to hide. Most Danes were downing glasses of beer in pubs, bars and even striptease clubs like Rosie Maggies and Disco Fever.

Night sightseeing in Copenhagen is always a spectacle. You would see the beautifully lit-up city while walking through its windy streets along the harbour with lights reflecting from the water. While passing by the lit-up sights like Nyhavn, the underwater Little Mermaid and the Parliament, you would also have the pleasure of seeing the beautifully illuminated Tivoli Gardens on weekend nights. But you require a good mood to see these illuminations. I was frightened, but in total control of my emotions. Local Danes were enjoying and some creating disturbances and fights as usual on weekend nights. Indeed, I knew they would engage with their nuisance most of the police officers, which would help me escape. Recent riots in Norrebro and Christiania had also engaged the police officers. This would further help me in this situation.

It was 3 am, a cool Sunday morning, when I finally came out of the hotel with my carry bag to try my luck for the final journey. After changing my lowers with a *dhoti* and wearing an additional *patka* and smearing my forehead with yellow paste I was totally disguised. Raja had already booked my flight to New Delhi. It was a little late, but we had no option. The Belgian flight SN2268 was scheduled at 6.35 am from CPH, which would reach Brussels at 8.15 am. Next it was Flight SN4129 from Brussels to New Delhi, departing at 10.20 am from Brussels and reaching New Delhi at 10.30 pm.

Weather is always unpredictable in Denmark. It started drizzling again as we moved in the car towards the 'Form' metro station to catch a train for the airport. I preferred to go by metro rather than in our own car to avoid any problem at Copenhagen airport. While Raja was driving, I took out all the money from my blue bag. I kept only 15,000 euro. Rest of the 65,000 euro and gold biscuits, I handed over to Saleem to divide them into two equal parts to support their families back home. Hearing this, Raja, who had a firm grip on the steering, gave me a grateful look through the back mirror. This really made me happy as they knew they could never earn such a huge amount even in five years working as unskilled labour.

In the back seat, I was lost in memories. As we neared the metro station I was pained to see two young guys peeing into the ATM mini machines of 'Danske' bank the way people pee everywhere in India. The true character of a man surfaces once half a bottle of liquor is down his belly. I could see several empty beer bottles smashed around on the main street of this most developed country of the world.

On weekend nights, Walking-Street and City Hall Square of the beautiful Copenhagen look dirtier than Dharavi, the biggest and dirtiest slum located in the heart of Bombay. This is perhaps the only adventure the young Danes resort to in their highly organised and systematic society. Fed up with their mechanical routine from Monday to Friday, they often throw all the laws to the winds and go berserk, painting slogans anywhere, smashing bottles, hooting and shouting till they get back home late in the night.

The poor immigrants and divorced women, mostly from Thailand and Indonesian, collect the empty bottles to sell and earn money.

These young Indonesian and Thai girls are brought here by local Danes for fun. They marry them and when they are fed up, they leave them. Some of them who are smart have opened their own 'massage centres' or Thai food centres. The 'Thai massage centres' mostly grow into prostitution centres. In Enghave Plads, in Copenhagen, there is a big colony of massage centres run by these girls. Middle-aged frustrated

Europeans are always attracted to the teenage East Asian girls because of their pretty appearance and sharp features.

At the back seat of the car while I was thinking about the destiny of these girls, Raja said, 'I can drop you at the airport around 5.30 after a breakfast of shawarma and fried rice, if you wish.'

'No, it is safer to go by train than in car. I will purchase shawarma drum on the way,' I said.

I was worried and had no urge to eat, although I had not eaten anything since the unfortunate incident at American Plads. Rain was getting heavier; I had no option but to kill some more time in the dark shady parking of the Form station near Frederiksberg Church. I sent two very important text messages from Saleem's mobile:

At 5.01 am, message to Gurinder in Delhi.

At 5.06 am, message to Guruji Suryaswami at Chamba.

The first message:

'Gurinder, God willing...reaching Delhi, late evening... flight no SN4129. Be ready—Jogi.'

The second message:

'Guruji...coming with final solution...have got the money...ready to give you as desired...be ready...will update the time and venue—Jogananda.'

'Salam Wallekum', I said to Raja and Salim, while appealing to them to send the money back home to support their poor families, of course, through illegal money transfer called 'hawala'. There were great chances that they might spend a big chunk of money on prostitutes in Istergade. Raja was fond of Thai girls.

'Don't waste money on five-minutes pleasure. Think of your families rather than your cocks,' I told Raja.

Saleem was a cool customer and was dealing with my hash contacts in Doda, Kashmir and Waziristan. So I said, 'In my absence, Saleem, you will make all important decisions and take care of the business. Don't forget to pay the rent for the 'Basement'. There are chances I may be caught at Copenhagen, Brussels or Delhi airports; if so, you will help me legally; try to keep some money spare with you.'

Saleem gave me a punched travel clip card required for Lufthaven, the airport in Copenhagen. He had managerial skills but no leadership qualities. When I was entering the elevator of Form metro station to catch the train for the airport, my heart was sinking. I found myself waving to Raja and Saleem. Criminals can also be emotional. Both had tears in their eyes. I could feel tears welling up in my eyes two. They knew I could be caught any time. I regretted my earlier suspicion of both of them.

Lufthaven—The Copenhagen International Airport

Emotionally weighed down, I got out of the elevator of the metro station of Forum and punched the travel card for my journey to airport station. M1, the metro train for Lufthaven was about to arrive in three minutes. I happened to see my face in the mirror at the platform. My face was miserable while my eyes were moist. Immediately, I cleaned my face with my scarf and adjusted the specs under the turban. The Metro train arrived at 5.20 am. While placing my baggage near the rear gate, I occupied the single seat to avoid any eye contact. The train left for Norreport, Kongens Nytov, Christiania stations and so on.

Although I was feeling strange and disturbed, I was ready with my plans.

Plan A: If caught, how I will be living the rest of my life in Copenhagen jail.

Plan B: If able to escape, what I will do to Guruji Suryaswami.

Feeling nervous, I went to the entry gate. At this crucial moment of my life, I realised the importance of the fear factor. All my theatre histrionics started to ditch me. Still I made sure that I had passport, travel tickets and money in my pocket. After placing my bags on the trolley, I walked ahead doubting even the cleaning staff and ordinary security personnel around.

Even though my get-up was perfect for deception yet I was tense and nervous. I was no more Mr Redne. A religious book in my hand further confirmed my skills in the art of disguising.

Suddenly, I found that everybody including the immigration officers were looking at me rather keenly, observing me from top to down. I got a little scared, but recovered immediately. I realised nobody was actually observing me. Immigration officials were doing their normal duty. It was entirely my own fear.

What fate had in store for me and my son, Aryan Yog, was foremost in my mind. I felt sure that Linda being a native Danish could survive with this system. But I doubted whether Saleem and Raja could work together. Would Wahid, the only son of Chacha, take revenge for his father? Hosts of negative thoughts were crossing my mind. Self-confidence was the demand of the hour. Believing in this *mantra*, I stepped forward to the immigration counter.

While I was trying to recompose myself, my boarding pass was handed over to me by a beautiful Danish girl at the counter. Luckily, she was fussy neither about my passport nor about my name Redne or Yogi. I was asked to proceed to terminal number three. Almost sure of being caught at the security check, I advanced hesitantly to the international terminal number three.

I was afraid to think that Danish Police might be carrying my photograph or a sketch based on the information with them from the American Plads shootout. As feared, I was stopped by an automatic scanning machine at the entry point. Thank God, it was nothing but only a can of pineapple juice detected in my carry bag. It was not over yet.

At the security check of terminal three while they were checking my passport again, my blood pressure shot up; I felt dizzy as I stood face to face with an immigration official named Jorgensen with big moustaches sitting at the counter. He observed me two times from top down while holding my passport before his eyes. I felt I was losing my control on my legs. The situation was utterly hopeless. Somehow, I pulled myself up, took out my cellphone and pretended to make a call, my right hand clearly trembling. To my great relief he stamped my passport.

Patka, the headgear, helped a great deal in matching my present looks with the photograph on my Indian passport. But later I noticed that this *patka* itself was creating some nuisance as I heard someone whispering 'Taliban-Taliban' in a subdued tone. Ironically, the *patka* was helping me in hiding my original identity of Redne but at the same time, it endangered my life. I even thought of going to the washroom to get rid of it, but it would have made the situation worse.

I decided to find a seat in a corner to avoid unwanted communication with anyone. Luckily, I found a seat in a remote corner. Now I shifted my focus from Immigration officers to Copenhagen police officers. After an intensive brainstorming session with myself full of questions and counter-questions I got a solution.

'Why the hell will they stop a person who is willingly getting deported from Copenhagen? They will definitely not.'

I was right; Chacha was not of national importance. He was only an illegal immigrant.

Officers were busy handling other pressure situations and did not give a damn about the murder of a notorious blacklisted foreigner. Feeling confident of my logic, I turned my gaze towards the security and the police area. To my great satisfaction there was no police officer at the Copenhagen airport. I felt relaxed and took out my most precious holy book, the 'Bhagavad Gita' from my bag and pretended to read verses, as if it was a part of my routine. This helped me a little bit.

Anxiety would not allow me to relax. Within minutes I started thinking again; this time about Brussels. It was the biggest obstacle, where I had to change my flight for New Delhi. I knew that the European Union had such an understanding that they could easily exchange information whenever they wanted. The fear of being caught cropped up again.

Like a pendulum, my mind was swinging between Brussels and Copenhagen when I heard a call for boarding. I rushed instantaneously to the queue for the flight. With all this mental wrestling, I got into a 120-seater, a relatively small Belgian aeroplane with mostly European passengers at 6.20 am.

When I was looking for my seat number 54A, I realized that my fellow travellers were avoiding me with a strange look in their eyes, usually directed to poisonous snakes or unsightly cockroaches. Why, I did not know.

I found my seat but felt like an unwanted guest, although Raja had paid the same amount of money for my ticket as was paid by the fellow travellers. Maybe, it was my mystic look or exotic *patka* that created the confusion.

Since the attack on World Trade Centre, people from the West are intensely scared of brown-black people. They often get anxious when anyone of us makes the slightest movement in an aeroplane as if there is going to be a hijack or the person moving is a suicide bomb. This travel of two hours from Copenhagen to Brussels was punctuated with memories of when I had first landed in the same costume and looks, with Linda Christensen, courtesy Guruji Suryaswami.

At Brussels, it was a two hours wait to catch the connecting aircraft for New Delhi at 10.30 am. I said to myself, 'If I am able to cross this barrier of Brussels then half of the battle is won for me.' The last barrier would be to dodge the corrupt greedy officials at the Delhi airport. 'Stray voracious dogs' is the best definition you can use for them. If you put a little piece of bread soaked in milk in their mouth, they behave like obedient pets. Thinking on these lines I walked straight to the dutyfree shop at Brussels airport and purchased some expensive perfumes, chocolates and two bottles of vodka.

Strangely, there was a lot of activity happening at the airport. My bad luck; all the Indian passengers flying to New Delhi were asked to make a queue to show their passports. My suspicion was right. I was running out of luck. In an effort to compose myself I tried to make immediate acquaintance with some co-travellers. I noticed a young Swedish pair going to Delhi, holding in their hands the map of India.

Briskly I initiated a conversation saying 'Namaste' with folded hands. I found out that Stefan and his girlfriend Anja from Gothenburg, Sweden, were looking for a man who could help them find some cheap accommodation and transport in Delhi. They were in search of either adventure or spirituality or maybe both. I tried to be friendly with them and promised to render local support. Later, I realised, in given circumstances it was not a good idea to remain with them as they were not supposed to be standing in the Indian queue.

I changed my attention to a Punjabi Sikh family who were the centre of attraction because of their jumbo size. Harbhajan Singh, a taxi driver from Amsterdam, along with his wife Gurcharan Kaur and three sons and five daughters were making more noise than the sound of a real jumbo jet.

The youngest of the girls was weeping and Bibi Gurcharan Kaur was slapping her in order to restore order. Sardarani was new to Europe and was not aware of the state rules of child assault. Seeing the mess as an opportunity, I took the baby in my arms and gave her a chocolate from my polybag. The trick clicked; soon the baby was happy and started singing some religious rhymes at my prompting.

I became a part of this already large family. Maybe, Harbhajan Singh was aware of the money you get as an incentive from the government if you beget more children in Europe.

I know one Afghan, Jamshed Gul, from Kabul in Copenhagen. He has 14 children. Gul works in a kiosk to make money whereas on records he is unemployed and getting support money from the Danish government. Parasite on society! Pia Kjæregaard of Danish Folk Party is right when commenting on the exploitation of the social security system.

Standing in the long queue I was relatively relaxed, my costumes and *patka* matched with the outfits of Harbhajan Singh and his three sons. There was tight scrutiny at the airport in Brussels. The officers were checking each and every individual minutely and were matching them with their passport photographs. They were also carrying some handmade sketches. I was sure they had mine. When my turn came I gave my passport to Harbhajan Singh and took control of his kids in my arms. Seeing 11 passports of a family, the officials at Brussels got confused.

Next minute I was in the 786 Boeing, a big aircraft,

echoing with divergent noise made by my exotic countrymen. Even though the seats are reserved in aeroplanes yet you could marvel at the terrible level of noise the Indians make while looking for their reserved seats. The level of their noise is equal to that of an unreserved train in Bombay or a local bus in New Delhi. Without any chaos, the charm of travel is lost. Sometime I imagine, if Indian beggars, snake charmers, dancers and singers are allowed in airways, they can make the 18-hour flight from Chennai to New York really a spectacular journey. India has talent.

Brussels to Delhi

In disguise as a preacher, I came out of the aircraft at Gate no 7A of the Indira Gandhi International Airport. Near the exit gate there was an assembly of airline workers, rude in language and forceful in behaviour. Mimicking their typical mannerism and dialect I opened the conversation.

'*Bhai ke naam hai tera*?' meaning what is your name?

The trick worked. He was thrilled and simply said, 'Sir I am Jakhad...I mean Jagatbir Jakhad, Guruji.' After little pause, he said, 'You seem to be our man Guruji. From where you belong?'

Instead of answering the question I hurriedly occupied the seat of a wheelchair and secretly slipped a note in his hand. He could not believe his luck. It was as good as his three months salary in Indian rupees. His facial expressions suddenly softened and happily he carried me to the final Immigration check point. With a single look he was able to understand my problem. How beautiful is this art of non-verbal communication! Experts in this art, cheats can communicate more rapidly than the normal people. They understand the language of eyes rather swiftly.

Jasbir Singh Jakhad was his complete name and he took me to a person who looked like his twin. Jhangra was the officer in-charge at the immigration counter.

People in this area have incredibly similar anatomy and physical appearance that you cannot differentiate one from the other in a single look. Seeing my outfit and a religious book in my hand, Jakhad addressed me as 'Guruji'—the most terrible word in my dictionary ever since I grew into a man from a teenage boy.

Within minutes I was in front of the immigration counter sitting on a wheelchair like a handicapped person. Even though there was a long row of passengers at the counter still, Mr Jhangra was completely poised and relaxed. He was having a cup of tea with police officers at the counter itself and cracking jokes. Delhi Police made me anxious. Without wasting a second, I handed over the bag full of perfumes and vodka to Jakhad. Accepting the offer, Jakhad said, 'Guruji give me your passport.' I slipped another note under the passport into Jakhad's hand. This time it was meant for Jhangra, the officer in charge.

While handing over the passport to Jakhad, Jhangra said

respectfully, 'Guruji, you can go. If you need any other service, we are always ready for you.'

He performed his job so respectfully that overuse of the word 'guruji' at regular intervals irritated me.

Jakhad and Jhangra—what a team, I thought!

This is called timing and a slice of luck. Jakhad pushed my trolley towards the exit gate. His language was totally rude when he was talking to other people but with me his tone was quite comforting. I saw the same Swedish pair struggling at the airport. We just smiled and waved as I was further carried in the trolley to the exit gate.

Pushing the trolley, Jakhad again said, 'Guruji, you need not ever worry at this airport. Everybody knows me very well. Officers are my friends. I will take good care of you.'

I felt very special. There was a long queue at the customs and security checkpoints. Some diplomats were trying to convince the Jhangra type of people that they were on a diplomatic mission, but it was not easy to convince them. Some labourers from Dubai were fighting and settling the bribe amount for their electronic items. Carefree travellers were searching for their bags at the baggage trolley. Thanks to Jakhad and Jhangra, I was out of IG Airport in a flash, safe and sound.

Sitting in a chair for the handicapped, I was the first person to get out of this crowd. My joy was like winning the Olympic Gold in a marathon race for the handicapped. It was a live demonstration of *chai-pani* in severe adverse conditions.

Jakhad called some taxi drivers. I said 'No' as I was

supposed to meet Gurinder in the parking area. To get rid of my lucky charm, I said: 'I am feeling a little better in my leg.' Saying this I got up from the chair with a little limp. I still pretended feeling some discomfort in my right leg to look like I had some signs of arthritis or fracture. I was not sure what he thought. I said, 'thank you, Jakhad sir…May god bless you!' He promptly responded, 'Come on, Guruji… I am not "sir", but your humble servant.'

He touched my feet according to the Indian tradition, though I felt a little uneasy. He went back quickly to help some other genuine travellers or the disabled.

To my irritation and utmost surprise, Gurinder was not seen outside the IG Airport. It was unexpected. Gurinder, in my opinion, was a well-organised guy who knew the value of time. Guruji Suryaswami wanted Gurinder killed, but defying all orders of the high command, I had spared his life.

I couldn't do much but wait near the airport parking. It was India! Forgetting about European discipline and punctuality I shifted my attention to the Indian sense of timing. It always and essentially meant half an hour late.

Many drivers made a futile attempt to negotiate the fare with me. Delhi looked cooler and modern in the night, with lots of recent developments like wide and clean roads, fancy and powerful street lights and, of course, the parking lot sprawling over some kilometres.

My excitement turned into a sad frown looking at a female beggar in the parking lounge.

I saw Stefan and Anja walking out of the airport. Who would teach them the art of 'yoga?' I thought to myself. I am a Brahmin, so I know the whole lot of them. They take years thinking and planning to transfer the treasure of knowledge to their own off-spring. How could these Swedes expect to learn anything in days and even months. Wherever in the world, people claiming to be yogis are frauds. At the most they might be teaching 'Hatha Yoga', a physical exercise like aerobics. The real meaning of yoga is meeting the Divine. Gurinder came up in his Maruti 800. It was 1.30 am.

Flouting all the rules of parking, Gurinder ran up to me shouting, 'Pa-ji, welcome to India.'

'Guri...relax, and why have you parked your BMW here in the middle and blocked the traffic?'

'No problem Pa-ji, not at all in India.'

He nearly snatched my carry bag and hugged me as if he had never done it before to anyone, shouting but in a rhythm – *Sat Nam Shri Vaheguru*. He wouldn't let me go of his hug for minutes together, showing all his gratitude and affection to me. It was a rare moment for me too.

'What do you say Guri, is Kamini ready?'

He smiled and nodded, carried the bag into the car, put it at the back seat; came back, carried rest of the luggage.

ॐ

Jugad

Rohini, a new upcoming gigantic housing-hub on the outer north-west of Delhi, was our next halt. Sangriya, my birthplace in the deserts of Rajasthan, was the last in my plan of action. It was en route this colony.

Gurinder was living in Rohini, and we had to drive about 20-km to reach his apartment.

He was settled in Delhi and was working as a copywriter in an advertising company ever since his escape from a murderous assault on him in the Himalayas. He had altered his name in Delhi to avoid any confrontation with Suryaswami, the influential Guruji. There was no need of changing his appearance as most Sikhs looked similar. Garry, Gulvinder Singh was his current name.

The city of Delhi looked fascinating in the night, with a lot of new multi-storey buildings, flyovers and the metro train. Recent additions of the two adjoining satellite towns, Gurgaon and Noida, had added to the beauty.

When we were about to enter Sector-7 of Rohini, Gurinder halted his car near Sai Baba Chowk for a while to purchase a packet of vegetarian food from a street vendor. He asked, 'What would you prefer?' I was not hungry. I said, 'anything, I don't need too much. I will share a little.' The Dutch Sikh couple had given me two big jumbo *paranthas* in the jumbo plane when I was elaborating the art of *chai-pani* to the Swede pair.

At around four, it was a moderately cool Sunday morning. Fresh breeze was flowing. Early mornings are always very special in India. You can feel the spiritual atmosphere all around when the priests of different religions start off with their daily prayer rituals in the morning. From one side you can hear the chanting of the *mantras* and the ringing of the bells from some Hindu temple, from the other you will hear a melodious *Azan* coming from a mosque on the other side of the road. *Shabads* from *Gurbani* in Gurdwaras are always intoxicating if you understand their meaning even if a little. You can hear sometimes even the bells of a church ringing if you are in a metropolitan city like Delhi. This last addition to this 'morning-musical-spiritual-orchestra' was contributed by the Europeans with the help of their missionaries long ago

langurs. On another side of the street there was a big crowd listening to a spiritual Hindu lecture. 'Katha' is a storytelling ritual in Hindus to get rid of the sins they may have committed in their life. This Hindu ritual continues for seven days with regular morning and evening prayers. It is performed by sadhus, saints and the gurus. While diverting Gurinder's mind from Guruji, I said, 'Do you know the inside story of these rituals? Each saint has his own expertise. While one is holding yoga sessions, the other is teaching about salvation. There are two sessions of prayers in a day, each session consisting of two hours in the morning and two in the evening. Morning session of two hours is further divided into yoga, meditation, musical *satsang* and spiritual lecture. Evening session of two hours is totally devoted to lectures.'

'Pa-ji, how do you know all these details?'

'Of course, I learned it all from Guruji as a teenager.'

'See, Guri, there are around 50 major gurus popular in India who are appearing on in national television network and having mass following, forget about gurus of small towns or villages. Each guru has a decent following of 5,000-10,000 people. It is next to impossible to count all the sadhus and saints in each and every street of India. Additionally, here we will have to also exclude the sadhus of the Himalayas. 'Nagas-the naked ones', who never interact with the infected humans, are also excluded from the calculations. It happens only in India.

'Pa-ji, do you believe there is a God?'

'Of course, Guri, God exists in India. Without God's help, I mean blessings… how can such an empire run on its own. God is somewhere, he is certainly hidden somewhere– in Himalayas or in deserts of Rajasthan or in the jungles of Tamilnadu. Maybe, He is enjoying somewhere on the popular beaches of Goa with our guests from abroad as everything is under control. Half the workforce of this country is sleeping and meditating, still the country is making waves in the world economy.'

It was an interesting walk in Delhi compared to the one in Scandinavia. Europeans are dying because of loneliness and solitude and Indians are dying because of narrowing personal space and attitudes.

We were back at home around nine. I was relaxed and focussed. While we were having dinner, Gurinder said, 'I have just got a call from Kamini, she is ready but more eager to meet you.'

'Sounds great, but first let me find my 'doctor-duo.'

'Doctor-duo?'

'Yeah, Dr Sandeep Chaudhary and Dr Nirmal Joseph. Both are doctors but of different kinds. They are going to help us a lot.'

After making a few calls I was able to find both of them. Guri was eager to plan the further course of action. He took long leave from his job. It was not so easy for Kamini as she was anchoring live news 24 hours. We decided to meet Kamini at her office in Noida, in a newly developed filmcity.

We woke up early in the morning. I had a long relaxed sleep without a single nightmare. To my utmost surprise, I did not get any call or even sms from Guruji or his associates. The ground under my feet seemed to be slipping away, with fear instantly gripping me for a while! CCTV cameras at IG Airport! I might have been captured! Guruji must have known about my arrival in India! What next?

I warned Guri to be more alert. It was better to meet Kamini in a lonely place rather than in the jam-packed film city of journalists in Noida.

'Guri, why has Guruji not responded either here or even in Denmark?'

I immediately rang up Saleem in Copenhagen from a different sim card and inquired about the recent developments. Surprisingly, there were no calls from Suryaswami or Saliulla Bukhari. Saleem and Raja were still hiding. In fact, Danish police were very happy at the elimination of Chacha Imam. For many years Chacha had been creating political nuisance by misleading the youth. Secret agencies were not much bothered about the murder. This made me comfortable further.

ॐ

Nirmal the Nomad

Nirmal and I had our schooling from the same St. Mary's School. He is the only son of a Christian widow nurse, Lucy, and belongs to Kerala. How he became 'Joseph' and his mother Lucy is an interesting and funny incident. When he was only three years old he got influenza. The deprived widow, his mother Lata, took him to a missionary hospital for treatment. After Nirmal was discharged, his mother 'Lata' became 'Lucy' and our 'Nirmal' became 'Nirmal Joseph'. Nirmal's sister was transformed from Anita to Eliza.

Nirmal Joseph went to Jeddah in Saudi Arabia as he got the job of an assistant mechanical engineer. Apart from his normal salary, he also accepted a lucrative deal, 35,000 Riyal, a pair of clothes and shoes for allowing one physical change in his anatomy. A little surgery was performed on his genital organ. His temporary job was now confirmed as permanent. Nirmal became 'Mohammad Nirmal' in the port city of Jeddah, 200 km from Mecca.

There is a reference in holy *Quran* that if you convert a non-Muslim, you will be blessed by Almighty Allah. Conversion to Islam is a way of adding brothers to the community.

Even a single marriage is quite an expensive affair in Saudi Arabia. The social strictures for women are very hard, but the luxuries accompanying the marriage are implausible. Each wife has her own personal car, a personal driver and a personal maid. It is the duty of the husband to provide all the facilities to each of his gorgeous wives. Hard-working maids are primarily imported from India, Pakistan and Bangladesh. The drivers are mainly from Sri Lanka or the Philippines. With the arrival of kids, the personal staff of the super-rich Arab Sheikhs increases day by day. The house, that looks like a pre-school, is not an easy affair to manage.

As a result of becoming Mohammad Nirmal Joseph, Nirmal got a further three-year contract from his Arab Sheikh Daud-Adul-bin-Ahmadini-bin-Abdul-Azeez'. Later, when he was back in India he got a job to construct a Sikh Gurudwara. He preferred to call himself Nirmal Singh. As he was born to a medical nurse, everybody called him Doctor in the village when he was a child. Now he called himself Dr Nirmal Mohammad Joseph Singh.

'Great Pa-ji, he is not a simple *jugad* but an illustrious *jugad*. I believe he will be a great help.'

Next day passed with no results from the mobile phone.

I wrote again, 'I am Yogi, back in India, want to meet you, Guruji.'

My second message read: 'Killed Chacha Imam in Copenhagen. Desperate to meet you to make final deal and take your blessings.'

Desperate to make contact with Guruji, I again made call to Saleem. There was a happy report from Copenhagen. My case had been referred as murder in self-defence. Same controversial newspaper *Jylland Posten* even published an article about Chacha and his terror activities, stating clearly that he was a corrupt fundamentalist and that he had no right to lead any spiritual or social organisation in Denmark. Common people were also reacting in the same manner. *The Politiken*, another Danish national newspaper, went a step ahead portraying me as a national hero or campaigner against all the evils and sins being committed in Copenhagen.

Now having heard from Saleem, I was certain that there was no character like 'Saliulla Bukhari' living any more in Afghanistan or anywhere. The scene, I am sure, was created by Guruji to get his money back from me, the money that I had received as final installment of my hash deal. This hash deal was the biggest deal for me as well as for him.

Guruji would certainly find me out to get his money back. There were many agents or touts working for him and they would supply the information.

Recent calls of Copenhagen made Guri anxious, especially about the multi-million hash deal. While he was preparing dinner he seemed more eager to know how I escaped and what I was planning next. He knew me well for the last ten years and was responsible for all my investments and did the job nicely. Somehow, he postponed his queries and focussed his mind on fixing my meeting with Kamini. He could sense the urgency. Finally, the meeting was fixed for the next day on the outskirts of Noida. I spent the whole day inside Guri's apartment in Rohini. I had already added two of my trusted friends in the plan: Dr Sandeep Chaudhary and the ever-reliable Dr Mohammad Nirmal Joseph Singh. I sensed many questions in the eyes of Gurinder. He even suggested to me to drop this idea of inviting Suryaswami at my place and instead go over to his ashram. He was stupid as it would be so idiotic to enter his den. Being one of the closest disciples of Guruji for ten years, I knew the outcome. Patience was the need of the hour.

Next day at 2.30 in the afternoon we left Rohini in our Maruti car to meet Kamini in Greater Noida. As usual, we had to wait for the traffic lights to clear at the Sai Baba Square.

I noticed disciples and organising committee members of the same Sadhu community frantically announcing their further plan of action to fool their devotees for the evening session. Distribution of free food and ayurveda tonic was their idea to keep this crowd attentive. Every moment they were scared of losing the faith of this crowd in their so-called spiritual mission. While driving, Gurinder was breaking all the traffic rules. Actually, there were no traffic rules. Whatever, I was terrified because of my own fears.

'How the hell are you driving, man?' I shouted at Guri.

"Pa-ji, relax, you are too conscious. If I follow all the traffic rules, we will never ever reach Noida. Any big truck can crush our little *jugad*."

Gurinder's driving irked me for a while because of my sense of road discipline developed in Denmark. Even the lanes meant for cycles in Denmark were bigger than this main business road of Punjabi Bagh. Cars, jeeps, trucks, military tankers, goods carriers, transport buses, school buses, matadors, different types of modern and old scooters, bikes, motor bikes, pedestrians, pigs, cows, donkeys, rickshaws, auto rickshaws and, of course, rickshaw pullers were moving ahead in the same lane.

Guri talked about Kamini—how she got the job with Network 24. She was anchoring a live bulletin, considered very big in media circles. Many years ago they were classmates in Pathankot and they graduated from the same prestigious school of mass communication and journalism. Two years back, when she was doing a desk job in the channel as a researcher, she was suddenly promoted to this lucrative job of an anchor, courtesy the bureau chief.

This revelation surprised me sharply. Such sudden jumps have always landed me in some or the other trouble.

'Should I trust this girl?' I said to Guri.

"Of course, you should," he said.

How can a girl grow like this? Maybe some connections! I always doubted this superfast career advancement scheme since our science teacher Smita was promoted from a kindergarten teacher to a senior science mistress. I had a superfast promotion scheme from vendor to dealer.

We ultimately reached 'Film City' in Noida. A hub of media activity, leading media companies had their head offices here. Every second person on the road carried an identity card around his/her neck declaring 'Press' in bold red letters. Expensive cars had press stickers on front and back glasses. Everybody appeared special and seemed to have airs.

Media vans were seen on both sides of the street. Each van was fixed with two to three umbrella-type satellite dishes. Some of the channels were doing a great job in educating the brown-black people to know their basic rights. BBC and CNN also had their offices here.

After passing through these multi-storey stunning buildings we entered an under-developed area of Noida where massive construction work was in progress. There was a tea stall at some height. There were lots of people having tea and were scattered in different groups. There was no meaningful road leading to this kiosk. So Gurinder parked his car at some distance. He took his mobile phone out and we started to move towards the *khokha*.

Near this stall, local labourers were freshening up for their further hard work to construct new extravagant multi-storey buildings supposed to be equipped with swimming pools and glass houses.

'Guri' kept trying to contact Kamini on his cell but failed every time. Luckily, there was none among the journalist fraternity in this mobile café. Maybe because of their social status as they never liked these cheap stalls. Tea was tasty and refreshing.

After failing to connect, Gurinder said, 'Pa-ji, she is not picking up the phone...if you don't mind, can you wait here. Sometimes...they are too busy...they don't even have time to go to the loo.'

'No problem, Guri, I am ok here.'

Guri walked down Kamini's office to meet her personally. I chose to relax myself with one more cup of tea and wait for them. My worst worry was that why I could not make connection with Suryaswami. I had sent several messages to his personal number, even on that number from where I had got the threats and warnings.

While diverting my mind from Guruji Suryaswami I focused on the discussion of labourers and asked for another cup of tea. They were discussing the local politics of this state and were criticizing the oversize sculptures of the elephants and the political leaders.

While soaking a piece of bread in his tea one said, 'What the hell these double sized concrete elephants are doing at each and every square.' Making hypothetcal estimation another said, 'With this much of cement and brick you can make at least ten primary schools and hospitals for our village.'

After gulping the soaked bread the first got agitated.

"To hell with hospitals and schools. We fucking labourers don't even have proper urinals. Fucking Elephants! What to do with these elephants? Tell me what to do ?"

There was silence among the labourers.

'Do we push elephants up our buttocks?'

'You better do it', said I bursting out with laughter. All joined me and the laughter doubled up.

Gurinder tapped me on my right shoulder.

'Here is Kamini,' he introduced her to me.

'*Sat Sri Akal, Pa-ji,*' she said respectfully.

I received her equally respectfully, wishing her *Sat Sri Akal.*

She sat close to me as if we already knew each other. She was quite tall and fair, about 21 years old, wearing blue jeans and white *kurta* with high-heel sandals. Her features were sharp and she had one bangle on her left hand and a trendy designer watch on her right hand. She was carrying a laptop and a purse held on her shoulder. She seemed full with confidence.

'How was Copenhagen?' she asked.

I felt irritated with Guri, believing he had told her everything about me, even about the murder of Chacha Imam. Guri spoke in place of me, 'Yeah, Copenhagen is always wonderful.'

'Come on Guri...Have you ever been there? I am talking to Pa-ji. Don't please poke your nose.'

Kamini asked, 'What do you do in Denmark ...I mean

your profession?'

Truthfully, this made me nervous. There was a big 'pause' which made the situation more awkward.

I promptly said, 'I am a painter.'

'Wah! Great! It's wonderful,' she exclaimed.

'What type of work you do in painting? I also like painting but in this media job it is next to impossible to find time to paint.'

She focussed her eyes on me for the answer. Meanwhile, a boy served three glasses of *chai*.

I mustered all my courage, cleared my throat and said, 'I paint everything, I mean everything on the earth, though I am not a great artist.'

'Wah! Majestic, Pa-ji, we will have great company.'

I said, 'See.. this is my hobby, sometime I even paint walls, roofs and even houses to make my bread and butter.'

She smiled. Gurinder immediately changed the topic, citing traffic problem in the evenings in Delhi and said, 'We are getting late, Pa-ji.'

When we were leaving, she said, 'I am with you, Pa-ji.'

Soon we were on our way back to Rohini. On the way, Guri stopped for a while at Bangla Saahib Gurudwara for blessings. He is rather religious minded and has strong beliefs, like Chacha Imam. Though I also have a huge respect for Guru Nanak Dev, yet we differ from each other in our ways of worship.

Besides Guru Nanak Dev, I like the philosophy of

Sant Kabir and Gautam Buddha. I always believed in their ideologies rather than their costumes, colours and rituals.

'Pa-ji, tell me the truth, do you believe in God,' Gurinder asked.

'Of course, if you believe there is God but if you don't... then *Sat Sri Akal.*'

'This is not the answer Pa-ji', he said.

'Man, spirituality is inside you… you need to discover it… a special Guru is required to help you realise it.'

'Like Guru Suryaswami', he laughed.

'He is not a Guru, but a '*Guru-Ghantal*'. Everybody is not lucky to find a true Guru. Some may end up like me.'

It was late in the evening we finally reached Rohini. There was still no message on any of our phones from Guruji. Guri was getting anxious. I could do nothing but wait. He was inquisitive to know about my life in Copenhagen, particularly about the ways and means of making so much money. Gurinder knew about me since I joined the ashram of Suryaswami. My earlier life, since I left my home and became a sadhu, was still a secret to Gurinder.

We had dinner together. Gurinder tried to ask me more and more and charged me emotionally to the extent that I really wished to share my life, my problems, my sorrows and sufferings and, of course, my joy and happiness with him. I strongly felt he was getting closer to my heart.

Here, finally and luckily, was Gurinder whom I trusted and loved to share everything with him. It was all the unseen hand of destiny that was working for me, I told him honestly. The fact was I was running away from pseudo-spirituality prevalent in the world, specially in India, in every home and society at large. The more I tried to escape the more strongly I was chased by it. It started at my home, with my pseudo-spiritual mother, Bhagwanti.

Guri said, 'I met you for the first time in the Chamba ashram. What made you become a sadhu and what was your life before that?'

'I did nothing to become a sadhu; in fact, I never did anything to become anybody. I am the result of circumstances pushing me this side and that, up and down,' I answered.

Guri said, 'Not really clear to me. You must have done something.'

'Well, you really need balls to listen and understand how all this happened to me; where I was born, how I was brought up; who thrashed me, why and where. I have been fucked up for whatever I did even as a child at home, student in a school, passenger in a train, refugee with a father in Bombay, disciple in Haridwar, servant in Chamba ashram and even a simple immigrant in Copenhagen,' I said.

'I want to; I really want to know everything and here I am waiting to listen in detail,' Gurinder said.

Unlucky Start

I was born as Jogender Dutt in a Brahmin family considered culturally rich, literate and pure amongst all the ancient castes of India. Everything was opposite in my case. I was born in a poor lower middle class family to Om Parkash Sharma. Mother Bhagwanti was extremely spiritual but totally illiterate. 'Bhagwanti' means blessed with divine luck. Bhagwanti was so unlucky that she was born with an underdeveloped brain and was forced to marry an alcoholic. Bhagwanti was beaten almost every day by her husband. He used to call her mad, neurotic. She was my stepmother. I don't have memories of my biological mother. She died of some chronic illness when I was three. There were rumours in our locality that she committed suicide.

Neighbours tell stories about the late-night fights between my mother and father in our little house in the deserts of Rajasthan. Om Parkash Sharma had studied ayurveda. He was working as assistant to Dr Meena to pay the fee of my English medium St Mary's school. Nirmal Joseph, Sandeep Chaudhary, Eliza and Wahid did their schooling from the same school. Nirmal later became Nirmal Mohammad Joseph Singh and Wahid the youngest Imam after the death of his father. Dr Sandeep Chaudhary is now a professor and head of the Hindi department in a reputed college of the region. Sandeep was a bookworm. He used to read film and sports books in the class. Once he brought a book full of porno photographs. We enjoyed every single page of this magazine while skipping the practical class of chemistry. This school had a big reputation of producing some great talents. Nobody excelled in academics but did great in their own fields. Many of them later joined the department of crime to make money thick and fast. Some of them are still in jail and the rest joined politics to avoid any police harassment.

My father was a frustrated medical practitioner who did not know a single word of English and modern medicine. His English vocabulary had only a few medicine words like paracetamol, brufen, multivitamin and antibiotics. That his senior, Dr Meena, was from the lower caste, a Sudra, was causing a lot of mental agony to him. How can a low-caste

Sudra be the boss of a Brahmin? This was prime on his mind. My father was a staunch supporter of ayurveda but it was slow to take effect. Patients, without knowing the true value of ayurveda, usually changed over to allopathy in frustration. This pained my father. When Meena was away from the hospital for private visits, he would abuse modern allopathy by lecturing on its side-effects. Patients ignored his claims and declared him a psycho like his wife Bhagwanti. I inherited all this frustration.

Our physical education instructor used to strike a wooden stick 20 times on our hands for not speaking English in the school. If he were in a bad mood he would strike it harder on our naked ass during the morning prayers. The rhythm relaxed his mind. There was a rumour in the school that PT sir's wife Smita Mam had an affair with principal sir. I was a regular offender and thus got beaten up almost everyday. Ironically, PT sir did not know a single word of English himself.

When I escaped PT sir, Dad would take revenge in the night. The stress made me to run away from home for the second time after a gap of three years.

The first time I left home, I was caught at the main railway station when I was about to board the train for Bombay. Local police informed my father. My father accepted his fault at the police station and promised that he would never ever assault me again. As expected, he became more aggressive and violent when we reached home.

Injustice to indigenous Ayurveda and Hindi done by his

boss Dr Meena was forcing my dad to consume half a bottle of alcohol before he returned every night. At home, he would get more stressed on seeing my neurotic mom Bhagwanti Devi.

Around 100 photographs of idols of each and every God available on the earth decorated the walls and floor of my mother's temple. Shiva, Rama, Krishna and Vishnu—the male Gods—were in the centre. Goddesses Durga, Kali, Saraswati, Laxmi, Vaishno occupied elevations according to my mothers' wish. Ram was with Sita and Krishna with Radha. Bachelor Gods like Ganesha and Hanuman had their respectful position and status in this temple. My mother believed in the philosophy of life that every living organism on earth deserved our love and respect because you never know which organism had God living in it.

I was influenced by the pseudo-spirituality practised by my ignorant mother. I was well-versed with all the rituals for every God and time. My maternal uncle Parkash also taught me what colour to wear on which day. Though he tried his best to teach *tantra*, *mantra* and ayurveda, it was difficult for me to understand and analyse these at my age. Parkash uncle would not give up. To memorise *shlokas* and *mantras* from the *Vedas* and *Puranas* was a demanding task for me. Bollywood's angry young man Amitabh Bachchan was more interesting and close to life than *jyotish*.

Parkash uncle introduced me to '*Krishna-Leela*', the most interesting drama from the Hindu mythology. I enjoyed it because of my taste for dance, music and theatre. My ascending popularity in drama performances was creating a sort of confidence inside me. Even my school was exploiting this inherent talent in me to turn their annual prize distribution function a smash hit every year. Parkash uncle was the man who nurtured this talent in me with all discipline. Parkash uncle also inspired me to read and analyse drama scripts. Memorising lines and imitating the characters came naturally to me.

Uncle was extremely strict on diction and speech. Sanskrit was so alien and difficult to speak on stage; still I had to memorise all the *shlokas* and lines correctly with exact pronunciation.

I followed the same methodology for English dramas in St Mary's. Enacting the main character raises your confidence to such a level that you feel like a king. This I realised later in my life. I was average in studies but exceptional in dance, music and theatre activities.

When I was growing up my mother showed signs of mental degradation. My father would rebel against English in his hospital in the day and in the evening would teach me a lesson or two in English. This contradiction confused me at that time. But now I realise it was perhaps his love for me that forced him to teach me something which he hated himself. He perhaps did not want me to face the humiliation he may have faced at his workplace for not knowing the language. After finishing my last examination of 12th standard I decided enough was enough and ran away. I was determined that I would not re-visit this town in my life, but had no idea where to flee.

Gurinder was mesmerised listening to my childhood story. He was more curious to know about my transformation to a Sadhu.

While we were having dinner, I got my first SMS from Guruji. I responded immediately.

'I am in trouble right now, police is after me. It is not good to meet at Chamba Ashram…better to meet somewhere else where I can deliver the money. Next time I will contact from different number.'

Gurinder was still engrossed in my story. He said, 'We will just follow you Pa-ji. Tell me, where did you flee? What happened to your mother and what is your father doing?'

Bollywood – The Angry Young Man

I decided to flee home. I had a feeling that with change in my location my destiny would change. Why did I choose Bombay? I did not know exactly at that time. Now I realise I just wanted to escape my miseries and my home town.

Bollywood and cricket stars played a key role in my decision. Idolisation of Bombay started at 'Shehensha-Saloon', situated in the centre of our village. Its barber Soorat Singh Chauhan alias 'Soorta' always dressed like Amitabh Bachchan. The signboard of the saloon had portraits of angry young Amitabh Bachchan and a beautiful Parveen Bobby holding a comb and a pair of scissors. Exterior gate had a poster of *Kabhi*

Kabhie with Rakhi and Amitabh lying on red roses. A little wooden temple hanging on a knob at the entrance adorned a small picture of Amitji along with Lord Krishna and Lord Rama. A zero watt red bulb always shone in this little temple as a mark of respect. Inside was a beautiful collage of posters: Amitabh and Dharmendra on a twin mobike, Amitabh and Rekha holding each other intensely, Amitabh sporting a rope around his neck. Mirrors magnified the saloon's interior design. On the other wall all looked so lively and real.

Soorta, the barber, in his mid-twenties, was our mentor, guide, and a best friend. He had a great sense of humour and was a lovely stand-up comedian. He had perfectly mimicked the haircut of Amitabh Bachchan and was as tall as Amitabh. Everybody called him *lamboo*. He always conversed in Amitabh's peculiar tone.

I was impressed with his dialogue delivery and conversation with customers. I can still recall some of them.

What an impression! I remember when he almost had a fight with bank manager RC Gupta at Sangria. Nobody liked Gupta in the village for his superiority complex. We were sitting outside the saloon when this incident occurred. Soorta was shaving Gupta in his cabin and was humming a song of *Muqaddar ka Sikander*. Gupta got irritated and Soorta stopped humming. We knew something was on the cards.

After the shave, Gupta threw a ten-rupee note on the dashboard near the mirror. Soorta became wild and in a flash transformed into 'Mr Vijay' of Deewar, his eyes red hot.

Clearing his throat and straightening his shirt, he said in a loud voice,

'Mein aaj bhi phenke hue paise nahin uthata Narang Sahab.'

This made Gupta furious. He asked, "What's the matter with you?"

Soorta thundered, *'Ye tumhare baap ka ghar nahin...Police station hai...is liye seedhe khade ho jao....'*

"What are you saying?" Gupta asked.

'Agar apni maa ka dhoodh piya hai to saamne aa...kutte.'

Frightened, Gupta tried to get up from his seat but sat down immediately on seeing a barber's knife in Soorta's hand.

While sharpening the knife, Soorta said, *"Sahi baat ko sahi waqt pe kiya jaye to uska maza hi kuch aur hai...aur main sahi waqt ka intezaar karta hoon."*

Horrified, Gupta got up from his seat and came in front of Soorta. Folding his hands like a begger, he said,

"What is my fault. What have I done?"

We peeped inside.

This incident became the talk of the town and consequently a depressed RC Gupta got himself transferred from Sangaria.

Back home, it was equally difficult for me to understand the difference between 'real' and 'reel' life.

Fascinated by Bombay, I was ready with my plan of action. The need of the hour was money. First, I stole money from my mother's temple. I thought I did not commit any crime as I had always seen a lot of unaccounted money lying at the feet of Lord Krishna and Rama. For years, gods did not show any interest in it while I was in desperate need. I collected all the money, seven hundred rupees (consisting of several coins and many currency notes of different denominations, some half-soiled with *ghee*) lying at their sacred feet.

My next target was my dad's pocket. The day he got the salary from Dr Meena was the day I planned this noble robbery. Why noble? Coz it kept my dad away from alcohol and apparent torture of my mom for at least a couple of days. I knew he used to hide his money inside the hidden pocket of his vest. I stole a thousand rupees.

I thought my dad and PTI sir had tortured me enough to harden me to any cruelty of the world. But I was wrong. The outside world turned out to be more vindictive than my expectations. I was too young, and I knew nothing apart from art and culture and Bollywood. I remember that once uncle Parkash, seeing lines in my hands and matching them with my forehead, said, "Bhagwanti, see, your Jogender has special blessings of God, I can see from his forehead he will one day become big."

Mesmerised, Guri asked, "What do you think now? Are there some supernatural powers up there?"

'See Guri, at this juncture of time in my life I accept the existence of some special powers. How is it possible that I got all the courage to kill Chacha and escape? How lucky I was that I found Jakhad who made my exit safe and smooth at Delhi airport. I do believe in predictions of uncle Parkash.'

In any case, Bombay was the best place to try my luck. I

left home with cash in hand plus all the embarrassment and memories of childhood. I was on my way to railway station to catch the all-important train to Bombay. I was afraid of being caught by the police. I had once been caught by a policeman at the same very railway station of Sangaria. That experience was still fresh in my mind.

'Fifty-rupee note is enough to handle any policeman in any part of India,' Sandeep Chaudhary had told me.

So I had four such notes in the front pocket of my jacket. The steam engine was hissing at Sangaria station. I was wearing blue pants and a cream shirt, my school dress was in my carry bag. When the whistle blew, it was the signal for me to begin a new independent life. I was sitting in a corner in the crowded compartment. It was a sunny morning.

The journey from my home town to Bombay was exciting and adventurous. Every city and town we passed, I grew in confidence. I was like a newborn chick breaking all the layers of its shell.

Gurinder asked, "Pa-ji ...what happened to your parents?"

'My mother died the same year I left home. It had nothing to do with me. She died because of her deteriorating mental illness. She never showed any feelings of happiness or sorrow and remained most of the time confined to her temple. Soul was supreme for her and soul can never die...'

"What about your father?"

'Sandeep Chaudhary told me that my father died because of a head injury in a fatal accident. It happened six months after the death of my mother. A jeep crushed him while he was returning home on his bicycle. Wine shopkeeper told Sandeep that he was perfectly alright when he purchased a bottle of whisky from him. The shopkeeper said my father was a bit drunk but was in a hot discussion with his friends. He was explaining to the shopkeeper that alcohol was a herbal drug which had great advantages if consumed in a right amount. 'Multinational vaccine manufacturer companies are a big fraud. They are murdering our original Tibetan and ayurveda medical practice. They are banning herbs gifted by the Almighty. Marijuana and opium are like gifts from God. People do not know advantages of these drugs. Lord Shiva was the only person who knew the real value of these drugs.'

Some said this was not an accident. Some even did not rule out the foul play of pharmaceutical companies.

I could feel my eyes moist while I remembered my parents.

I controlled my emotions and continued, 'I was in the train. Till that day in my life I was an obedient boy and had always followed the orders of my parents, teachers and even others. But in this train to Bombay started a new journey where there was none to object or command me.'

Stranger

Stranger-1: Father Goodwin Utarid

Bollywood, my destiny, was now only 45 minutes away. Our train halted at Vasai, a suburb of Bombay. There entered in the compartment a boy around six years and a girl about one year younger, singing melodiously a popular Bollywood number. They looked innocent in their tattered clothes, barefoot and with ruffled hair.

Opposite me happened to be sitting Father Goodwin, about 58 years, six feet tall, wearing a pure white robe, designer specs with golden rims and a book in his hand. He had been engrossed in the book since he boarded the train at Delhi.

Suddenly now he was looking at these child entertainers. The girl was singing at her highest pitch and the boy was performing the famous moon-walk of Michael Jackson even in this crowded compartment. Some passengers appreciated their performance or maybe out of pity gave them some coins.

Father Goodwin appeared visibly moved, fished out an apple from his bag and handed it to the boy. He further gave a ten-rupee note to the girl. I was impressed with the performance of the children and, of course, even more impressed with the kind gesture of Father Goodwin.

He offered me also an apple as he noticed me looking at him appreciatively. With a smile I thanked him. It was our first direct interaction, though we had been together whole day and night and met each other several times while going in or coming out of the common toilet in the compartment.

Everybody was packing up but I had nothing, no luggage to get down and didn't know what to do. The train halted at 'Bhayender' train station. Father got up to take out his suitcase from under my seat and my legs. The next minute the train started and I heard him say,

"Are you sure where you are going?"

I tried to ignore him.

He had perfectly understood that I was a runaway.

"Get down with me at Meera Road, the next station," he said plainly.

After five minutes the train halted at 'Meera Road Station'. I followed him like a dog on the platform over the bridge and then down through the tunnel on the main road.

The scene was amazing for me, a simple village boy. I was at a loss to make out whether we were following the crowd or the crowd was following us. From the station to anywhere and everywhere it was a sea of multi-colour males, females, eunuchs, vendors, salesmen, beggars, rickshaw pullers, auto-rickshaw walas, scooterists, bikers, cars, buses and what not.

It was late night. We left the main road and walked into a narrow street.

"What's your name?" Father asked without looking at me.

I immediately changed my name slightly and muttered, 'Sir…Jog…I mean Jogeshwar Dutt.'

"Where are you from, my son?"

'Sir,… Ganga Nagar. I mean…a village 'Sangaria' in Ganga Nagar district, in Rajasthan.'

He stopped and said, "Are you a vegetarian or non-vegetarian?"

'Sir, hundred per cent vegetarian.'

He entered a shop. There were multi-storey buildings hundred times taller than our simple houses in Sangaria. I hadn't seen even a double-storey house except in films. Father came out with two 'tiffins'. Giving one to me, he said, "This is vegetarian."

We reached his three-storey apartment building, 'Sarvagya', yellowish and pinkish. He opened the main gate and we entered. I followed him upstairs to his flat. Outside on a plate was written Father Goodwin L Utarid.

The drawing-cum-guest room was small but cosy with a bookshelf, sofa-cum-bed, two chairs and a small round table. There were many pictures of Christ with frames or without, two candlesticks with a Bible placed on another table, besides an almirah and a hanger for his clothes and hat.

While eating our dinner he suggested that I should go back home, if not, I could stay with him as a domestic help. At the same time, he said that further education was really important for me.

Following his advice, I picked up the plates from the table and went into the kitchen to clean them, wondering whether formal education was meant for me or not. It had never been. I always preferred informal tutors like Parkash uncle.

He pulled the sofa into a bed for me and got out a blanket from the almirah. With an affectionate kiss on my forehead he said, "Good night, my son." And went to his room.

All the acquaintances whom I knew in the past started appearing on the screen of my mind one by one. I tried to take my mind away from my mother, but the vision of my father flashed with a bottle of whisky in one hand and a stick in the other. Surprisingly, he was not in his dress of a doctor but in the sports dress of PT. I tried to sleep but Nirmal Joseph and Sandeep came up with porno photographs of hot actresses. Then I felt somebody was beating me. It was again PTI sir who was striking his cane on my buttocks in front of the railway station. Smita mam was laughing instead of helping me out. Parkash uncle had joined St. Mary's School. He was teaching

English instead of ancient philosophy while principal sir was memorising Sanskrit *shlokas*. My mother was the chief guest of the annual prize distribution function. All the teachers garlanded her as a token of respect. I performed a soliloquy of Othello on the stage in front of my mom. Soorta was in role of 'Cassio' and Eliza as sweet 'Desdemona'. There was a huge round of applause and cheers when I finished my monologue.

Next I found myself running away furiously with Eliza in school dress. We ran away to catch the train to Bombay. It started and suddenly stopped in a second. I looked outside the window. The same inspector who had caught me when I was 13 years old appeared on the platform. He saw me sitting with Eliza in the train. He came to us and caught me by my neck, slapping me on both my cheeks. When Eliza protested, he slapped her as well. She started crying.

Thc pain and the sound together jolted me out of the dream.

I found myself lying on the sofa-cum-bed. I was perspiring all over and trembling. It took me time to recompose myself.

I pulled up and declared to myself, 'None in the world can even touch me.' I dozed off again into deep slumber. The trouble started again; it was worse than before. PTI had already pulled down my pants. He was also trying to pull down my underwear. He was completely in a romantic mood, though I had always seen him in a commanding mood.

"Jogeshwar pl…ease, lower your pants," he whispered coaxingly.

Then he slipped his hand under my pants. It was totally

strange and unexpected. I held his hand tightly and gave a twist to it. He tried to convince me but I further twisted his hand with force. During this tug-of-war my dream crashed. At once I realised it was not a dream. It was Father with his hand under my pants. He was naked and had bared me also. I happened to look up—at the bottom of the portrait of Jesus Christ was written: *We are born to serve others.*

I slapped that dirty messenger of God, hitting him on his back with my right foot so hard that he fell on the floor. I ran away from his flat.

He quickly put on his clothes and ran after me shouting "Jogeshwar, Jogeshwar, please stop: I didn't mean…I didn't mean…" Instead of listening to him I just ran down the stairs pulling up my pants.

Wandering through the slums all alone, barefoot, I reached Ambedkar Colony.

Stranger-2: Ali Murtaza

Sandeep and I used to look at the girls in the school and appreciate their bodies, even discuss the relationship between Smita mam and principal sir. What the hell was Father Goodwin going to do to me! I had never ever imagined that sex could be possible between males.

I walked into a narrow lane and saw a group of boys of my age playing cards. Sheepishly I went and squatted beside them. One of them looked up and said expressionlessly,

"Hey, do you know 'sheep'?"

'Yes, I do.'

"Got money?"

'Yes.'

"Well, shuffle the cards and distribute."

I wanted to be an actor but became a gambler on the very first day in the slums of Bombay. Ali Murtaza and I were on one side while Kamlesh and Guddu on the other. Kamlesh was thin and tall while Guddu was bulky and round. I played well, thanks to Dr Sandeep Chaudhary, who had trained me in the game of cards over a number of days behind the boundary wall of St Mary's School. They pronounced the game 'sweep' as 'sheep'. After two rounds, Ali was quite happy at my performance.

Ali and I won 20 rupees each and went straight to the *vada-pao* vendor. It was around 12 noon. I hadn't eaten anything since the previous night. The famous *vada-pao* with fried green chilly tasted really great.

I faced problems communicating with them. They were speaking a mixture of Marathi, Urdu and Hindi. I immediately followed the PTI sir style: 'Speak less, communicate with gestures'. I felt sure Father Goodwin had no chance to reach here and if he dared, my new rowdy friends wouldn't spare him.

"Would you like to see cinema? It's cheap, only five rupees," Ali asked.

In desperate need of company, I said promptly, 'Why not?'

Ali was a generous guy, with a lovely heart. He took me to see the matinee show. A large hut was improvised into a cinema hall and they were showing a Bollywood film on a VCR. This makeshift cinema hall was almost house-full with slum dwellers. It was extraordinary entertainment. Guys danced with every dance number and the operator even rewound the song '*Hum premi, prem karna jaane*' twice on public demand. Amitabh as a police inspector mesmerised the slum-dwellers. Crowd clapped and yelled every dialogue like a live show. Forgetting the past, I truly felt like a free bird. When we came out of the hall, it was cricket time in the Ambedkar slum. Ali joined them and forced me too.

By evening I had become an integral part of this huge family of slum dwellers; all teenagers became my friends and Ali Murtaza my best friend. Most of these guys were unemployed and school dropouts. Some of them had never been to school. They all were child labourers involved some way or other in the massive construction projects around the city.

Night was approaching and I got worried. I had nowhere to go to. I thought of sticking to Ali. He was ready to share with me whatsoever he had. His '*jhuggi*' was made of waste materials, polythene bags and jute and had nothing except mass of discarded polythene sheets beautifully improvised into a carpet to sleep on but was free from any disturbance. We had left-over *biryani* to eat for dinner.

Ali Murtaza Khwaza Hussein, 16, short, brownish-black, long-hair, outrageous rowdy slummer became my room-mate. He was doing a part-time job of a cleaner in a restaurant.

I was trying to sleep beside him but couldn't. I turned to him.

'Ali, are you a local? I mean where are you from? Where is

your family?' I said

"You can call me local", he said, "Originally I belong to Hooghly, a district in West Bengal."

'Which town?'

"It's village Chapera but sorry I have only faded memories of my home town."

'Why so?'

"My father Yusuf and mother Sabina migrated to Bombay when I was only one. My father died of cholera and his body was taken to Chapera. This is the only memory I have of my ancestral village."

I felt sad to hear this. He continued, "Soon after my father's death my mother eloped with Jamal Khan. She was a whore and never cared about me. Although Jamal was my dad's friend yet I never liked him. Jamal and my mother stayed together for a short time and then separated because of their own differences. Jamal was a chronic drunk. He used to abuse and thrash my mother every night. One early morning I came to know that my mother had committed suicide. I lost both my father and mother by the time I was nine. No one supported me. I became a child labour a and was exploited by fat builders and contractors. Now I am all alone but happy. This is my life."

When he asked about me, I truthfully disclosed everything including the incident with Father Goodwin.

I was still talking about my misadventures when I noticed he had fallen asleep.

It was my second night in Bombay.

Ali woke me up early next morning. It surprised me as I

knew he had nothing to do, not going to school or working anywhere. There was not a single toilet for these slum dwellers. These poor fellows, including women, had to walk a long distance carrying beer bottles of water away to the open fields to defecate. Ali always kept three to four empty bottles hidden outside his hut. We went to the fields swinging bottles in our hands. Ali warned that we must go fast otherwise farmers would pelt stones at us.

After defecation we went straight to the mosque. Free breakfast of *biryani* was awaiting us. Muslim *mazars* serve free *biryani* to poor people every morning in special months. We ate our fill. We followed the same routine the next day, playing cards, seeing films on VCR and chatting about cricket and Bollywood. The routine was burden-free and relaxing. There was no need to bath, wash or even change our clothes. Most of the guys had only a single pair of clothes. They would change only after they found a new one, which was very rare. When we got bored of playing cards it was time to play cricket with our self-made bats the narrow passage through slums. Days passed.

One night there was supposed to be a night-long celebration called *Mata Ka Jagran* at Kamlesh's house, a musical ritual offered to the mother goddess by the Hindus. Our group was excited, expecting delicious food. So, all the young slummers gathered in front of Kamlesh's house. We slum-dwellers looked so similar that it was impossible to differentiate on the basis of our religious identity. 'Durga Jagran Group' started their performance with a Ganesh Vandana. Then it was the turn of religious songs based on Bollywood tunes. A few members of the family started dancing. Slummers also joined them. Regular supply of free tea never stopped. Outside the *pandal*, seniors of our group had occupied the empty seats of rickshaws parked in the open ground. They were drinking and smoking and waiting for the free food. Bhoora was the undisputed boss and the ring-leader of the seniors. At midnight, the organisers started distributing the food. I gave a packet to Bhoora and he said, Thank you, Angrez."

Everybody laughed. 'Angrez' means 'British' in Hindi. It was all because of my North Indian Hindi accent and use of some English words. The night passed off with great fun.

Many slept on rickshaws, hand-carts, corners and platforms and even with the dogs along the walls of the mosque and the temple. I also learnt the art of sleeping like a free bird anywhere with or without any blanket or mattress, forget about pillow. For me, the fantasy was gone. The difference between real and reel was clear. Jobless, I felt lonely, bored and sad. Ali was busy doing his petty job in 'Hazi' restaurant in the evenings.

One day Ali came back with two *vada-paos* and yelled, 'Hey Jogi, our problem is solved, man. Great news for you and me.'

I sat up.

"Man, I am offered the job of a painter, 170 rupees per day…no strict time-table, no hassles, because you know… my boss is my friend. Wooo… how fantastic."

'Wow! Congrats.' I exclaimed. 'What is the other news?'

"You can get into my job now at Hazi restaurant. What a chance!"

We both laughed and high-fived.

"But," he said. "Your wages could be low, only 130."

'No issue...you get me the job right now. Is there anything particular about this job, you may want to tell me? I think it is only about helping in the kitchen, *na*.'

"Wait, I will tell you everything. Eat your *pao* first."

He continued, "Do you know what 'Halal' means?"

'Halal?'

"Halal means a kind of butchering, inch by inch."

'What do you mean?' I frowned.

"Yep, it's a little arduous for people like you but actually very simple and easy. You have to chop a chicken by cutting its neck while humming some particular Arabic *'aayats'* from the holy *Quran*. It's a spiritual ritual and only performed by Muslims."

'How then can I get this job? I'm not a Muslim but a Hindu,' I said.

"Idiot, you don't need years or millions to change your name from Angrez Singh to Ajaz Mohammad. Secondly, they wouldn't pull your pants down like Father did to see whether you are a Hindu or a Muslim", Ali said with a mischievous laugh.

I was convinced and he trained me in learning and reciting the important Arabic verses recited during Halal. Finding it difficult to understand, I singled out a waste leaflet from the garbage and wrote everything precisely. When I asked about the meaning I found Ali didn't know.

I was a bright student of Parkash uncle who had memorised the most difficult verses in Sanskrit. Hence, memorising the Arabic verses was not difficult. Chanting '*Bismillah...Allah hu Akbar*' was easy but keeping my identity a top secret was a frightening task. Killing a living creature was the most difficult thing to do.

I was at once reminded of the religious atmosphere at home. Being a Brahmin, even a thought about killing a living creature was considered heinous and an unpardonable crime. Forget about killing, my mother used to feed insects and birds every morning regularly. Thirsty birds and hungry insects used to gather in front of our house. My father was always angry with my mother for these strange rituals.

Once angry, Dad said, "Why are you feeding them? These crows and insects are not going to become the SDMs (sub-divisional-magistrates) of the city and deliver social justice in this country. Why are you wasting precious water? These eagles are like American agents helping the world pharmaceutical mafia."

There were two opposite ideologies confronting me, scientific outlook of my father and the blind faith of my mother. Both these divergent outlooks of life confused me always. Desperate to find a job, this time I preferred to be on the side of my father. I made up my mind and decided to give it a try.

After about 45 minutes, Ali came in with a sharp knife and a *ghiya* (bottle gourd). He held the knife in one hand and a '*ghiya*' (bottle gourd) in other and started the demonstration like a biology dissection class: Lifting *ghiya* up like a chicken in his left hand and knife in his right, he said, "See, hold the bird the way I hold this bottle gourd from its tip. Now push it solid on the hard surface. Start cutting its 'blood pipe' from its neck slowly inch by inch without giving a jerk, it's very simple; remember, never cut the '*bheja* pipe' then it will be 'haram' instead of 'halal'. Mind it, you have to recite *Allah hu Akbar* in the end in a high-pitched tone."

So here in this *jhuggi*, I learnt the art of butchering from my most trusted friend Ali Murtaza. I found him truthful and sweet. I understood what he meant. Blood-pipe was 'jugular vein' and *bheja*-pipe the 'spinal cord'. He also taught me '*salaam wallekum*' and '*khuda hafiz*'.

Next day, after '*jumme-raat*' prayers, we went to Hazi Restaurant situated on Delhi-Bombay highway at a distance of two kilometers from the Ambedkar Colony; and open 24 hours all days. It was an all-Muslim area and smelled strange. Goats, chicken, pigs, cows, pigeons and parrots were wandering and flying freely on the streets. Women in burqas and long-bearded men without moustaches further confirmed that we were in a Muslim colony. It was clear that the restaurant used to cater primarily to truck drivers and locals. There were cots called *charpais* spread outside the restaurant for drivers and their conductors to take rest.

We went inside and met owner Hazi Barkat Khwaja, in his mid-forties, wearing a white Muslim cap. I introduced myself as Ejaz Mohammad alias Angrez. The trick clicked not because of our smartness but because of the emergent need of child labour in the restaurant. Barkat was least bothered about my religion or anything else.

"Do you know what you gotta do?" Barkat asked.

"Yes Chacha, I have told him everything," Ali said.

"Ok Chhotu, you start from today. Mind it, it is 130," said Barkat.

Chhotu is a common name given to the child labourers at small roadside restaurants or tea stalls in India. Chhotu means 'small'.

Ali got engaged in talking with Barkat. I went to the kitchen. As told by Ali, everything including the big knife was well placed but not my heart and self-confidence. I thought killing a live bird would be more painful and hateful than getting into the lustful hands of Father Goodwin. But now it was the time to test my grit and I looked at the chicken and then knife. My blood pressure was shooting up and a sense of disgust was killing me.

I opened the cage to pick the bird but suddenly an image of my mom came in front of me feeding sparrows at home. My legs started trembling and face sweating. Closing my eyes dreadfully I held the bird directly by the neck and got it out. The frightened chicken squawked with a loud harsh cry and started throwing its legs and wings in every direction. I was about to cry but with a force controlled the bird, applying additional pressure from my chest. While cutting the neck of this pitiful bird, I again closed my eyes. My heart was full of guilt and I was about to vomit. Still, I said to myself that I cannot go back. I held the knife in my right hand and a bird in my left. Even though my hands were shivering, I collected all my strength and said loudly '*Allah hu Akbar*' and butchered the first creature in my life. My hands and face were sprinkled with blood. This loud chanting of *Allah hu Akbar* convinced everybody inside and outside that I was 'Ejaz Mohammad' not 'Pandit Jogender Dutt Sharma'. After killing about 10 chickens, I became a seasoned and skilled butcher.

This is how 'Chhotu' alias Ejaz Mohammad, the butcher was born on this fateful day of '*jumme-raat*' (Thursday) in the month of June on this highway connecting the two major cities of India.

Life was beautiful in Ambedkar Colony with an earning of 130 rupees per day for only four evening hours and the rest of the time was to explore Bombay.

Growing self-confidence and the company of friends made me forget my dreadful memories of the past. I got rid of my North Indian accent and started to speak the local language fluently with heavy abuses and idioms. The basic of this dialect was to start a sentence with an abuse and by chance if you failed then you could end with a mighty abuse. *chootia* and *gandoo* were the powerful words and *kaiko khali peeli* the soft *behan-chhod* was almost compulsory. These conversational skills were a far shot from what I was taught by Parkash uncle at home and by my teachers at school.

I and Ali started travelling in local trains without tickets. He showed me almost every part of the city. We travelled through Borivalli, Malad, Kandivalli, Goregaon, Jogeshwari, Andheri and Bandra. Ali took me to the coast of Worli in southern part of Bombay where two important monuments were situated.

Haji Ali, a mosque and Mumba Devi, a temple near Zaveri Bazar, were the best places to have free food any time; just had to wait there for a few hours. Muslim beggars outside the mosque and Hindu beggars outside the temple never hesitated to rush to either side for better begging at peak hours.

These are considered auspicious holy places for new immigrants in this metropolitan city. Before settling down in Bombay, immigrants must pay a compulsory visit here.

"Ask Haji Baba anything, he will certainly give," Ali said.

'Of course, I will.'

I closed my eyes I could sense a special feeling of confidence which was soon interrupted by a beggar when he pulled my shirt. Though I was myself nothing less than a beggar, I gave a coin to him. I found beggars in Bombay quite smart. Many of them had turned into 'fortune tellers'. Quite experienced in palmistry, courtesy Parkash uncle, I said, 'See Ali, I can make huge money here.'

"Yeah, I know, you are a brilliant actor," he said.

'No, I know the art of palmistry.'

Ali laughed and said, "Then tell me about my future, Mr Angrez. When will I become rich?"

'Seeing your forehead, I can predict that you will, one day, certainly.'

I was very clear about myself becoming a Bollywood actor and prayed for this. But I desperately needed a professional photo-session to try my luck. It was a very expensive affair. So I decided to give it a try after six months, saving some money from Hazi restaurant. Meanwhile, Bhoora the boss noticed a great talent of cricket in me.

"Angrez, if you work a little hard on your offspin, you can be an all-rounder of our team," he said.

I started feeling very special in these cricket matches. Captain Bhoora always celebrated each and every win of his team in his own inimitable style. Young slum cricketers would eat different kinds of dishes and sweets while the seniors would booze with different types of country liquor and a variety of hash.

It was always fun at the post-match team meetings. Apart from discussing cricket, we also discussed about up-coming starlets and beautiful girls of the slums. What a life full of fun!

'Guri, I still rate those days spent in slums of Mumbai as the best days of my life. I have got everything in life, but I miss the charisma of Bombay. This night at your flat in Rohini, in New Delhi, I am sharing all those wonderful days of my teen life with you.'

"Pa-ji, don't you need a cup of coffee or tea? I want to know more and more about you. I never even imagined that you had such a stressful childhood."

'You know, I would have been butchered if Sardar Rounak Singh hadn't appeared on the scene...'

Stranger 3: Sardar Rounak Singh

I was enjoying my job at Hazi restaurant. Four hours would pass happily as I would think, plan and sometimes even talk to myself about joining my friends in the evening, gossip, discuss films and girls with them and play cricket.

One day it so happened that Bhoora came unexpectedly to the restaurant to take me for our slum cricket match. He did not know I was 'Ejaz Mohammad' at the restaurant. He used to call me Angrez. Some people were sitting inside the *dhaba* eating while some others were waiting. Majority of them were local Muslims. Truck drivers and their conductors preferred to sit outside. It was lunchtime. Barkat was preparing curry at the counter.

"Chacha, where is Angrez? We have a very important cricket match today, can I take him along." Bhoora said to Barkat in his own typical style. "We have no Angrez working here," Barkat said.

"Come on Chacha, I know that North Indian Hindu boy who speaks English, has been working here for the last three months."

"You mean Chhotu… he is Ejaz, not Angrez."

The Muslims inside became alert. They realised I was a Hindu and not a Muslim. Immediately, the '*halal*' chicken turned '*haram*' for them. They became restless. Sensing the gravity of the situation, I came out.

I said sternly, 'Hey Bhoora listen, I cannot join you guys for today's match. I have a lot of work to do in the kitchen.'

As I turned to go in, two of the Muslims got up and caught me by my collars and said: "Hey, who are you? Hindu or Muslim? What's your name?"

Barkat intervened, and said, "Stop, let me explain."

One of them slapped his face, the other one pounced upon me, hitting me in my stomach. The first one also turned to me, held me by my hair and hit my head on the table. I was bleeding. He didn't leave me, pulled me up, and shouted, "What meat are you compelling us to eat? *halal* or *haram?*"

Frightened, Barkat tried to clarify, "He is Muslim and his name is Ejaz. That's why I employed him."

The guy who was holding me released me at once and went straight to Barkat, standing helpless behind the huge containers of chicken and mutton. Barkat gestured, suggesting that I should slip out from the back door. First, the guy hit the huge container with his foot and later smashed it with an iron rod. Holding Barkat by his collar, he pulled him over the container and hit his face on the wall. He was bleeding. "This guy said 'Ejaz' and you believed him. Do you know what a sin you have committed by allowing a Hindu to Halal chickens for us? You have insulted Islam. Do you think you are a Muslim? Shame on you!" the mob shouted at Barkat.

The scene turned ugly and violent. Barkat was helpless and shocked, seeing his *dhaba* badly destroyed, chairs and tables hurled here and there, cooking ware including huge containers for meat, chicken curry and *dal* thrown about. I was badly thrashed. My eyes met Bhoora's and a message flashed between us. I held the butcher's knife in my hand. With my chest puffed up, eyes burning red hot I stood up erect, shouting ugliest abuses while holding up my knife as if I was ready to kill all of them. They were least scared, rather they turned to me more violently, shouting even filthier abuses.

Barkat shouted, "All of you must know the holy *Quran* says that if anybody even once in his life declares that he is a Muslim, then he becomes a Muslim. Leave this innocent guy, for Allah's sake." The mob was in no mood to listen to him and wanted my life.

Suddenly; a thundering voice was heard. The chaotic scene turned silent. Everybody made way for him as he was approaching me.

"Get aside, all of you. I say, let me see who is this motherfucker telling lies and fooling us."

He was a Sikh truck driver, Rounak Singh, a six-footer; about 130 kg wearing Taliban-style blue turban, white *kurta* and chequered *lungi*, rocket-size moustaches, a few thick hair jutting out of his nostrils and a few other standing erect on the edges of his ears.

He looked smart with sharp features but with a horrible pot-belly, enough to hold 10 *tandoori* chickens at a time. The sizeable upwardly hooked tips of his shoes were so hard and piercing that when turned frontward for an attack they would surely cause a deep hole in the opponent's chest.

He thundered, 'Motherfucker, who are you? Why don't you speak?'

He snatched away the big knife and caught me by my collar. I was frightened and speechless. Hitting and slapping he hurriedly dragged me out of the hotel up to his truck, still mouthing abuses at me. He finally slapped and pushed me on to the seat beside him.

I was scared as never before in my life, not knowing what this stallion would do to me. Even Bhoora, my captain, and Barkat looked helpless in front of this enormous man. Then he did the most unexpected thing.

Rounak got into the driver's seat and started the truck. Sitting on the driver's seat with a knife in his hand he shouted, "If anybody tries to come in my way I will tear him like a piece of chicken; I am taking this guy away." With some resistance and jerks, the truck moved off, emitting columns of heavy smoke. He was so sure and confident throughout the act that nobody dared follow him. A few minutes later he put the truck in top gear.

I was getting away from my city of dreams. Bhoora ran after us but stopped after some time. He had to... I could understand... in me he had lost a dashing opening batsman-cum-leg spinner of his dream team. The truck was heading in the direction of New Delhi or somewhere in north India. Sardar-ji was changing gears of the overloaded truck with thunderous sounds.

I was feeling sad and emotional. Images of Ambedkar Colony were flashing before my eyes. Rounak was silent. After a long while, he slightly turned to look at me. Overwhelmed with a deep feeling of gratitude, I tried to pass a glance of thanks with a nod and a smile on my face. He acknowledged it with a nod; then broke the silence after an hour by switching on his tape recorder. He started singing after the song and tapping on the steering, creating nearly a perfect rhythm…

I did not have the courage to ask him to drop me somewhere on the way. After about an hour he got bored with Punjabi music and changed the cassette. At this point he gave me a little smile, and said, "*Kake*, how do you feel?"

'Feeling good', though I was not. I was badly confused as I did not know what would happen next. I was so scared that I could not speak further.

The tape recorder was running too fast. He withdrew the old broken cassette and then hit it gently on the dashboard three times. With this magic trick, the cassette started to play properly. Now the music and lyrics were clear. This is how I learned the art of fixing any little machine by shaking or hitting it gently on the hard surface.

The song that was playing was a *bhajan*.

With curiosity I said, 'Sardar ji, what is this song about? It sounds similar to Saint Kabir's.'

"*Khotey*" (donkey), he said, "This is not a song but a verse from *Gurbani*, a collection of reflections on life by various saints of India. How do you know about Kabir? You seem to be an intelligent guy. Listen, *Guru Granth Sahib* is written by great saint Guru Nanak Dev. The *Granth Sahib* includes the writings of the great saints of India including Saint Kabir. This '*shabad*-verse' means there is only one God though the paths to reach Him are different."

Pushing on the accelerator a little harder, he said, "What made you work at Hazi Restaurant? Don't you know the locality is dominated by Muslims? It is riot-ridden most of the time."

'Sardarji, I didn't even think about it. All my friends are Muslims', I said.

"I also have many Muslim driver friends but all are not the same. What the hell is this *halal* and *haram*! Kiling is killing; How can one kill an innocent bird to please God. Food has no connection with Him. I don't know much about these things. Honestly, I don't know if there is any God or not. But I can easily understand that there cannot be many Gods on the earth. Power hungry, selfish politicians and so-called religious leaders are killing communal harmony. Hell with them. If *Sacche Patshah* (Almighty) blesses me with power I will poke the eyes of these motherfuckers with this screwdriver. *Sacche Patshah* has saved you today."

He looked through his side window and shouted some abuse at the driver of a truck overtaking from the wrong side, turning back to me at the same speed.

I cooked up a story so that he would drop me at a safe place. He was ready to drop me home, but I refused.

Though I did not know where I was heading, I strongly believed in the destiny as predicted by Parkash uncle that I was blessed with special powers of Ma Kali and Hanuman.

We might have travelled more than 150 miles. I felt comfortable and was enjoying the company of Sardar Rounak

Singh. On the conductor seat, I was now reclining at the open window and looking at the occasionally passing by villages, trees and vehicles.

I enjoyed imagining myself as his assistant driver. The conductor side is called 'calendar-side' by the truck drivers as these simpletons can't pronounce conductor-side. It was 8.30 in the evening and Rounak Singh was feeling hungry. I hadn't eaten anything except a '*vada-pao*' since morning. He parked his truck at a roadside *dhaba* where lots of similar trucks were already parked. It was Daman, a port city.

Rounak, the stallion, walked up to a cot and sprawled on it, his palms joined as pillow under his head, his heavy and hairy legs stretched out, unmindfully exposing his balls to the cleaners and the waiters passing by.

Outside the *dhaba* there were many truck drivers relaxing, eating, brushing their teeth or carrying bottles to the fields. They simply had no time-table in their life and followed their moods for loading and unloading of trucks as well as themselves.

Rounak fished out another quarter from under the folds of his *lungi*, pouring it into a jug already containing some water and gulping it down in a single shot, pretending as if drinking water. Besides the pungent smell of this *desi* liquor, I could easily identify the smell of what Bhoora smoked in the slums.

It was sulfa, marijuana or hash! Many drivers and their conductors were smoking the same stuff.

I was aware of the power of sulfa. With just one puff of

the original Afghan hash, the truck drivers were ready to take on any challenge on the brutal roads from Kashmir to Kerala at a stretch.

Dal fry and *kadhi* seemed the *mast* and must items on their menu. They ordered *matar paneer* and *malai kofta*, when they were in a mood to celebrate or when they would get their salary.

'What do you want to eat, *Kake*,' Rounak broke my reverie, asking me rather loudly.

I said *matar paneer*.

While eating my preferred dish, I recalled my mother, who specialised in preparing *matar paneer* for my uncle Parkash as and when he visited us during our summer vacations.

This was 'Fauji Vaishno Bhojnalya' similar to Hazi Restaurant but more spacious and, of course, cleaner.

I felt rather happy at my luck, eating *matar paneer* after a gap of five years! But I felt sad at my bad luck of losing Barkat and my cricket captain Bhoora. Coincidentally, one of the drivers initiated a conversation about the recent cricket match between India and Pakistan.

Loud and angry, he said, "What the hell is Chetan doing in the team! Couldn't throw the last ball in his senses. Javed Miandad hit it off for a sixer in Sharjah. Where do we stand? Taking Pakistan lying down? I was feeling so let down that I couldn't drive my truck for three days."

Cricket fever is rampant all over India. Here also some of the drivers and conductors were finalising the future cricket team of India. Coming from different parts of the country, they seemed like cricket selectors assembled to finalise the national team to play some crucial international match.

Without any rhyme or reason these drivers abruptly changed their discussion from cricket to politics while their assistants were busy checking the water and oil levels in their trucks. All of them agreed on their prediction that whoever came into power at the top rung must be a thief and a confirmed liar. They also agreed in one voice that anybody who gets into power anyhow never loses a chance to make money by all means fair or foul.

Before the discussion concluded, we were startled to hear a bang. All eyes turned to the highway. An overloaded truck had broken down, maybe its axle had given way, with a loud crash. There was an unexpected pot-hole and a long stretch on the road in rather bad shape. Automatically they switched to abusing and cursing the state government for constructing bad roads. Instead of constructing proper roads, contractors construct their own big houses. The anger extended to the corrupt state police for taking bribe from them for silly excuses such as 'show your pollution certificate'. Drivers were fed up of the corrupt road police and traffic road inspectors for their unending greed and lack of regard for the rules. Inspectors were openly looting money from these illiterate but hard-working and low-paid drivers.

Rounak thundered, "Motherfuckers! We get only ten per cent for the roads, where is the rest 90 per cent?"

I was surprised to hear these drivers talking sense even

though they were drunk. "Ok, now I understand why I have to change the tubes of the tyres all the time. God! Please... save us from these corrupt officials and badly broken roads."

As a matter of routine, they changed the subject soon to sex and the pleasure it gave.

One of them tried to share his own trusted and tried method of enjoying perfect sex.

He said, 'Shilajit, a Himalyan herb, has 10 times more stimulant power than Viagra. If an old man takes even 5 gm of original 'Shilajit' he can satisfy a tigress, forget about a woman."

They were happy sharing their self-discovered postures and positions of love-making, without any reference to '*Kamasutra*'.

Before these drivers dispersed each to his own truck, their assistant drivers ensured that the air pressures of the tyres was right. They hammered a big screw-driver on the tyres to hear its sound.

Conductors and helpers were supposed to fill up the empty bottles of Coke or Pepsi with drinking water before they left. Free water served by this 'Fauji Vaishno Dhaba' was one of the major attractions apart from the availability of country liquor and grass 24 hours.

We were ready for our onward journey. My boss, the driver in chief, was sure where he was heading; but I, his assistant driver, wasn't.

The heavy goods transport trucks have ample space to sleep above the cabin. The cabin itself resembled our *jhuggi* which I shared with Ali in Ambedkar Colony. Bollywood actors with guns and actresses in see-through clothes in swimming pools are a similarity between the two as far as their interior decoration is concerned.

Twisting his moustache upwards at the corners, Rounak Singh said, "*Kakya*, you go up there and sleep. It is a long night's journey. We are about to enter Madhya Pradesh; then we will cross UP (Uttar Pradesh). I will drop you at a safe place in the morning."

It was not a suggestion but an order from Sardar-ji. I had to obey him as he had saved my life. The sleeping space for drivers was meant for keeping baggage and tools but Rounak had improvised it to serve as a single bed. Two people could be accommodated if they were in a relationship. Listening to different romantic tunes of Bollywood, I tried to sleep leaving everything to destiny and the wish of God. I was wary of Rounak a little but certain that this driver could not be as inhuman as Father Goodwin. I dropped into a deep sleep dreaming about my past and unpredictable future.

In the dream, Bhoora, and his cricket team, were thrashing the Muslim fanatics at Hazi *Dhaba* with their hand-made cricket bats while I was giving severe blows to the man who had pulled hard at my hair and dragged me.

Suddenly, I was jolted out of the dream with a loud horn.

To my surprise, I found myself alone in the truck. I looked down from the floor but Rounak wasn't there. The clock in the truck was showing 3.35 in the morning.

I gulped some water from the bottle I had filled at 'Fauji

Vaishno Bhojnalaya'. I got down from the truck to look for Rounak. There were many trucks, maybe 50 parked on the left and right side of the road.

I saw lights on the road at some distance and also heard some noise and babble. Obviously, I headed in that direction though I couldn't see the path ahead of me. It was dark except for those lights. As I neared I could make out that it was a small colony. Then I thought Sardar-ji might have taken a break for a cup of tea after continuous driving for seven hours. Surprisingly, there were no tea stalls or restaurants either.

But unintelligible female voices could be heard louder over others. It was definitely not an accident, but something more compelling. There were mounds of sand on either side. It was a place somewhere in the deserts of Rajasthan. I could hear music coming from some houses. Just as I entered a street well lit with colourful lights, a beautiful young girl held my left hand and said, "Hey, hero....want to sleep with me? Only 500 rupees."

I went blank for a while, believing this girl to be Zeenat Aman in film *Qurbani* because of her dress, features and height. At once I composed myself, disentangling my hand I stepped ahead but I was surrounded by three others looking like top heroines of Bollywood, in western outfits and even more beautiful.

These dazzling girls of the most under-developed area were wearing dresses of international brands. One was showing big cleavage in a top with the logo of 'Abercrombie and Ficch' pasted just over her breast. Another was carrying a handbag of expensive Gucci and showing beautiful hips with a big sign of 'Lee' on them. She was also wearing Rayban sunglasses even in this dark night. Another's Wrangler jacket hardly covered her assets. These unfortunate girls were the failed models and actresses who couldn't prove their talent in their proper field. So, now they were encashing their talent in this remote colony in a desert.

I was sure that Rounak Singh was somewhere in this colony with the girls. Overdose of alcohol and romantic melodies must have led him to explore romance and entertainment. He had been away from his wife for the last three months. I walked ahead and saw colourful lights mainly red, green and blue flickering on top of each door of the room made of concrete walls with a thatched roof. The care takers were sitting on benches outside sipping tea, smoking *hukkas*, gesturing and welcoming the customers with a phrase *Aao Sa Padharo* into the room. As Vasco di Gama was welcomed in Calicut in 1498.

Beside them outside each room was standing a beautiful girl under a spotlight luring the customers with singing and dancing. Some of the girls were inside their huts with customers. I didn't want to risk my luck in the light of my past experiences. I thought it wise to slip away. I turned back and made fast to my truck.

At the start of the street was a signboard which read in bold letters–Primary Health Centre, village Sodavas, Distt. Churu, Rajasthan. It is a unique area connected with three big states Rajasthan, Madhya Pardesh and Uttar Pradesh. This under-developed village was a leisure spot for the hard-working transporters, who were shaping the future of the country without knowing anything about HIV or AIDS. It was 15 minutes before Sardar Rounak Singh came.

Seeing me awake he said: "*Kake*, why aren't you sleeping? I was feeling sleepy. To freshen up I went to have a cup of tea. Do you also want tea or want to sleep?"

'Thank you, Sardar-ji I will sleep,' I responded in a sleepy tone pretending that I had just gotten up.

'Which place is this Sardar-ji?' yawning I asked.

"*Kake*, it is a small village Sodavas famous for a Shiva temple and tea."

The first part of his statement was right. The second part was as wrong as Pakistan declaring it would bring an end to Islamic terrorism.

It was four in the morning. After cleaning the windshield of his truck with a soiled piece of cloth, Sardar-ji mounted on his seat. First of all he lit an *agarbatti* in front of Guru Nanak Dev and then bowed before several small portraits of gods and goddesses fixed on the dashboard. He started the cassette player and song *Yamala-Pagala-Deewana* started playing. He immediately ejected the cassette and inserted another. It was time for spiritual music after a good round of romantic melodies. He himself started humming the verse. How fantastic was Rounak Singh, changing music according to his time and mood!

At about nine in the morning we halted at another *dhaba*

like Hazi's along the highway. We had breakfast; I tried to pay, but Rounak didn't allow. I felt like a seasoned assistant driver. I had completely withdrawn into myself thinking it was time to depart. He could drop me anywhere.

We reached Mathura, the city of Lord Krishna and got down for dinner. We had had our lunch somewhere on Delhi-Jaipur highway. I was in no mood to leave this truck but Haridwar was the best option for me; I had already been there once with my mother Bhagwanti.

"*Kakya,* you had better stay here. Mathura is mainly a city of Brahmins. I am going to Rishikesh, my last destination, and if you wish I could drop you at Haridwar. There you will have plenty of free food and some shelter as well," suggested Raunak.

We reached Haridwar, the house of God, next morning. The town has more saffron-clad *sadhus* than common people.

Parting is always painful. Emotionally, I pleaded with Rounak to keep me with him as his assistant driver. Equally emotional but objective, he said, "*Kakya*, this is not my truck; I am going to hand over the keys to its owner as soon as I download the goods at Rishikesh. It is my last day with the truck. I will be on a long holiday in my own village with my family in Gurdaspur district. If you want to be with me you are always welcome."

I was touched by his offer; I could feel in me a deep feeling of gratitude for this lion-hearted man from Punjab, who had blessed me with a new lease of life by saving me from fanatics at Hazi restaurant. I got down at the square near Har-ki-

Paudi and tried to touch his feet, but he stopped me short. A traffic police-man couldn't wait to disturb us with his repeated warning, "Hey… you go from here; you are blocking the traffic; get lost with you and your truck."

Rounak sped away. I still regret I never met this lion-hearted Sikh in my life again.

HARIDWAR AND MASTANA

I was standing and wondering what to do at the main square in Haridwar. Haridwar holds the same importance of a religious place in Hindu mythology as Vatican in Christianity and Mecca in Islam.

Seeing a crowd going in the direction of Har-ki-Paudi, I started moving with them. Within no time I was at the banks of the Ganga river. The scene was amazing with clusters of people performing different religious rituals like *upanayan*, the initiation ritual, *mundan,* the head tonsuring, *asthi visarjan,* immersion of the ashes of the dead and *shraddha*, appeasing the departed souls of their ancestors.

I could remember one of the childhood stories often narrated to me by my mother at my bedside to help me sleep, dreaming about the past religious glory of India. King Bhrithari had come to Haridwar and meditated on the banks of the holy Ganges. When he died, his brother Vikramaditya (1st century BC) constructed this *ghat* in his name, which later came to be known as Har-ki-Paudi.

The atmosphere was so religiously charged that I felt as if I were at home. I looked around and was naturally drawn to an impressive figure of a middle-aged, mystic sadhu with black long beard and equally black long hair standing and singing *satotras* (holy verses) loudly and rhythmically while playing on a harmonium hanging around his neck with a long strap. He was bare-chested and had smeared ashes over the upper part of his body. He was the centre of attraction. I was spellbound with his magical voice. Without caring to look around to see what was happening, I made for the mystic musician sadhu with my eyes fixed only on him. I had nearly reached him when suddenly somebody took hold of my right hand and pushed me down to the ground. The other forced me to sit properly in a line with some other people. I looked up to find that he was a bald man around 60 years old wearing a white *kurta-pyjama*. He was surrounded by his family members and a priest (*panda*), head shaven except for a thick knot of hair in the centre of his head.

I looked on my side to find 10 people sitting in a line. They needed just one more to make the number complete, like a cricket team of 11, for this *shraddh* ritual—a Hindu ceremony of feeding to minimum of 11 people on the banks of the river Ganga to please the souls of their forefathers. The *panda*, that bald man along with the members of his family members started chanting some *mantras* in chorus. The whole activity was going faster than expected. In no time each one of us 11 had in our hands *puris* and a handful of *chhole*. Then the bald man asked us to eat fast.

All the 11 'cricketers' including me started to stuff the free food and *halwa*, a special Indian sweet dish. Only two of my team members were eating while others were busy stuffing the *puris* into bowls and bags. I was hungry and finished it in no time. Before I could clean my hands, I had 101 rupees placed on my palm. The same was done to others. The *shraddh* ceremony was over and we were getting up to leave when somebody else forced us down. This time we were 21. The ceremony started again. The *mantras* included names of the man's father, grandfather and his forefathers being chanted at a fast track. The same ritual this time did not take much time. I was richer now with an offering of 201 rupees but couldn't stuff any more *puris* into me. Others, quite experienced, were frantically collecting money and putting it safe in the inside pockets of their cotton jackets. They were totally focused on the money, counting it and leveling the notes in a numerical order, though they were still pretending to be eating in a rather slow motion. It was clear to me that I should slip away or I would be forced to eat again and again. My unknown colleagues were experienced and could manage any amount of *chhole-puri* the whole day.

Somehow I managed to slip out of their clutches and looked for the mystic musician. He was nowhere to be seen.

I had eaten to my fill and thanked Sardar Rounak Singh. He was right telling me that no Brahmin can go without food in Haridwar. After struggling through the crowd, I made it to a lesser crowded place called Braham Kund. I felt some relief. Standing on the bridge I could have a broad view of the scene. Ever hungry for food and money, my new colleagues and *pandas* were eating less but counting aggressively.

It was *Sharad Poornima*, a special day for them. Vedic *mantras* and *dakshina* were in full swing.

I knew well through Parkash uncle that in Hindu mythology, after the death of someone the family takes the ashes to Haridwar for immersion into the Ganga. The family then serves free food to Brahmins and donates money according to their financial status. If the food is good and Brahmins are more than 51, then it guarantees them the status of a rich family. The poor serve food to only 11 Brahmins and donate only 11 rupees each. But in anarchy like this you cannot differentiate who is a Brahmin and who is not.

Being a Brahmin by birth, I was the natural choice for this ritual. I was wearing a white *kurta* and *pyjama* gifted to me by Hazi Barkat Ali. This costume was perfect for me to enact the character of a Brahmin.

Once during the rehearsal of *Ram Leela* we needed 11

actors to act as Brahmins to complete a scene of *shraddh* of King Dashratha but were short of seven actors. I remembered Parkash uncle telling me that no fixed number is required. Even one Brahmin is enough. This figure of 11 Brahmins enables Brahmins to feed themselves and their coming generations without doing any work. Every Hindu family is supposed to come here on a pilgrimage once in lifetime. I could see the *bhandaras*, a ritual to distribute free food, going on all around. There were more suppliers than takers.

I was happy but not content. I somehow still yearned to meet that mystic sadhu. I set out to find him. I finally reached Bheem Goda, which has a reference to *Mahabharata*. A legend goes that while going to the Himalayas through Haridwar, prince Bhima drew water by thrusting his knee (*goda*) to this rock. I realised that the day was almost over. I made it fast to Har-ki-paudi.

That evening at Har-ki-Paudi was exceptionally special, religious, spiritual and mystic for me, a scene that I would never forget in my life. There were hundreds of lights reflecting in the calm water of the Ganga. The scene was a unique blend of sound and colour. Several floral floats could be seen bloating on the dark holy water. The temple nearby appeared to have descended from heaven. The *aarti* had just begun, with hundreds of devotees standing wherever they were, in the temple, on the steps, on the bridge, etc., with their hands folded, humming *'Om Jai Gange Maiya'* in a sweet melodious chorus while the main *panda* was leading the prayer facing the holy Ganga.

I hadn't even remembered God since I fled home, but now I felt it naturally coming to me. I folded my hands and joined the chorus. I prayed to God to finally help me out of my bad days.

People from all over India come to Haridwar to pay their homage and to get their sins dissolved in the purifying water. I had no desire to have a dip, because I hadn't committed any sin. There was no question of purifying my soul, although I desired the company of somebody like me.

Unbelievably, I saw the same mystic sadhu playing on his 'harmonium' and singing *Dil De Diya Sat Guru Pyare Nu.* I couldn't resist running through the crowd to the steps where he was sitting, with many pilgrims at his back and on his side, some standing, others sitting and clapping in rhythm. I went closer and seated myself beside him. There was a *dafli* (a one-sided drum) lying with some coins and rupees on his saffron-coloured improvised bag, called *jhola* in their dialect. He glanced at me though he was completely lost in singing. I found it the most opportune moment to touch his feet reverentially. It was a gesture of appreciation for his talent. I picked up the *dafli* and started with the beat required for the moment, and took up the refrain on the same note *Dil De Diya Sat Guru Pyare Nu.* Our voices sounded like two in one. He was quite pleased; glanced again at me and nodded with a smile.

This immediately resulted in more people coming up and

more coins dropping by the *jhola*. Tired as he was singing so loudly, he slowed down. I didn't lose a moment, stood up and started singing at an even higher note but not losing the rhythm.

The performance was finally over. The crowd silently dispersed. A few sadhus along with us were left to spend the night there on the steps of Har-ki-Paudi. The mystic looked at me, his eyes piercing mine. I felt a little sensation in my third eye. He stood up to go.

I could hear a voice from nowhere: I am Mastana. Follow me, Yogi.

I picked up the harmonium and *dafli* and followed him, not knowing where and why.

Baba Mastana was walking ahead with a long *danda* (stick) in his right hand and the *jhola* hanging in a sling on his left shoulder.

It was dark except for the soft light of the full moon on *Sharad Poornima*. We moved out of Haridwar to the mountainous path leading uphill to Neel Kanth. I followed the Baba to a hut at a considerable height. It took us more than on hour to reach here. On entering the hut, he lit a lamp on the side of the door. The hut, including the roof, was supported with rocks on all sides except for the door. A concrete kind of platform was raised along the back wall, big enough for two people to sleep on. There were two pitchers placed together on one side along with two suspicious-looking bowls beside them. I could see a *hukka*, *chillum* and some tobacco lying in a human skull improvised into a kind of box. A pair of saffron *dhotis* were hanging on a line over the pitchers. There was a hole on top of the door improvised into a ventilator. As I looked up, I heard a loud rustle of some feathers. At once from the hole two eyes stared at me, a beak opened up and shrieked shrilly. It was an eagle! I lowered myself to the floor. In a flash, I found some *puris* in my hand. Like a robot, I started eating. Mastana was busy preparing the *chillum*.

In a day, I became familiar with Baba Mastana's routine. I would follow him to the Ganga. We would play and sing together. Pilgrims would assemble around us and place their offering happily in the form of money, food, clothes etc.

Baba could challenge any popular singer of the country as far as the knowledge of Indian classical *ragas* and *raginis* was concerned. Ahir Bhairav, a morning *raga*, was his favourite. His presentation of this *raga* was undoubtedly a masterpiece of Indian classical *'Khayal Gayaki'*. Once he started he would take at least 20 minutes for the *allap* and half-an-hour for its *mukhda*: *Jago jago re mohan pyare*. Unfortunately, he was no teacher. Although I had passion for music and the opportunity to learn from him, he never bothered to help me. However, he would encourage me to keep listening to him as long as possible, and I did so quite religiously. I tried to know many things related to religion, spirituality, Haridwar, *akhadas, pandas* and Nagas. He answered many of my queries. So, I got to know many things that Parkash uncle could not explain. To be honest, I liked Baba Mastana and wanted to serve him in my own small way. I would wash his clothes, clean the vessels, give him massage and get ready his *chillum*. Lately, I had discovered that the tobacco was actually a mixture of tobacco, marijuana and some unknown mysterious herbs. After he had one or two hard puffs at the *chillum*, he would reveal his esoteric beliefs. In one such mood he disclosed to me that whatever I saw around and the whole world was a play created by Lord Shiva with his third eye. He would always conclude his spiritual conversational talk with '*Har Har Mahadev*', his arms raised up, eyes half closed and corneas rising up to his third eye. He would also tell me that marijuana is just not a herb but a key to the treasure of the divine expanse of knowledge.

The days passed. I was happy serving him and he seemed to accept me in his life.

One afternoon while he was relaxing he talked in a sarcastic tone about Haridwar:

'You may call it Hardwar, Haridwar or entry to heaven. It all depends. Har means Shiv and Hari means Vishnu. It hardly matters what you call this holy town. A few drops of elixir accidentally dropped here while Garuda was carrying *amrit* (nectar) over this place. It could have happened anywhere and you would then call that place Haridwar.'

I asked him why were there different categories of sadhus seen in Haridwar.

"Yogi, your question is as silly as they are: *Akhadas* are centres of politics, power and embezzlement. Their heads are chief embezzlement officers (CEOs) and chief fraud officers (CFOs). Only the rich and politicians have access to them. They want their empires to flourish and care a damn for religion. If Adi Shankracharya happened to see his *akhadas* today, he would hang himself at Har-ki-Paudi out of shame and regret."

Babaji, What about these pot-bellied *pandas*?

"Well, they are really hard-working, maintaining and managing unmanageable records of the Hindu genealogy since centuries or to be precise, since time immemorial. These poor fellows can tell you the name of your great grandfather in a second without a computer or a calculator. People from Kabul and Karachi come to them even today to know about their ancestors. They are really soft-hearted and soft-bodied, gorging on anything that is made of milk and sugar. Liquor is banned in Haridwar, so at the end of the day they go out of the town, a kilometre or so, and booze and smoke to relax after performing their feat of maintaining their record, worth an entry in the Guinness Book of World Records. My blessing are always with these inexhaustable and harmless gluttons."

Who are these Nagas, Babaji?

"Get me the *chillum*." He sat up, caressing his long flowing beard with his left hand, closed his eyes for a moment and advised, "You shouldn't ask about them, their age, their religion, what they eat and what they do. Let the time come and you will get to know yourself. They are the real sadhus."

Mastana never told me anything about his past, though I tried many times to probe. I found him living in the present, not relating any action to his past or future. He was busy preparing himself to join Sant Samagam (religions conference) to be organised in the Himalayas on the occasion of *Guru Poornima* in the month of July. This Sant Sammelan was supposed to be organised in Chamba beside the river Ravi. It was an exchange programme to study and share religions and different thoughts. Many knowledgeable sadhus from around the country were invited to participate in this religious conference.

Mastana as Aghori

Mastana accepted me as his disciple. Many incidents touched me and passed. I absorbed everything, but what happened on that particular full moon night surpassed every other experience of my life.

In the third phase of the moonlit night... I suddenly found that Mastana was awake and doing something different. He was totally naked... I was about to scream, but controlled myself in time. His eyes were bulging blood-red and he had covered his face with yellow turmeric paste. He was humming some *mantras* in low tone. These were similar to Shiva *mantras*. Mastana was slowly transforming into a different human being altogether. There was a fire-like aura around his body. Slowly he got up and left his *kutia* (hut) with a *khappar* (vessel) in his left hand and a big *danda* (wooden rule) in his right. I was left alone. Fear gripped me from head to toe. I decided to follow him out of fear and anxiety. At the same time, I was curious to know what he was going to do this dark night.

He was slowly getting down from the mountains and approaching the river Ganga. Mysteriously, all the jackals and wild animals of the mountains started to behave like his pets. Instead of attacking or barking, they followed him wagging their tails. The scene frightened me.

For my safety, I picked up a wooden stick. I knew the stick was nothing in front of these wild dogs and jackals. Even a leopard had been reported in the area. Fear resulted in leak of a few drops of urine. Still I followed cautiously, holding my breath with all my might. Naked Mastana was approaching a Hindu graveyard on the bank of the river Ganga, with a brigade of wild animals. Hiding myself behind a bush, I noticed three dead bodies burning close to each other in the graveyard. Mastana made a gesture with his hand and all the animals except one dog disappeared from the scene. He slowly walked towards the burning bodies. One was fully burnt almost to ashes while the other two were half burnt. There was complete silence in the graveyard; even the dog was mute. There was no chance of my going back. I tried to make a minimum noise and kept a safe distance from Mastana. I hid myself behind a bush.

Naked Mastana took a long dip in the chilly cold water of

the river Ganga three times while humming *Om Namay Shivah*. The whole city was sleeping while Mastana was collecting ashes from the remains of the dead body. He segregated the burnt human bones in one corner and the ash in another corner. I held my breath in disbelief when he retrieved a human skull from the ashes.

Slashing his thumb with the sharp edge of his cane, he drew some lines on the head of the human skull with his blood. He upraised the *khappar* in his hands and brought it to his lips. Next moment he gulped down the *khappar* full of *som-ras* (a kind of whisky). His body started shaking while he was humming Shiva *shlokas* with full force. He started to smear the ashes of the dead body all over his body. I was about to faint. He was not just a begging saint. He was sitting totally relaxed with a human skull in his closed hands in front of the flames of the burning human body.

A beautiful naked woman appeared from behind the flames. Mastana stood up. In the soft yellowish light of the flames she looked a perfect beauty. Her long dark hair reached full length down to her rounded buttocks, while her fleshy mounds of breasts pointed to him.

Mastana reached for both her breasts with his hands, slightly and softly massaged them and nipped at her right ear lobe, kissed at her eyebrows and slowly reached for her left ear lobe; he started sucking at the hollow of her left collar bone.

Suddenly, she jumped up to his groin encircling her legs around his waist; her lips were entwined with his and she pushed him down on the ashes beside the other two burning bodies. Their bodies were completely merged and covered with the human ash. To my horror and disbelief, Mastana was thrusting up and down his lower body in the air as high as one foot. The dog stood motionless looking at them. He wagged his tail slightly once; closed his eyes; dropped loose his erect ears and howled abruptly but loudly in respect of the divine copulation. They were making love so furiously that I was about to faint.

Away from all the sounds and crowds of Haridwar on the banks of the river Ganga, this love scene was in progress and high-pitched repeated sound of Shiva and Shakti were coming when I fainted. I recalled the story told by Parkash uncle that during the annual festival of Jagannath Puri, temple prostitutes played the role of "the wives of the god-king", and had sex with him in order to evoke Varun, the God of rain to bring down the seasonal rains. When I looked up the sky there were no signs of clouds, forget about rain. It was the last visual that I can recollect. I do not know what followed the love scene.

I came to my senses when he called out, "Jogi! What are you doing behind the bushes?"

Pointing to the skull, he said, "My son, bow down to Shiva."

The human skull was still burning with flames and Mastana started eating half-burnt human flesh of the dead body. I felt nauseated but couldn't do anything out of fear. I don't know why I didn't faint or run away. Surprisingly, there was no woman around. Instead, I saw a column of dark intense smoke swirling and rising up from the spot nearby.

Mastana gestured and I lay prostrate before the burning skull. When I got up, Mastana put his right hand on my head and said aloud, thrice: "*Om Namay Shivah*".

"You are a Shiva sadhu now," he said.

Suddenly, the dog stirred, his ears erect, his neck stretched upwards, mouth open and he barked in a peculiar manner that sounded like *Om Namay Shivah*.

Slyly, he looked towards me for a moment, closed his eyes, ears down and went back into the same posture.

I still shiver whenever I recall that night in the graveyard. How Mastana knew I was hiding behind a bush; why he did not call me earlier; why the dogs didn't bark and what happened to the woman will always remain a mystery.

Mastana was trying for an entry card to the Sant Samagam, a saint conference to be organised in Himalayas. Fortunately, he got it one day from the Juna Akhada.

I was excited about seeing the Himalayas but I didn't have an entry card. I was nobody; secondly I was not 21.

Moreover, Mastana wasn't interested in taking me along although he was happy to leave his hut to me. Such people, once gone, never return to the same place. It was whispered that once he went somewhere for three days and returned after seven years.

"You better forget it," he said. "It is not really a question of arranging an entry card for you. The fact is our train to

Chamba will pass through Jallandhar, Amritsar and Pathankot, and you know these are the major centres of Sikh extremists."

I was so engrossed in telling my story to Guri in his drawing room at late at night with bowls of tomato soup waiting for us on the table that I completely forgot the reality.

"What a turn of events! This is how you became a child sadhu. I am curious to know how you reached Chamba even though Mastana tried to detain you in Haridwar," said Guri.

'You know I have always been on the run. This time an overcrowded train wouldn't allow me to disembark before it started. Destiny or what, I can't say.'

I must know how it happened, Gurinder said.

'This is nothing mysterious compared to what the Punjab Police did to me. If I hadn't used my brain, today I would have been Shukhvinder Singh Rada alias Sukha of Babbar Khalsa International, courtesy the Punjab Police.'

ॐ

Indian Rail

Sant Samagam was scheduled to commence at Chamba Ashram in the Himalayas on the day of Guru Poornima in the month of July. Baba Mastana left his *kutia* with his customary bag, *kamandal*, *chimta* and the small harmonium early in the morning. The weather was pleasant as it had been drizzling in the night. I was accompanying him to the railway station with a heavy heart. A big crowd of sadhus was also heading towards the station. As we crossed the bridge over the Ganga, we were joined by many other groups of sadhus.

Outside the station the sadhus largely outnumbered the local passengers. At the ticket window, there was a total chaos, passengers were struggling for their tickets; surprisingly there was not a single sadhu trying for a ticket.

Sadhus, inside and outside the station or anywhere around, were relaxing and puffing at their *sulfa-chillums*. Some in small groups were singing religious songs. Mastana joined them, playing on his harmonium. The whole atmosphere smelled of *sulfa* and *bhang*. Sadhus were lost in the religious ecstasy caused out of these natural gifts of Lord Shiva.

Saints of India have no idea of reservation of seats in the trains. They catch any train, no matter how crowded. Express and superfast trains are never ever liked by them. Speed they hate the most in their life. These sadhus were ready to wait for days at this railway station of Haridwar. In between their *bhajans* and *marijuana chillums*, they roared: '*Bole Bum Bum Bum Har Har Mahadev*'.

After about a 90-minute wait, a slow and totally unreserved passenger train came like a fractured elephant and halted, heaving heavily.

It was the most indirect train going to Jammu which would cover almost the whole of northern India. It was already overcrowded when Mastana and I entered the compartment.

Mastana found a small container skillfully improvised into a seat near the lavatory. Two sadhus had already occupied this seat, but out of compassion and saintly discipline they agreed to accommodate Mastana. I managed to keep standing with my hands, head and shoulders loaded with a harmonium, a *kamandal*, a *chimta*, a *jhola* and a stick. I was worried about how

I would hand over the things to Mastana and get down when the train started.

After a long wait, finally a long whistle from the guard declared that the saffron-coloured mega train full of sadhus, beggars, entertainers and salesmen and a few passengers with legal tickets was ready for an exotic journey.

The whistle blew, and the engine hissed and pissed. I was standing sandwiched, my ears touching the ruffled hair of a sadhu, shoulders rubbing with a salesman, my back feeling the erection of a milkman. A baby around nine months old was holding onto my little finger with his left hand. In her right hand she was holding firmly the mammary glands of her mother.

Mastana smiled as if he knew I was not getting down either here or elsewhere till the destination.

We were heading towards the capital of India. With passangers getting down at every passing station, the train got lighter and lighter. Slowly it shed the weight of daily passengers, milkmen and their heavy milk drums.

As we were about to enter the state of terror-hit Punjab, the train looked more civilised, no overloading and passengers sitting on their seats. However, the signs of fear was visible on the faces of the passengers. There had been incidents when Hindus had been isolated on trains and gunned down. Since the passengers included many saffron-clad sadhus, the risk was manifold.

As we entered Punjab, we could hear the slogans—*Raj Karega Khalsa Baki Rahe Na Koi* (only Sikhs will rule the world, others may perish).

Out of fear, the conversation in the compartment took a serious turn. Our team leader, the seniormost baba, Malang Baba, also joined the conversation though he was mute through the journey so far. Soon they shifted their discussion from spiritualism to militancy in Punjab. Sadhus started talking about the root cause of militancy. They didn't seem to be against Bhindranwale but they were clearly against the government policies.

We were now at the railway junction of the biggest industrial town of Punjab called Ludhiana, the Manchester of India. A heavy police contingent was deployed at the platform for security of passengers. It started raining profusely with occasional thunder. More thundering was the news that recently many Hindus were pulled down from the train and gunned down at the Gurdaspur railway station itself. We were supposed to get down at Pathankot, the last point of Punjab from where road service to Chamba valley was available. Our train was halting at each and every minor station, increasing our heartbeat.

After around 45 minutes, the train stopped with a shocking jerk. It was dark and there was no sign of a station. I found myself breathing heavily. I could feel the sadhu standing beside me control his urinary bladder.

We heard a threatening voice.

"Open the gate, you motherfuckers. Why the fuck have you locked the door!"

Nobody reacted. The door was forced open. We held our

breath. Suddenly, there was a sound of the door opening from the opposite side too.

"Balvinder, *check karo salon ko*."

"Yes sir", responded the constable. It was Punjab Police. Seeing these naked and half-naked saints in the train made them uncomfortable. What to search from these empty handed people!

Meanwhile, sadhus enchanted in unison, "*Bole-Bum, Bum-Bum-Har Har Mahadev.*"

Punjab Police was making best of the terror-hit time. Since they were given special powers to tackle terrorism, most of them were misusing their power to smuggle narcotics, beat up small-time thieves and drink with high-profile smugglers.

We were singing '*Govind Bolo Hari Gopal Bolo*' at a high pitch. As the train neared Pathankot, all the sadhus with one force rounded off the *bhajan* with '*Bole Bum Bum Bum–Har Har Mahadev*', their excitement showing on everybody's face and voice.

Punjab Police

It was platform No. 3 of Pathankot railway station late at night. Monotonous screaming of *chai-chai* again gripped the station. It was windy and cold on the platform. We really liked it as it was scorching hot back in Haridwar. There were two prominent colours visible on the platform: khakhi and saffron. Saffron outnumbered the khakhi. Thunder and lightning in the sky further intensified the atmosphere. Majority of the sadhus were long bearded and ruffled-haired, but I didn't even have a full-grown moustache. I immediately covered my face with the *patka* I always carried.

Outside the station, a huge tent-cum-*pandal* was pitched

up in a vast square of the market, with several shops along the three sides of the platform gate. The tent served as reception and refreshment for the sadhus. There were some vendors, with some passengers and taxi drivers drinking tea, eating snacks and smoking. It was late night and drizzling.

The *pandal* was lit with several milky bulbs. Sadhus were ordered to move out to the other side in a single queue passing through many barricades for their identity card verification by policemen specially deployed for this purpose, provided with metal detectors and scanners at different gates. There were hoardings of 'Sant Samagam' all around the area. Everybody going to Chamba was interrogated and searched thoroughly.

I was standing in a big queue of sadhus along with Mastana near the reception centre. We had already crossed two important barriers without any meaningful queries, maybe because of our saffron outfits. Still, it was a long wait. Fortunately, the rain stopped as we stepped ahead. At the next checkpost, police were taking too much of time asking about minute details. Reason behind this was the recent shootout at a Nirankari Sant Sammelan.

From the display boards and hoardings I could make out that this conference was going to be organised by Shri Shri 1008 Mahant Shri Suryaswami ji Maharaj Juna Akhadewale, most powerful and popular saint of India. Two mercury light bulbs were specifically focused on the picture of Guruji standing in a posture showering blessings. On one side, Mastana and I were struggling to get through to the barrier number three, on the other some people were getting direct entry through the final barrier. Participants from powerful rich communities were directly reaching the last barrier in their expensive cars. It was clear that the conference was going to be a lavish affair because of the participation of high-profile sadhus. Mercifully, even common sadhus could participate provided they had the entry cards.

Naked sadhus who had nothing to hide were searched but rich people with loads of baggage were getting special treatment. Nobody was searching their belongings. The search was just a mockery as I saw a policeman opening Mastana's bag and inquiring about his harmonium.

We were at the final security barrier and were supposed to be loaded in big trucks like sheep and goats for our final journey to Chamba. Luck favoured me. After brief inquiries from our team leader Malang Baba, we were asked to stand in a queue. The police checked only his identity card and ignored rest of us. There was a truck waiting. First of all, Malang Baba got into it. He then ordered Mastana and all of us to follow. There was a big noise around. One by one sadhus were loaded in the truck by the police officials and volunteers.

I was happy to see that IDs were not being checked. My *patka* unfolded when I was about to climb on to the truck. A policeman noticed me and shouted,

"Hey young Baba, show me your identity card."

'Sir...'

"Show me your card or stand out there," he thundered.

I was helpless. Mastana standing in the truck also looked helpless. Everybody else boarded the truck and the policeman locked the back door. Within seconds the truck was out of my sight.

The policeman walked up to me and shouted again, "Oye...where is your entry card? Who are you? Speak the truth."

Without giving me a chance to answer, he caught hold of my neck and dragged me towards a makeshift police post where I heard a group of police officers laughing full-throated and applauding a joke cracked by their boss. The post was at about 100 metres from the exit gate. It was made of bamboo and tarpaulin and lit by an LPG gas lamp. A big table was placed in the centre and six to seven officers were sitting around it. The boss was occupying the chair in the centre. In the dim light, it was difficult to differentiate the officers from one another as they looked very much similar with their red turbans, *khakhis* and, of course, their identical moustaches. A police van with a red light flickering on its top, was parked just at the entry of the post. Two young guys with their hands folded were standing helpless in a corner outside in the veranda. They were shivering although the rain had stopped.

The policeman then saluted the officers with a big click of his boots and gestured me to stay outside with the other two guys. He joined the conversation. One of the officers was cracking a joke. Even though it was not hilarious, the junior officers laughed and appreciated it. I exchanged a look with the guys.

One of them got up and said, “Great sir, excellent sir, marvellous!” He looked red hot in the red flickering light of the siren.

“Saab, this child sadhu has no ID,” he said.

“Satnam, take down his details,” the boss said.

Pulling me by my ear, Satnam took me inside the tent and said to another: “Preetpal, search him thoroughly.”

Within seconds, Preetpal searched me from head to toe and found nothing. He ordered me to sit in a corner.

I spent the whole night at a police post seeing the trucks leaving for Chamba Ashram. Early morning some other policemen took over the charge.

I was sitting as if I were the main suspect responsible for terrorism in Punjab. The officer who was laughing abruptly got up from his chair and violently struck a cane on my ass. “Son of a bitch, who are you? Why are you wasting our time?”

I couldn’t react. I knew I was the son of Bhagwanti Devi. Never had imagined that a comic scene could turn so violent. Clearing my throat, I tried to say, ‘Sir…actually….my age’

“Actually.”

He slapped me hard, started delivering kicks and blows on my back, legs and everywhere. He ran out of breath, stopped and ordered, ‘*Chal – murga ban.*’

‘Actually…sir I am Jogi, Jogender Dutt. I have come from Haridwar to participate in the Sant Sammelan. I am telling the truth. I sincerely want to know about religion.’

He got irritated and shouted, "*Saale*, you are speaking English."

My fluent Hindi sounded like English to him.

He became more aggressive.

"Liar, speak out the truth and spit out the name of your organisation?"

At once one more constable joined him. I could not make out whether they were two or three as my head was lowered down in the posture of a *murga*. I only felt blows on my back and lower back. He came, sat in front of me, and said, "Aren't you from Babbar Khalsa?"

'Sir, I hear this word first time from you....'

I felt more helpless than the chickens at the Hazi Restaurant. One of them got hold of my hair and the other started beating me both with his hands and legs. I shrieked like a chicken fluttering under a knife when being butchered. Many people started gathering around as I could see many feet approaching towards me. A huge crowd of sadhus also were witnessing this live torture show. They were continuing with their free style beating when the ASP came and said sarcastically, "Sure, you don't have an identity card."

'Sirji, please leave me, I am only a child. Out of curiosity I just came along with these sadhus to see the Sammelan.' I started crying bitterly.

He pulled me up and greeted me with a solid slap, and said, "Don't speak English...spit out the truth, you dirty pig."

I felt dizzy. Before I could recover, the buffalo-mouthed

black DSP intervened. He had been witnessing the whole drama for six hours.

"What is the problem Gurdayal?" he inquired.

"Saab, chhota sadhu taan angreji bolda hai."

Holding me up by my shoulders, Gurdayal said something in Punjabi.

I was standing with my hands folded and tears rolling down my face. Mastana had already told me about the fake encounters by the Punjab Police... young, innocent guys from the villages picked up and later killed in fake encounters. Often they threw the dead bodies in the fields. Babbar Khalsa sent a shiver of fear through my body. I was sweating all over as I visualised my bloody end near a mustard field in Amritsar. Seeing my end so close, I don't know what power gripped me. I shouted at the highest pitch. 'I am a sadhu, not a terrorist.'

Two policemen dashed to get on me but I was more agile. In a flash I picked up a rifle lying on the table and darted out of the door, shouting louder to attract the attention of the sadhus.

This unexpected move alerted them to stand still with whatever they had in their hands. They were drunk and made a failed attempt to catch me. Knowing not what to do, I jumped into a Maruti van, pointing and waving the rifle at them. Satnam, the constable, who had first isolated me from the truck, tried to hit on my legs with a long stick, but I got hold of it and hit him on his head.

More than 50 people including sadhus, drivers, shopkeepers were standing at a safe distance to know what the matter was.

I could see big pandemonium. The situation became more volatile when the head constable caught me by my leg and tried to push me down from the police van, but I hit the butt on his head.

I felt more confident, with the crowd looking at me and started shrieking like a monkey. Meanwhile, a white Ambassador car screeched to a halt at some distance, and out came a tall and handsome white-robed gentleman.

I was suddenly possessed by my father, Dr Om Parkash Sharma. Imitating his style I started shouting in English,

"You cheats, cowards, dirty drunken bastards…I am not a terrorist. I am a sadhu…if you have the guts, catch the real terrorists. I will gun you down, each and every one of you… and then I will shoot myself."

The man walked towards us. Seeing him, the ASP stepped forward and persuaded me again with his gestures to calm down, but I continued,

'You fucking cowards…I will burn you and this police car. You are the terrorists, the eunuchs. Don't touch me any of you bastards.' I was yelling while the gentleman walked close to the van. All eyes were focused on him rather than me. There was no sound. The policemen saluted him. I was confused. He gestured to me to get down. I followed his order, though reluctantly.

He said to the policemen, *"Ise chhod do"* and to his assistant, *"Ise apna card de do."*

He was the same Sri Sri 1008 Suryaswami ji maharaj, Juna Akhadewale, whom I had seen on the hoardings at the pandal.

He shook hand with the DSP. The constables saluted him again and touched his feet. They were avoiding eye contact with me. Silently, I thanked Guruji Suryaswami from the bottom of my heart and touched his feet.

Guruji was fair, 5'10" tall, with shining hair falling down to his shoulders. His broad forehead had three horizontal lines drawn with turmeric across the middle. His eyes were hypnotic, his lips juicy red. A mystic aura surrounded him.

I got into one Ambassador car in the big convoy of cars. There were three identical white cars in the centre, with same registration number plates on their back. Nobody could know in which car Suryaswami ji maharaj was travelling.

Celebrity treatment was given to me, a juvenile sadhu. Instead of travelling in a truck like sheep in the company of Mastana, I was in a luxury caravan of the most powerful saint of India.

What a transformation!

Chamba Valley and Ashram

Destiny was visibly playing its role in shaping my future; for good or bad was yet to be seen.

Chamba was 125-km away, showed a roadside signboard. Jeeta, of my age in saffron, was driving. On his side was sitting Bala. I was seated with Murali on the back seat in the Ambassador. Too happy and immature to understand the reason why I was saved from the Punjab Police criminals and why Guruji Suryaswami allowed me to be a part of his caravan, I turned to look at the beauty of the hills and the valley. Sadhus on foot in small groups, and many women, some even carrying their children, were walking up the hills to the ashram. Besides, many others were going in their own vehicles and also some trucks belonging to the ashram were transporting many more devotees. All of them were chanting in full devotion *Bole Bum Bum Bum—Har Har Mahadev*, carrying in their hands small saffron flags. Each flag was prominently painted with the picture of Suryaswami and the sun.

The spectacular beauty of the snow-clad peaks left me spellbound throughout the journey to the Chamba Valley, popularly known as the Ravi valley. Small villages and hamlets were scattered over the landscape. On the way we crossed Chakki, Banikhet and Khaziar. The ashram was situated in Chamba valley touching the border of the Shivalik mountains 996-m above sea level on the south bank of Ravi. Murali opened the conversation.

'Hey Bala, do you know how this name Chamba came into existence?'

'Chamba is Chamba, *chidiyan da Chamba*,' said Bala.

'Wrong, it is Champavati's Chamba named by King Sahil Verma after his beautiful daughter Champavati.'

Murali looked towards me and smiled, showing his vast knowledge. He noticed that I was feeling cold. He took out a jacket and gave it to me. I fell asleep. When I woke up, we were at the front gate of the ashram.

Guruji Suryaswami was received and escorted in by Swami Shivananda and his huge following of sadhus and devotees. We stayed outside, as Bala was supposed to ensure arrangements of lodging and boarding for the sadhus, participants and devotees arriving for the conference.

Ashram authorities had already booked all the hotels, guest houses, *dharamshalas* and government schools and colleges, but that was not enough. Finally, I stepped in the all-important Chamba Ashram with Murali and Bala.

Anand Ashram was situated in the foot-hills of the Himalayas beside the river Ravi. It was a magnificent huge white building with many additional blocks, surrounded by green hills and plateaus. The view of the valley with this ashram, an architectural wonder made of white marble, appeared like the palace of Lord Indra in the heaven. Preparations for the conference were in full swing. Sadhus were erecting the gates and giving final touches to the preparation.

Bala was busy inspecting the arrangements. Murali softly held my hand, slightly pressed it, smiled at me and said, "Want to see the ashram?"

I nodded 'yes' with a smile. He again held my hand, smiled and looked into my eyes. We saw the sleeping quarters, the kitchen, the sheds for cows, the yoga hall, the dance hall, the dispensary, the library, the Vedic school and the school for poor children. When we were back on our way to the main ashram building, I happened to see a signboard marked 'Kundali Jagran Hall'. I could not see any entry or exit to it. It made me curious. I tried to find the entry but Murali stopped me at once.

"You can't go in! Young sadhus are not allowed. Kundali

Jagran Hall is meant only for the seniors for advance deep meditation."

I was more curious and said, 'How do the *sadhaks* get inside this hall!'

He explained, "It is an underground hall connected with the main building of Anand Ashram with a tunnel. Only Guruji and some special disciples go inside. You just forget about it and don't ask further questions."

After eating *jalebis* (sweets) with cow's milk, we went straight to *shyan-kaksh*. Murali went for a bath and I closed my eyes for a while. Tired, I immediately fell asleep. I still remember that I dreamt I was carrying a rifle in a police van and all the Punjab Police officers were begging in front of me. At this point Murali said, "Hey, baba, get up and take bath. This is your new *dhoti* and *kurta*."

Each ashramite was doing his/her duty in the evening. I also assisted in cleaning and serving water to guests. There were different departments for different work. Sadhus were classified as Mahants, Acharyas, Rishis, Vidyarthis, Sadhaks, Sevadars and Sevaks, Brahmacharis, Sadhus and Sadhvis.

Beside Indians there were westerners who were doing the *seva*. Prominent among them were from Germany, France, England, Italy, USA, UK, Canada, Australia, Sweden, Norway and Denmark.

I came to know some unbelievable facts about these Sadhus.

Mahant Omananda Brahmachari had not eaten even a single grain of cereal for the last 50 years and was looking younger than 30 years old. He had been eating only one apple a day since last three decades. You could see him either in *Padmasana* (sitting posture with crossed legs) or in *Sirshasana* (head down and legs facing sky).

Maharishi Chaitanya, an exponent of water-burial, was in deep waters of river Ravi since the last three months. He was doing *jal-samadhi* for self enlightenment. Earlier in his life, he had remained in water for six months.

Kali Baba was hanging from a tree for the last six months and was in deep meditation. Kali Baba had never used a vessel or cup to eat in his whole life. He had improvised his lower lip in the form of a cup.

Neeleshwarnanda was sitting in one corner with sacred ash all over his body. Deep layers of holy ash were acting as clothes for this naked saint. He was in *maunvrata* (complete silence) ever since he came to the Himalayas. Maybe he was also an 'Aghori' like Mastana. He also had a human skull improvised into an eating vessel.

It was late evening. Everybody assembled in the prayer hall. A short prayer was offered to the Almighty. Sounds of vessels in the kitchen confirmed that food was getting ready. Delicious vegetarian food with sweets was available for all. Sadhus were sitting in rows. We were ready to serve. I noticed Mastana with his harmonium sitting in the middle row. He was singing the same song that I listened to at Haridwar: *Dil de diya sat guru pyare nu*. It was his favourite.

Serving water in glasses, I went to him. He had closed

his eyes and was singing in low tone. I also started singing the same song. He opened his eyes and smiled at me. What a transformation! He was eating like a guest and I was serving food like a good host.

Now it was time for the evening prayers *Sandhya*. I also closed my eyes for a minute and remembered Parkash uncle, my mom and Dad. I never did *Sandhya* since I left my home. You can never ever forget your childhood. It was really refreshing to perform *Sandhya*.

Sadhus from almost every part of India were there in the ashram. Some were speaking Tamil and Malayalam while others were speaking Oriya and Bengali. Hindi was obviously the language of communication. It was a cosmopolitan ashram.

There was a store-room near the *'shyan-kaksh'* where hundreds of blankets, pillows and quilts were stored. I was helping Murali in taking them out for the guests as well as for us.

"Be ready at six in the morning for Guruji's blessings, session starts rather early."

He went to sleep immediately. Sleep was elusive for me. A new place, new people and, of course, a new room-mate.

I had been on the run ever since my school days. Whole of my life I was running and running. Where was I going? I had tears in my eyes and prayed to God to let me stay at the ashram.

I was excited but restless. I looked outside the window of the second floor of this ashram. I started asking questions to myself. Where did I go wrong? What was my mistake? I was only permitted to stay till the convention. Only Suryaswami ji Maharaj could extend my stay in the ashram if he wanted.

I wondered why Guruji rescued me.

Shri Shri 1008 Suryaswami Ji Maharaj and Conference

It was morning. Conference was about to commence. In the opening session Guruji Suryaswami was to deliver his welcome speech. I was standing beside him as his personal assistant. I felt very special, clad in saffron, and most close to Guruji. I was number two in the ashram after him. Sadhus started humming Vedic *mantras*. I escorted Guruji on the stage and he whispered some words in my ears. I said, 'Guruji, no problem, I will take care.' He smiled and blessed me, raising his hand in the traditional posture and straight went on the podium. I sat in the front row and Guruji started his speech.

"Get up! Get up! Hurry up! You are getting late, man," somebody was shouting and pulling me.

'What are you doing man? I am busy in the conference,' I protested.

"Get up! Conference will start in half-an-hour. Take bath, we are getting late," said Murali.

I heard the sounds of temple bells. Hurriedly, I took a bath and got myself ready, but the morning prayer had already begun. I was late. Murali was punctual and reached the temple on time.

Day 1

At 6.30 am we were at the main square. Everybody looked up at the first floor. Right then Guruji Shri Shri 1008 Suryaswami ji Maharaj appeared on the balcony to initiate the day with his blessings. He smiled, raised both his hands in a posture of showering blessings and muttered *Om Shanti, Om Shanti* and went inside.

People were still waiting outside in a queue to get into the ashram. Meanwhile, the ashramites took up their duties for the day.

A *shamiana-cum-pandal* was beautifully designed and set up with a platform and a decorated huge seat on it. People were sitting on red mattresses and chanting in chorus *'Om namo sachhidan shri krishnaye namay.'* Kirtan was in full swing.

After one hour, from the back door entered Guruji Suryaswami in a very slow and graceful manner, hands loosely folded and wide smile on his face. He sat on the cushioned seat and began his speech with a Sanskrit *shloka*:

Sachhidanand Rupay, Vishvoudpatyadi Hey Taye.
Tapatre Vinashaye Shri Krishnaye Vayam Numey.

"Courage is thy birthright, and fear not; peace is thy divine heritage, but not restlessness. Immortality is thy birthright, but not mortality; strength, but not weakness; health, but not disease; bliss, but not sorrow; knowledge, but not ignorance. Pain, sorrow and ignorance are illusory; these cannot live. Bliss, joy and knowledge are true; these cannot die. You are the architect of your own fate. You are the master of your own destiny. You can do and undo things. You sow an action and reap a tendency. You sow a tendency and reap a habit. You sow a habit and reap your character. You sow your character and reap your destiny. Therefore, destiny is your own creation. You can undo it if you like – destiny is a bundle of habits. Purushartha is self-exertion. Purushartha can give you anything. Change your habits. Change the mode of thinking. You can conquer destiny. You are now thinking: 'I am the body'. Start the spiritual anti-current and think: I am immortal, diseaseless, sexless *atman*. You can conquer death and attain the immortal seat of supreme splendour."

It was a great speech full of wisdom and knowledge. Everybody was spellbound. I still remember some of his lines told in a magnetic but sweet voice.

The introductory session was full of lectures by different

distinguished guests, speakers on religion, humanity. Speakers from different parts of the country lectured on different interesting subjects like *karma*, yoga, meditation, ayurveda, *tantra*, *mantra* and *kundali-jagran*.

Many scholars from different thoughts, viz, Hinduism, Buddhism, and Sikhism shared their insights on religion and humanity. There were hundreds of participants in the conference; I was the youngest and observed everything keenly. Every speech of the conference was full of wisdom.

Day 2

Proceedings next day started rather very early. It was Sunday and the session was focussed on ancient medicopathy. It was more practical and entertaining than the first day and was further followed by a special ayurvedic medical session.

A huge crowd had assembled in front of the gate. People had come from far-flung areas. It was a great display of amazing ancient Indian medicine.

In one corner, a South Indian saint, Pt Ram Naidu Joshi, was ready with his assistants. He was asking the patients suffering from asthma to engulf a live tiny fish in their mouth. He declared that once this magic fish was in their stomach, their respiratory problem will be cured for ever. This little fish was placed on a sweet dish made of cow milk. A woman declared that the fish was extra-ordinarily potent. She had thrown all her asthmatic inhalers in the dust bin after consuming the magic fish.

In another corner, Mahant Giri was treating jaundice

without any medicines. Giri had only one mantra and a little yellow fluid in his armoury. Satisfied patients were excited and thankful. Hepatitis B or C had no existence for Mahant Giri.

Bapuji was inserting a black powder called 'Snake Surma' in the eyes of the patients. He challenged that he could remove even contact lenses. Many people claimed that after using the magic 'Snake Surma' they were freed from glaucoma.

Kazi Karimullah, a Muslim saint from Dungarpur, was removing gall bladder and kidney stones with a knife without making surgical cut in the body. It was beyond imagination. Kazi had proof of all this unique blood-less surgery. Gall bladder and kidney stones of different sizes were displayed on his examination table. Even old patients were showing their ultrasound reports before and after these exotic procedures. People from different sections of the society, including a US-returned cardiologist and a retired Indian surgeon, approved this mysterious avascular surgical technique.

Swami Shivananda was suggesting some spices and oils to middleaged infertile females. Ma Nirmala was assisting Shivananda in this infertility clinic. Spices and magic oil were also recommended for impotent males. Inside his consulting room, there was a private ward where Shivananda was examining the difficult but overexcited females with the help of Ma Nirmala. Women seemed satisfied after the detailed examination. In scientific terminology it could be referred to as spiritual in-vitro fertilisation. A Tibetan physician was also challenging the science of gynaecology.

Western devotees from Canada and Europe were deeply engrossed learning 'black magic' from a Bengali Brahmin Sumantha Bhattacharya. Australian pair Adam and Neena were focussed on the science of palmistry, while an old German couple was enquiring about the role of *'pranayam'* in avoiding bypass heart surgery. Reiki master and hypnotherapist Sachidevta was selling his pyramids of different colours like indigo, pink, red and green.

People from all classes and categories were there in a queue to take spiritual blessings. They included highly qualified administrative officers, bureaucrats, politicians, film stars and sport stars. Guys who graduated from the best British or American schools were also in long queues and were waiting for their turn. There was a big demand for transcendental meditation.

Near the basement meditation centre, an assistant to Shivananda was guiding people about the use of particular exercises (*asanas*) to have prolonged coitus. He was also suggesting some herbs to improve the quality of sex. Shilajit was the herb in big demand. Middle-aged males were dying to get even a gram of original Shilajit.

Ayurveda was in my blood, courtesy my dad. I always was in a conflict about the system of medicine. I remembered my dad and really felt sorry for him. I thought he was right. He had some great formulations of herbs but nobody had faith in him. Undoubtedly, there was some divine magic in this ancient ayurveda, *tantra* and *mantra*. By evening the mind-boggling session was over. Most of the devotees and the invitees had departed from the ashram. I was asked to help in the kitchen. I was cutting vegetables, sadly thinking I would be leaving the ashram tomorrow, the last day of the *samagam*.

Day 3

It was around 8 am. Devotees started to assemble in the *pandal*. A cool Himalayan wind was blowing. The sun was playing hide and seek. The final proceedings of this conference were about to start. Guruji was supposed to deliver the concluding lecture. Everybody was waiting for him. The session was focussed on ancient art and culture. At the end, ashramites were to perform the *ras-leela*, a Krishna dance-drama ballet. The schedule was known only to the inmates and a few special guests. Murali told me about it.

The day started with Vedic Mantras. A group of 51 Brahmins clad in white *dhoti* and sporting *janeu* (sacred thread) around their neck and arm pit were seated in a big circle and chanting *mantras* from the *Rig-Veda* in a loud chorus based on only three notes Sa, Re and Nee (C, D and B in western notations). It was spiritually refreshing; the whole ashram vibrated with the hymns.

Guruji Suryaswami appeared on the stage in a maroon robe. His radiant face with a round vermilion *bindi* and a yellow spot within it on his forehead set him apart from anybody and everybody present there or anywhere I had seen so far. A white silky *patka* adorned his neck with its side-falls reaching down to his waist. A brown Rudraksh *mala* added to his charm and personality.

Guruji commenced his lecture with chanting of *Haribol* and *Bole Bum Bum Bum—Har Har Mahadev*. Then he started his speech:

> One who loves God's creation, truly loves Him, and is a true human. 'Humanism' is the true way of living and is called religion. Who imbibes humanism is religious in the true sense. But devoid of humanism one cannot be regarded as religious. Unfortunately, instead of following the teachings of love and non-violence of Lord Buddha and Mahatma Gandhi, today people have become violent not only in India but throughout the world. Today, man's thought, speech and action reflect violence. It is really sad that India, which taught non-violence to the world, is itself the victim of violence. There is a dire need of love and fellowship. Giving importance to love, the devotees contribute to fostering peace and happiness. It is so because they themselves have realised God and inspire humanity to do so. God is stated to be indescribable, formless, merciful and loving and gracious. He is the eternal giver, creator, doer, fearless, without hostility, in transcending time and never born.
>
> "Foolish persons were following their own wayward mind and not followings of their guru. They waste this opportunity in pursuit of transitory

> gratification. This is *maya.* Lust, anger, greed, attachment and self-will are impediments in realisation of God. A skill of the mind and body only enhances one's ego unless one has understood the guru's word through God's mercy. Guru's help is utmost important in understanding the purpose of life and the way to eternal joy in God. Meeting the true guru can only come about through God's Mercy. Merely reading and reciting the scriptures, going on pilgrimages, bathing in holy rivers, fasting, renunciation of the world, celibacy, various yogic routines, charity, etc., are all useless exercises."

The hall vibrated with *Bole Bum Bum Bum—Har Har Mahadev* at the end of the *samagam.* It was 3 pm and was getting dark. Rain was about to pour. Arrangements had been made for the devotees, sadhus and participants to go to plains or the railway station of Pathankot. Others were leaving in their own vehicles. Mastana along with hundreds of sadhus was waiting for the truck at the main gate. He didn't show any interest in me. I knew he was on his way to Amarnath Yatra.

By evening, the ashram looked deserted but peaceful and silent. I was not sure what will happen to me! I felt lonely and sad.

Ras leela ballet was scheduled to begin in 'Shiva Hall'. Murali was to perform.

I went to the green room and saw Murali adjusting his headgear in a corner. I picked up the eye-liner paste and with my ring finger put a little black spot on the top of his right cheek. He hugged me softly and planted a soft kiss on my forehead. VIPs were invited, welcomed and seated on the mattresses in the front row of the hall, with Guruji Suryaswami sitting in the centre. All the ashramites in saffron also assembled at 8.00 pm in the hall.

With the beating of the drums, melodious sound of pipe organs, harmoniums and high-pitched *alaaps* of the vocalist, the curtain opened. It was a great opening scene. Lord Krishna came as a king and asked his friend Udhhav to go to Vrindavan with his divine message for *gopis*. I understood everything as I too had performed in my childhood under the direction of Parkash uncle. I was dying to go on stage.

In the next scene there was a conversation between Uddhav and *gopis*. It was a masterpiece of knowledge transfer. The scenes kept changing and finally reached the final act.

In the third and concluding act, the performance reached its peak. It was *'Maharas'*, full of dances and choreographies. Indian and foreign dancers came in their joyful mood. Everybody stood up and started clapping and dancing. The drummers doubled their tempo and the dancers followed. They were chanting and dancing:

'Hare Rama Hare Krishna - Krishna Krishna Radhey Radhey.'

As it reached the peak, the vocalist changed the verse into:

Radhey-Radhey-Radhey-Radhey,
Krishna-Krishna-Krishna Krishna.

Everyone followed:
Radhey ki jay-jay Krishna ki jay-jay
Radha-Raman Hari Govind jay-jay.

Singing the last *kirtan* loudly, the accompanists stood up merrily with their instruments hanging round their necks or in their hands and started playing, dancing and jumping on the stage. Big bells started ringing. Performers went wild and started throwing flowers at each other and on the crowd. Shiva Hall was afire with fragrance and music. An announcement was made for anybody to come on the stage and join the *Maharas.*

Big horns, pipes and sirens were blowing. All devotees were dancing and chanting. *Masti* and music reached a crescendo. I could not resist and jumped straight on the stage and started dancing at my best like a trained classical kathak dancer. I could see appreciation for my dance mainly in the eyes of Murali and two girls, one European blonde and the other an extremely beautiful girl, nearly the same age, equally tall, shapely.

Taking a fast step forward I gestured to the *tabla* player and initiated a typical kathak *tukda* in perfect rhythm with tapping of my right and left foot in quick successions, with my arms delicately rising and falling in tune with the rhythm of my feet and the beat of the *tabla*. I increased the tempo; the beat of the *tabla* increased simultaneously. Everybody on the stage moved back while clapping to the beat.

Thanking my Guru Parkash uncle, I started the masterpiece of kathak the *chakkars* – circular dance movements. With grace I completed 54 *chakkars* and ended with a *tihai* (a kind of bang). Everybody was mesmerised. The two girls started imitating me. The European, whose name I later found was Linda, could not sustain long, though she was performing Indian classical dance so beautifully. The other one, whose name was Bhawna, continued dancing with me till the end, nearly perfect and that was the deciding moment for both of us to become friends and play Radhe and Krishna in the *Maharas*.

At the end we posed as Radhey and Krishna, the same as depicted in the pictures. The hall echoed and vibrated with '*Radhey ki jai jai Krishna ki jai jai*'. Everybody turned to go, their attention diverted from us. I found my arms softly encircling her waist. Unknowingly she moved closer; Linda smiled and clapped. I turned to look at Suryaswami for his reaction, but he was gone.

The VIPs were supposed to leave. A few others were also packing up to go. I had nothing to pack except my saffron *dhoti* and *kurta*.

I was not at all ready to leave this place and go back to Haridwar or Bombay or even home. After everybody had left, Guruji Suryaswami was standing at the main gate talking to Swami Shivananda. It was already late night. Seeing me standing anxiously with other young sadhus he gestured me to come towards him. He smiled and put his hand on my head. I laughed within and cried. Destiny was again showing up like the rising sun.

Next day I was given a new name according to the traditions of the ashram: 'Bal Jogananda'. 'Bal' means young and 'Jogananda' was just a suffix to my name. Jogi was my short name for my sadhu friends. I started to work with more energy and confidence—the most wonderful years of my life were spent in the ashram.

I learned a lot about Hindu mythology and Vedic literature and became one of the most loved pupils of Guruji. My inherent music skill was an added advantage. I led the morning prayers chanting musically and at my highest pitch. I became friends with Radhey, Linda, Shyama, Bhawna, Bala and Jeeta. But Murali Manohar became my best friend.

Extensive religious study and spiritual discipline helped a lot in transforming a raw unskilled Jogeshwar into a spiritually skilled 'Jogananda'.

Chamba became my home and Guruji Suryaswami became my 'father-cum-guru'.

"I know you today. All my queries are answered. I salute to you for your patience," said Gurinder, taking pity on me but feeling love and respect at the same time.

'You know nothing, idiot.' I told him affectionately.

Guri was feeling sleepy. Of course, he knew many things about the ashram, he came to drop Bhawna at the ashram the day before the conference commenced. But not everything.

Gorgeous Linda and Bhawna

Green-blue eyed, blonde Linda was an exceptionally beautiful Scandinavian girl. She was 30 years, 5 feet 7 inches tall, extremely talented. Linda Charlotte Christensen was her full name. When she hummed the Vedic *mantras*, listeners were charmed with her voice. She was from Copenhagen, Denmark and had come to this ashram in search of spiritual piece. She was always seen with Ma Nirmala, head of the sadhvis in the ashram. A journalist by profession, she was keen on learning many new things, including *tantra*. She was working with a leading newspaper *Politiken*, published from Copenhagen. She never skipped her class in the ashram.

It was her second stay at the ashram. She was always the first to reach for the morning prayers and for the Yoga class held in the Ganesha Hall. She always carried a notebook, a pencil, specs and a camera in her bag.

She was cut out for dance. I would play the harmonium and she danced in a ballet called *Radha Krishna* in the Shiva Hall. We performed together in *Maharas*, a favourite Indian ballet of the Europeans. Linda had the curves, the flexibility, talent and beauty to mesmerise anybody. Besides what I knew, she practised meditation in the basement called Kundali Jagran Hall, access to which was not allowed to me.

One day after the morning prayers, we assembled in the Ganesha Hall. Most of the ashramites had gone to attend a function in the plains. Only a few were left in the ashram. The day was cold and windy. We were only a few in the class.

Linda was practising '*Mayurasana*' – a peacock posture, one of the most difficult *asanas* where you have to posture like a peacock, your whole body weight on your hands and thumbs like the claws of a peacock. I was expert in performing this *asana*, trained as I was by Parkash uncle.

I was about to leave when she said, "Yogananda! can you wait for a while."

'Yeah, Leena, of course...what's the matter?'

'Leena' was her Indian name given by Guruji Suryaswami.

"Can you make me peacock, I mean can you train me for this *asana*?"

'Male or female?', I said mischievously.

She thought and then laughed loudly.

"Ok, female peacock will suit better."

In a flash she lay down flat face down the mattress and asked me to support her body.

"Come on, Jogananda, I'm trying."

Palm on the mattress, she made a valiant effort to support her body on her elbows. Unsure of the balance, she quickly muttered,

"Hold me…hold me from under my legs. Come on fast."

I was nervous. Beads of perspiration could be seen on my face. I had never touched a young girl, so beautiful.

I held her under her thighs. The touch was electrifying. Her legs raised up, her skirt was rolled over her round fleshy back. I was aroused. My hands trembled and she collapsed. I was breathing heavily, trying to compose myself.

"Why did you let me fall?" She protested. "Let's do it again."

We tried the second time, the same view. I closed my eyes and held her tight. She succeeded and held this posture for a long 30 seconds. Confidence was all over her face and I was shivering. Linda jumped in a victorious mood, danced a little, hugged me, planted a kiss on my right cheek and said:

"*Tak*."

I said, 'What?'

"*Tak* means…thank you very much in Danish."

'Now let me teach you three words in Danish. 'Hi' means Namaste, '*tak*' means thank you and '*farvel*' means bye bye.'

She was happy, chirping like a bird and went to other things.

One day she said to me, "Jogananda, can you teach Jesper also?"

'Who is Jesper'?

"My boyfriend, he is expected to join us any day."

I felt a kick in my stomach. I wanted to get closer to her. Jesper would soon replace me. I was drawn to her for her beauty, innocence and her visible energy and involvement in all her activities of the ashram.

I got to know from Linda that she would be staying with Jesper in Hotel Mountview, a mile from the ashram. Meanwhile, I was promoted from '*sadhak*' to '*sevak*' because of my devotion, commitment and discipline. Sevaks used to distribute *parsadam* and food to the outside devotees. Maybe my English communication skills helped but it really helped me to explore the beautiful enchanting valley of Chamba. Most of them were lodged in hotels and some of them as paying guests in the town. Mount-View Hotel where Linda and Jesper were supposed to stay was situated at the end of the main street facing the river.

Over two weeks or so, I became friends with the local shepherds. Mohan Chandel, 17 years old, from nearby village Jaito, became my best friend. I would give him and his friends food and sweets left over after regular distribution. If Linda was pretty, winsome and appealing, then Bhawna was endearing, charming, angelic and divine. Bhawna means feeling. It was quite evident on her face. The Mehta family had one more important member in the family. He was young

Sardar Gurinder Singh, now snoring in front of me. Guri was five years younger to Bhawna. Years back, their mother Jagmati Mehta had a nervous breakdown and fell seriously ill. Local doctors could not diagnose the disease and prescribed general sedative sleeping pills to calm her down. Even the best of psychologists and psychiatrists could not treat her properly. She was getting sicker and thinner day after day when finally Bhagwan Dass brought her to the Chamba ashram for spiritual blessings of Guruji Suryaswami at the recommendation of his friend Ramji Dass Chugh. There was a rumour in the ashram that she was 'half-mad' when she came for the first time. She had even thrown stones at the saints. Once she entered the main building of Anand Ashram, opened her hair and created a scene, shouting, "I am not mad…I am a goddess, I am Ma Kali, I am Goddess Ma Kali."

With spiritual blessings from Guruji and special healings from Swami Shivananda, she returned to a normal state of mind. Within weeks, she became healthy and totally religious. The following year she even took voluntary retirement from her job of lower divisional clerk in PWD (public works department) in Punjab and joined the ashram as a full-time devotee.

If Jagriti was outspoken, then Bhagwan Dass Mehta was a man of a few words, a 'yes-man' to his wife. He always had a sad, forced smile on his face. Surprisingly, he called his wife Mataji (Mother). Maybe he was more inspired by the silent saint of the ashram Omananda.

Bhawna was also a kind of a rebel. Even after topping the

university examination, she declined to become an engineer or a doctor. She was adamant in pursuing further studies with exclusive focus on spirituality and religion. Maybe she also inherited this unconventional trait from her mother.

As Ma Jagriti stayed in the ashram most of the time, the Mehta family visited her regularly on all special occasions and customary celebrations. Well versed with Indian culture, she already knew many things which we were supposed to learn. She discussed only '*Vedas*' and '*Puranas*', nothing else. In her spare time she was seen around Omananda and Kali Baba. I was amused... what she was learning from the mutes?

While playing harmonium, Bhawna never looked down on the keys. Her fingers moved faster than mine, of course, her voice was the most melodious. Whatever the topic of discussion, she would easily and logically relate to Indian philosophy. This really impressed me. She gave hard competition to Linda in all the activities of the ashram, including cooking and preparing *moong halwa* for the ashramites. The sadhus vied with each other to attract her attention.

One Monday afternoon, Swami Shivananda as usual asked me to go down and distribute the Parsadam in the Chamba valley to the visitors of the ashram staying in hotels. I was ready with my young brigade of sadhus. There were two groups of boys and girls, Bhawna leading the girls' group. Ashram authorities never allowed the young boys and girls to go together, but they didn't know the truth. We always started as two groups but became one after some time. I found my best friend Mohan and his friends waiting for the free food and *parsadam*. It was Monday and there were special prayers of Lord Shiva. We hurriedly distributed the *parsadam* to the ashram visitors in the hotels as directed by the Swami. Then we gave food packets to the beggars. We still had plenty of time left to go back. I asked Mohan to help us see the valley. Sadhvis also liked the idea and promptly joined us. Mohan showed us the famous Rang Mahal. I was leading the group and he was helping as a guide as he knew all the short-cut routes. We finally made it to the ashram on time for the evening prayers.

In the days that followed, we would visit some or the other temple. Foreigners also joined our group with permission from ashram authorities.

I have sweet memories of Chamba valley in the company of Linda and Bhawna. Here I met Gurinder for the first time. He stayed in the ashram for a day. He was in school at that time and was wearing red tie and blue blazer. I still remember he called me 'Pa-ji'.

Jesper Hansen

Jesper Hansen, a Danish national and boyfriend of Linda, was finally arriving in Chamba. He came with his Spaniard friend Andreas. They said 'Namaskar' to us. Both were wearing the same hats on their heads and carried rucksacks on their backs. Andreas had a camera in his hand. Without wasting a minute, Andreas started clicking photographs of the exterior gate of Rang Mahal.

'Woh…it's amazing...man!' he exclaimed.

Then he shot the cows who were struggling to find food in the centre of the street. We went inside the Rang Mahal. Jesper slipped in a corner with Linda and what he did was most amazing for Indian sadhvis and me in particular.

He hugged Linda, picked her up encircling his hands around her waist, made swirling circular movements in the air and placed her softly back. Not caring about our presence, Jesper pushed her to the wall and locked his upper lip on her lower lip. I tried to look aside and found Bhawna looking at them. She immediately cast her eyes down. Her face turned crimson red. Linda held Jesper from his head and started stroking his hair wildly with her hands. The palace walls were lined with exquisite wall paintings depicting the life and times of Lord Krishna and Radha in romantic moods. We left for the ashram, Linda and Jesper for the Mount View Hotel.

Next morning, Jesper and Andreas came with Linda to the ashram. She told them about the ashram activities. Andreas clicked the photographs of different yogic postures.

As I entered the Ganesha Hall, they welcomed me with the customary 'Namaskar'.

"Hey, Jogananda…will you please teach *mayurasana* to Jesper," she said.

'Of course, why not?' I said like a beaten rat.

I pulled my mattress to start but found Andreas almost

jumping out of the window.

"What are you doing, man?" I cautioned him.

"Capturing the Himalayas," he said.

'Ok... please take care…the window is cracked.'

Scandal in the Ashram

It was the most scandalous, wicked day of my life. Being Saturday, special prayers were offered in the ashram to please 'Shani Devta'. Shivananda gave me a list of hotels that I had to visit with no food but only *parsadam*. It was early morning and I was all alone for this job. It was easy to carry the small *parsadam* packets in a bag.

I stepped through the narrow passage and headed down to the valley where hotels were situated. As usual I was walking and singing to myself the hymns of Shani Devta '*Om-Pram-Preem-Prom-Sha-Sanishchraye-Namay*' meeting the local folks on the way, shepherds, beggars and newly made friends.

They wished me 'Namaskar'. The scene of Linda and Jesper smooching was on my mind. I decided to go to them at the end of my round.

Expecting another love scene, I composed myself, stepping up the stairs and stood in front of room No 102 on the first floor.

As I was about to ring the doorbell, I heard strange, loud sounds from inside the room in an alien language. I could not make out what they were saying, but it didn't seem normal. I stood speechless. Some English words made it clear that they were fighting. I heard Jesper saying, "Fuck you, I am going right away." Then there was a crashing sound of a glass with Linda shouting back 'go to hell' and the door opened. Jesper came out wearing only jeans, saw me with a small packet of *parsadam* in my hand. I said 'Namaskar'. He said nothing, instead went again inside and started shouting furiously in Danish. I was half in and half out of the room.

Linda appeared hyper. She was in a loose silky half pant and a short T-shirt. While shouting Jesper held his shirt on his shoulders. The room smelled of pungent cigarettes. Empty and half-filled glasses confirmed they were drinking. With wild eyes, Linda yelled at Jesper, pointing towards the door. Jesper said '*Tak*' and picked up the glass full of beer and smashed it on the table. Linda's eyes were red hot. She pulled out an artificial bouquet made of iron and hit it at his head. Jesper was wounded at his chin and bleeding. Immediately, I rushed towards him for help, but he pushed me aside with his full force.

Furious, Jesper said, "Hey, you get aside… get lost."

I was about to leave when Linda said: "Jogananda, don't go."

Jesper went out shouting abuses at her. She started crying. I was speechless standing near the table. I started picking up the broken pieces of glass. Linda was still weeping. I asked her permission to leave.

Linda wiped her tears with a hanky and stood looking at me. Unexpectedly, she hugged me and started weeping again. Next few minutes were pleasantly difficult. She was not in a mood to let me go. To cool her down I opened the bag and got out the *prasad* pouch. She took a small piece of sweet, ate half a bite and smiled, inserted rest of it in my mouth. Then she singled out a small black pouch hidden under the sweet and strode towards the couch.

It surprised me. I didn't know what that was! She took out a black piece, scratched off a part of it and started mixing with tobacco from a tobacco pouch placed on her side table. I was stunned, as the smell was similar to what Mastana used to smoke and Sandeep Chaudhary rolled into a cigarette and Bhoora smoked in Ambedkar Colony. It smelled almost similar but more pungent. In a flash, I understood what Shivananda was distributing to foreigners in the hotels.

Linda singled out a white shining paper out of a cigarette paper flap and placed it on her lap, plucked a piece of scratched hash and started burning with her lighter. Then she mixed tobacco with hash on her palm and finally placed it on the white paper. Wrapping it well like a cigarette, she fixed it meticulously with her saliva rotating her tongue from left to right like an experienced customer. I couldn't believe my eyes. How could she mix hash with her devotion and spirituality! She lighted the cigarette and inhaled a long puff, throwing the lighter on the side table.

Sitting carefree on the sofa, she again puffed hard at the cigarette, looked slightly up, letting out spirals of smoke and offered the cigarette to me without uttering a word. I couldn't decide what to do. She looked straight into my eyes and said: "Come on Jogananda, this is nothing but meditation. Take it, come on, honey," she said in an intoxicating tone.

I gave a harder puff to prove that I was really somebody and not just a typical orthodox Indian. Imitating her, I made an attempt to create spirals of smoke. Instead, spirals started erupting in my stomach. I started coughing violently, tears blinding me. I picked up my bag and somehow made out of the door. I hastened down the steps straight into the lawn inside the hotel breathing heavily for about five minutes till I came to my senses. Usually it took me 25 minutes to reach the ashram but today it was different. I didn't know why. It might be the effect of hash or of Linda. I was thinking about Shivananda, Linda and even Guruji. I doubted everybody, wondering whom to believe and whom not to!

As I reached the main gate of Anand Ashram, I found it was closed. I had never seen the gate closed. Seeing me, the guard opened it. Inside I heard some female screaming. Many ashramites had gathered and were looking up. Bhawna had loosened her hair and looked weird. She was shouting and yelling from the balcony. She was about to jump. Sadhvis were controlling her and Ma Nirmala was monitoring the situation. Pushing aside those two sadhvis, she ran down the stairs into the temple and started ringing the temple bells vigorously. Sadhvis followed and again tried to get hold of her but looked helpless. Bhawna picked up a *trishul*—a sharp trident of Lord Shiva. Sadhus came out of the kitchen and thought of ways to control her. I joined them. Shivananda moved forward to catch her but she pushed him aside, pointing the *trishul* at him and shouting she said, 'This is not an ashram but a prostitution centre. Suryaswami is a fraud; he is a rapist,' she started crying violently, her nostrils flaring, eyes red, her hair messed up. She said, "You can't do it to me. Fuck your mother, you son of a bitch. You ruined my mother. You better kill me or I will kill you."

Ashramites had gathered all around, including the foreigners, though they could not understand what was happening. Shivananda asked Bala to take the foreigners to Ganesha Hall.

She was uncontrollable and could do anything. Ma Nirmala pounced on her. Bhawna took hold of Nirmala's hair and threw her aside screaming, "You whore! How dare you touch me!" She was abusing Shivananda. Looking at me, she warned, crying loudly, "Jogananda, run away from here. They are rapists and criminals, don't spare even their daughters. I will tell you everything. Jogananda, you know nothing."

Shivananda stared at me. It really made me uncomfortable. We were not allowed to intervene in the ashram affairs. It was the second time she included my name. Shivananda forcefully pulled her by her hair and dragged her into the basement, the so-called meditation centre. Ma Nirmala and her girls followed him.

Looking at the young sadhus following him, Shivananda shouted in anger, "Hey you, get lost and resume your duties." I was about to leave with the sadhus, when he looked hard at me, again, and said, "Jogi, you stay here till I am back."

Bhawna was screaming, yelling, crying and weeping. Sad and helpless, I was looking at her till she was pulled down to the basement. I waited but Shivananda didn't come back.

It was evening. Everybody was tightlipped but inside they knew what had happened. Nobody had the guts to say a word. Meanwhile, a rumour erupted among the ashramites regarding Bhawna. One sadhu revealed that Bhawna had been molested by Shivananda like her mother.

I was worried why Shivananda asked me to stay and why he didn't turn up again. What did he want from me? I was being trapped for no reason.

Murali understood my problem but the poor guy was not in any situation to help. He was an orphan and dependent on the ashram.

I could not sleep the whole night. The world looked cruel again. I could not believe anybody on this earth.

I was half asleep, trying to get away from all this. Linda

and Jesper; their love scene; their fight, and now Bhawna, so innocent and talented, fighting for her life. Forcefully, I closed my eyes, Shivananda then appeared on the screen of my mind: Rapist! And a smuggler! Restless, I got up again and gulped down a jug of water. I went up to the window and looked outside; it was dark. I thought about Guruji.

Where was he? And what was he doing? Why is he not coming out?

It was the most devastating day of my life.

Enormous Kundali-Jagran Hall

I felt lonely, completely cut off from the sea of humanity. Nobody belonged to me; I belonged to none. I had no plans. Everybody had questioning eyes but none dared to converse. As expected, Linda and Bhawna were absent in the morning yoga classes. I had no way to find out where Bhawna was lodged. Shivananda didn't show any signs of regret and remorse. He asked me after the morning prayer, to go and distribute *prasadam*. Bhawna had openly accused him and Suryaswami of raping her. Why didn't he react? Where was Bhawna? I couldn't ask anybody. Days passed with suspicion and suspense.

A few days later, Linda appeared in Ganesha Hall for her yoga class. She looked dejected and depressed. Even with me she was not normal and instead focussed on reading.

Two weeks later, Bhawna was seen with Ma Nirmala and Ma Jagriti in the hall for the evening prayers. She was not at all her natural self. Impulsiveness and spontaneity was lost. She looked different. Even with me she was indifferent. I could easily make out that she was mentally deteriorating day by day. It seemed that she was forced to stay. Ma Nirmala and Ma Jagriti and other girls had a surveillance over her. Still, she managed to disclose that she was planning to escape from the ashram.

In contrast, Omananda and Kali Baba were still meditating in the ashram. Krishnanada was mute as ever. They believed in their *'karma'* and gave a damn about *'maya'*. Still, you could hear thc sounds of screaming and shouting coming from the basement of the ashram. It was torture or a healing procedure, I didn't know at that time. I had completely lost respect for Shivananda and Ma Nirmala, still I greeted them every day the way I was accustomed to.

Same day, at night a blue car entered the ashram gate. I came out to see it like other sadhus did.

Bhagwan Dass Mehta got down from the front seat of the car followed by a young Sikh wearing a red turban from the back seat. It was Gurinder. Bhagwan Dass went up the stairs and Shivananda welcomed him with Namaskar mid-way. Ma Nirmala also joined them accompanied by Ma Jagriti, Bhawna's mother.

They discussed a little and then Nirmala gestured the girls at the first floor window to come down. I saw two girls stepping towards her holding a girl whose face was covered with a cloth, a kind of veil. It was Bhawna wearing clothes she hadn't changed since many days. She looked half-conscious and unable to stand. Her mother was helping her. Shivananda was composed but there were signs of anxiety and nervousness on his face. Guruji came from nowhere. This was the first time I saw him tense. Young Guri was seeing all this with his innocent eyes. I felt he knew everything but didn't have the courage to speak.

Suddenly, she jerked away and stood on her own and said, "Don't touch me, get aside." Her mother came forward; she pushed her hard and starting yelling and accusing everyone. Her mother tried to close her mouth but failed.

She yelled, "You all are cowards. Nobody has the courage to speak. This is not an ashram."

While pointing to young ashramite sadhus, she said, "Run away, I am telling you the truth."

Bhawna half opened her eyes and happened to see me, though I was standing at a long distance.

"Goodbye Jogananda," she muttered and tried to wave her hand at me before she was seated in the car, with her father on her one side and her brother on the other.

Sadhus first looked at me and then at Bhawna. I exchanged a look with Bhawna. I had tears in my eyes. It was terrifying as I had no role to play except a bond of lovely wonderful friendship.

Guruji Suryaswami and Shivananda declared that it was all because of bad spirits. In a minute, the car was gone.

I completely lost my interest in the ashram. Though there was nothing special between Bhawna and me, yet I was missing her like anything. With Bhawna gone, half my life was gone from my heart. I missed her.

Kundali-Jagran Hall

Next day I was summoned by Shivananda to meet Guruji Suryaswami. Worried, I asked, 'What happened Swamiji ?' He said nothing, instead gestured for me to wait. He went straight to the basement while I was waiting alone. Negative thoughts gripped my mind. I was sure that as usual destiny would play a trick. He came after 15 minutes, each minute like an hour. He said nothing, just gestured I should follow him. He was heading towards the basement and I was following him. I was eager to see the mysterious 'Kundali Jagran Hall' but fear gripped me all over. When we finally entered the basement, I could not believe my eyes. It was as huge as the ashram outside, with modern architecture and facilities.

We walked past many halls. Crossing a long mysterious passage, Shivananda entered a big air-conditioned hall, a kind of a retiring room where yogic *kriya* was in progress with sounds of 'Shiva' and 'Shakti.' Suryaswami was in 'Natraj' posture wearing a white gown. Many foreigners were sitting and watching as if in a trance. He was performing '*Shiva Tandav*', a special form of dance, a bit similar to Mastana's, which I had seen on the banks of the river Ganga in Haridwar.

Standing on his left leg, with a trident in his right hand, he was dancing and chanting with intermittent force on the words, '*Jata Tavi Galai Jvale Parvah Pavitasthale.*' His eyes were raised up to meet in the centre of his forehead, and his dance movements had double momentum, as swift as a tiger. He looked wild and possessed. Even the disciples in the hall looked different, lost or maybe hypnotised. I regretted my doubts and believed in the supernatural powers of Suryaswami for a while. As I was looking at them intensely with guilt inside me, all closed their eyes and went into a deep mode of meditation.

I stood away in a corner with Shivananda. Finally, Guruji Suryaswami sat on a big cozy chair and started his discourse:

"Sex has distinct and separate purposes. The male and female are conjoined physically, and represent 'Shiva' and 'Shakti'. Beyond the physical, a subtle fusion of Shiva and Shakti energies takes place, resulting in a united energy field. On an individual level, each participant experiences a fusion of one's own Shiva and Shakti energies like procreation, pleasure and liberation. Those seeking liberation eschew frictional orgasm for a higher form of ecstasy, as the couple participating in the ritual locks in a static embrace."

I stood listening. I felt deep compunction and remorse. He went on:

"Sexual rites may have emerged from early Hindu *tantra* as a practical means of catalysing biochemical transformations in the body to facilitate heightened states of awareness.

These constitute a vital offering to *tantric* deities. Sexual rites may have also evolved from clan initiation ceremonies involving transactions of sexual fluids. Here the male initiate is inseminated or ensanguined with the sexual emissions of the female consort, sometimes admixed with the semen of the guru. The *tantrika* is thus transformed into a son of the clan (*kulaputra*) through the grace of his consort. Although popularly equated with *tantra* in its entirety in the West, a minority of sects historically practised such sexual rites. For many practising lineages, these *maithuna* practices progressed into psychological symbolism."

"Now practice the divine *kriya* of Shiv and Shakti."

Devotees in pairs commenced the *kriyas*. They were so erotic and hot that this made me befuddle initially and spellbound later. Suryaswami then called Shivananda and said something in his ear. They moved out to the corridor. Shivananda called me to join.

Suryaswami said, "Don't get confused with this '*tantric maya*', Jogananda. You had enough experience of ashram affairs. I know, '*tantra*' is still a secret art for you. Don't worry, you will soon get to learn it. It is an advanced exercise practised in the tutelage of a special Guru. I will teach you all. You need to understand sex in order to understand *tantra*. The poor girl, Bhawna, couldn't understand. May God bless her!" He raised his arms.

I bowed down and touched his feet. He blessed me.

"Listen, Jogananda...Don't waste your time with

Omananda and keep away from girls."

I was taken aback.

"I know you are young, these things happen, but don't mix with Bhawna too much...ok...maybe Linda," he smiled.

'Yes, Guruji,' I said, stunned.

"If you want to stay in the ashram then follow Swami Shivananda and Ma Nirmala, otherwise you will have to go to the same place from where I rescued you. Don't forget Punjab Police. Keep your mouth shut and help in ashram affairs. I don't want to hear any further bullshit about Bhawna."

I nodded.

Finally, he said, "From today you are promoted to sevadar of the ashram, follow the orders of Shivananda. May God bless you, my son!" he turned and went inside.

I was upset with Bhawna and angry at Suryaswami. Bhawna committed a mistake by openly alerting me about the ashram.

Sevadar was a promotion from sevak. I was not interested in it but there was no choice.

Sevadars had a different lodging facility. It was an independent room with attached bathroom and television. Shivananda showed me all and strictly told to keep the secret from the sevaks. I had tasty and healthy dinner in the basement. I had not imagined two governments existed at the same time at the same site.

Murder, Mystery and Suicide

Being sevadar of the ashram, I was free from paltry jobs of cleaning, helping in the kitchen etc. I had some special powers. I was free to move anywhere in the ashram, even in the mysterious *kundali jagran* basement. Many things unfolded as I assisted Shivananda in his underground activities. *Parsadam*, I learnt, was a mixture of sweets made with cannabis, which was giving the hallucination effect of meditation. The black packet beneath the sweets which I used to distribute in the hotels, was charas, a type of Himalayan hash. With my sense of smell, I could differentiate Kashmir and Afghan hash. Within days, I became an expert delivery boy and a henchman of Shivananda.

He was operating this huge network of drugs with the blessings of Guruji Suryaswami. Ministers, police officers, bureaucrats and army officers were involved in this racket. Hidden farming of cannabis and marijuana in the adjoining areas was flourishing up to Pakistan-Kashmir border. Smuggling across the border was a silky smooth action carried out specifically in Doda and smuggled to India. Topmost army officers on both sides of India and Pakistan were at peace on this issue though they had strong disagreement on the international border issues. Everybody involved was making good money.

Saliulla Bukhari, an Afghan national, the main supplier of opium and marijuana, had his own farms in Kandahar. He had control on hash farming in the western province of Pakistan and even in India. He was the biggest supplier of opium and marijuana.

It was now clear to me how huge money was flowing in the ashram. Earlier, I thought that the money came only by donations but I was wrong. Young sadhus including Bala were helping in smuggling hash. Strongly built guys acted as musclemen. All was hidden and underground. The whole operation was managed in an old building adjoining our ashram building. From outside it looked a dilapidated old house, inside it had different exit gates from the ashram. Most expensive cars of the world were parked inside it.

Three weeks later, a local newspaper report created a stir in the ashram and the areas around. It was a scandalous story about Suryaswami and Bhawna with some pictures in the local dailies. They even published an interview with Bhawna.

By evening, a youth brigade of the ashram was ready to take action. In the leadership of Shunty, the strongest young man, four jeeps started off to the plains of Pathankot. I was also a part of this party. I was sitting with Bala. We stopped at the outskirts of Pathankot where the office-cum-press of newspaper *Sach Ka Sapna* was located. It was late evening. Shunty hit the glass door with a hockey stick and the glass fell into pieces. He thrashed the security guards. Two more came but after looking at the scene, they ran away. Within minutes, all the computers, keyboards, printers, etc were thrown out into the street. Smashing the rest of the accessories, Shunty and his accomplices then jumped back into the jeep.

Shunty yelled, "Off to Aggarwal."

We followed his jeep. The jeep scratched to a halt in front of the house of J J Aggarwal, Editor-in-Chief of *Sach Ka Sapna* in Friends Colony.

"Come out, Aggarwal," Shunty screamed, kicking at the door. It opened.

There was standing a sobre-looking man of about 50 years, shaking in his legs.

"Are you Aggarwal of the newspaper?" Shunty asked.

"What happened?" he said, hands folded.

Holding him by his collar, Shunty dragged Aggarwal onto the back seat of the jeep where two guys were already waiting. He got on the front seat. The driver reversed the jeep like a circus driver and sped off. We followed him instantaneously.

We dashed back to the ashram and entered through the back door. Shivananda was already waiting for us.

"Got him," Shunty said, pulling Aggarwal down, Punjab Police style.

"Take him upstairs," Shivananda said.

Thus was kidnapped the owner-cum-editor of a local daily published from Pathankot. Local reporter Bharat Rishi Ram had published this report on the basis of his interviews with Bhawna and Gurinder. The headline: 'Ashram a centre of sex and drugs'. In another news box the paper said, 'Bhawna is pregnant.'

Suryaswami came in and said, "You wrote this shit?"

"Guruji, I don't know, the report was submitted by Bharat Ram."

"Who the hell is this Bharat Ram?"

"Guruji, he is a new reporter who joined us last week. I was on leave when he committed the blunder."

"Do you know what you have done and its consequences?"

Aggarwal stood up, fell on his knees and said, "Pardon me, Guruji, I promise, I will correct everything. Give me two days."

"Fix everything in the next edition, otherwise you can imagine the result for you."

"Guruji, I will manage, and I will fire that bastard Bharat Ram today."

Aggarwal took a complete U-turn and Guruji promised him help in his business.

The paper published a completely changed version of the story the next day. It explained that Bhawna was psychic, eccentric and a crazy girl. Ma Jagriti, her mother, claimed that her daughter Bhawna was sick and depressed. She supported Suryaswami and the ashram, elaborating that she herself was an ashramite for the last 20 years and no such thing had ever happened. Bhagwan Dass Mehta stated that his daughter was not pregnant. It was a bogus story cooked up by the newspaper.

I didn't know who was right and who was wrong but the last part of this incident was shocking. The brave journalist Bharat Ram died in a road accident near Pathankot next day. This was a clear-cut murder. None out of the leading newspapers reported anything about Bharat Ram. People in and around Pathankot were openly criticising and condemning Suryaswami and his ashram.

To defuse the tension, Guruji ordered Bhagwan Dass to bring Bhawna back in the ashram. Late in the evening, Bhawna's mother Ma Jagriti with the help of Ma Nirmala forcefully brought Bhawna to the ashram.

I knew their plan. Abortion. A loud thud with a long shriek was heard at about 3 am. We rushed out of our rooms into the open. Bhawna had jumped from the top floor of the ashram. She lay in a pool of blood, dead.

The first to reach was Omananda. As expected, he was mute and expressionless. Ma Nirmala joined him soon. Krishnananda was weeping. All the ashramites were shocked and most of them were weeping. Blood-stained Bhawna was lying in the centre of ashram between the temple and stairs. I could not control my emotions. I realised my hidden love for her even though we never expressed our feelings for each other. Soon Shivananda came, and instead of showing any grief gestured to Bala to go somewhere. Soon he went out with Ma Nirmala.

The dead body was kept in the ashram and everybody ordered to go back to his/her room. Shivananda was seen making preparations to transport the dead body. Bhawna was taken to her ancestral village Dudike Kalan for cremation.

Before dawn, we started our painful drive to her village. Except Omananda, Malang Baba and Krishnanada and a few others directed by Shivananda, everybody else got into cars, trucks and jeeps. Guruji intentionally allowed everybody to reach Dudike Kalan to show off his following and supremacy.

We reached the village. Bhagwan Dass Mehta was already waiting at the crematorium with his close friends and relatives. The village folks who had heard about the tragedy gathered too. The atmosphere was heavy and tense. As we got down, her relatives and friends screamed and cried. Surprisingly, Bhagwan Dass and his wife looked blank, expressionless.

Bhawna's brother, young Guri, was standing aside, his face stony, his eyes burning with revenge. Sadhvis covered the dead body with a white cotton sheet. Petals were showered all over. Ma Nirmala placed a garland of red roses. Finally, the body was placed on a heap of dry wood. One local priest started humming the Vedic *mantras*. The eldest of the Mehta family,

Gulshan Dass, consigned the body to flames. The entire crowd contributed small pieces of wood to the burning body and folded their hands in 'Namaskar' as a mark of respect and final goodbye to the departed soul.

Suryaswami started his condolence speech.

"Death of Bhawna is the biggest personal loss of my life. It is the hardest day of my life. I have lost everything. I pray to Almighty to give peace to the departed soul. I have lost my daughter and the most talented girl of our ashram, I am feeling guilty that it has happened in my ashram."

Suryaswami acted smartly as his crocodile tears showed up in his cruel eyes. Revengeful eyes of Guri were observing every action of Suryaswami. I was observing both.

Suryaswami continued, "I will not remain silent and will find out what exactly had happened in the ashram. I know some mischievous element has done all this to bring a bad name to the ashram. I will not remain mum and the person responsible for this heinous act will be behind bars, I promise to one and all present here."

All of a sudden Gurinder picked up a burning stick from the flame of dead body and hit Suryaswami on his head, shouting and abusing–"Son of a bitch, you are a liar, you are a rapist… you killer. You have killed my sister. I will kill you, bastard."

I jumped in between and controlled Guri. Others followed me.

Furiously, he shouted, "I will not leave him Pa-ji. He is nothing of a Guru. This rascal is a rapist and a murderer…;

leave me alone. I will burn this dacoit right away."

Gurinder was getting uncontrollable but we were many to overpower him. Shaken, Suryaswami declared that the ceremony was over and got into his car with his personal security. In the next jeep were Shivananda and Ma Nirmala. We also got into our respective jeeps and cars. Nobody was talking. Our caravan of cars, jeeps and trucks was on its way back to Chamba Ashram.

Back to Pathankot Jail

When I woke up in the morning, I was not in the ashram, I had a severe headache and felt numb. Where the hell was I? It was a police station. I couldn't believe my eyes. Who brought me here and why?

When we came back to the ashram from the cremation at Dudike Kalan, I got out of the car with Murali at the main gate. I was not at all in a mood to eat anything and straight went to my room. Tired, I immediately went to sleep. Before that I only ate one sweet *laddu* offered to me by Shivananda, I could not refuse though I was not hungry. I didn't remember anything else.

I had been sleeping continuously for 48 hours. My cell had

a mattress and a jug of water. I gulped down one full jug of water and cleaned my eyes, then I heard a sound of footsteps approaching my cell. It was dark inside the cell.

A drunk policeman opened the door. Without any preliminaries he said, "Drop your pyjama."

'Sir!' I pleaded.

"Do as I say," he thundered.

'Why? Sir?' I asked.

He pulled my hair, pushed me to the wall. Then he started slapping me with both his hands one after the other, keeping up perfect timing.

The flap on his shoulder said, 'Punjab Police'.

Within seconds, I dropped my lower.

'*Bainchhod... murga ban.*' (sisterfucker, become a chicken).

Without delay I turned into a chicken.

This policeman had two table tennis-like rackets. Holding me by my hair, he smashed these rackets on my protruding naked ass one after the other with full force, power and vigour.

I jumped up in the air and lost my balance.

He gestured again, *'Murga'*.

Tears in my eyes, legs trembling and body aching, I somehow managed to pose as *murga* again.

Spitting on my ass, he struck the racket with herculean power again. An electric current like sensation flashed through my body and I was lying flat on the ground. He kept hitting till he got bored. Then he said, "You rapist, terrorist, son of a bitch, I will see you later," and left the cell.

My headache was turned into a total body ache. It was clear to me that I had been implicated in the Bhawna suicide scandal.

Next day, I was remanded in the interrogation room. Around 20 young boys were already standing in a row when I joined them. Officers were writing the reports and getting them signed. Most of the guys had beards and turbans. The police showed the photographs of dreaded extremists to all. Everybody denied. When my turn came, one officer said, "Sadhu Baba, you might be knowing someone of these."

I simply said, 'No sir, I don't know, I am from Haridwar.'

After interrogation, I was asked to move into another room. Two policemen were already waiting. It was the torture chamber. They asked me to take off my clothes. One policeman started beating me like an animal, so ruthlessly that my feet and fingers started bleeding. He tied both my hands and legs on a special wooden board and passed electric current through my body, stretching my legs apart to extreme limits. He finished his job in 10 minutes as he could see my urine and blood all around. From the adjacent rooms, sounds of crying and screaming were heard, indicating that the other people too were being tortured.

Now it was the turn for the other policeman, who raised the temperature of the machine to a point where it became miserably hot and then he suddenly brought it down to freezing cold. Finally, he opened my hands and legs and said to the first, "Get another ready."

I collapsed on the floor. There were bloodstains on the ground. All were not mine.

He shouted, "Clean them and get out."

I cleaned the bloodstained floor with my underwear and got out of this hell limping and crying. Another guy was thrown in for the same procedure. I was back in my cell, specially designed for the suspected militants of Kashmir and Punjab.

Wicked experience forced me to stop believing in the existence of God or any character like this on earth. I was made a scapegoat by the ashram authorities. Alone in this cell, I was cursing my destiny when a policeman threw in two *chappatis* in a bowl. Hungry, I picked up one but couldn't eat the whole of it, I was crying so much.

Four weeks later, I became used to it. I learnt the meaning of life; even the worst memories of my past seemed sweet. I was lucky in my saffron. The officers were not as cruel to me as they were to others. I even escaped the traumatic pethidine injection procedure by police which made guys crazy, half mad and schizophrenic. No FIR was lodged as there were no terror allegations against me. I became friends with other boys called terrorists. When the officers were tired of inflicting torture they enjoyed their drinks in the police station itself. Because of my good behaviour I was assigned the job to serve these officers with water and tea in the night.

When the police was boozing, the detained people talked. Sufferers shared their miseries.

I thought of Sandeep Chaudhrary. There was no FIR lodged against me. Sandeep could be the one to get me out from here. I became hopeful. But how to contact him was the question. I knew his permanent home address but the most difficult thing was to smuggle a postcard into the jail. I endeared myself to all of them with my sense of humour and dramatic skills.

The day I got the postcard, it was a great moment. I felt I had some chance. All alone, I wrote a letter in my cell. Bhola, a water carrier, and big fan of old Hindi songs was ready to drop the card at the nearest post box.

I was wrestling with my mind, when I heard '*Bole-Bum-Bum-Bum*' outside the police station, similar to our ashram sounds.

Footsteps were approaching my cell. I immediately hid the postcard under my clothes, closed my eyes and pretended I was sleeping.

I realised someone had come near my cell.

"*Oye khada ho... Guruji Aaye hain,*" some voice said.

Suryaswami was standing right in front of me.

Putting all my histrionics to the test, I started weeping. On my knees, hands folded, I started pleading, 'Guruji please save me, please forgive me. I swear, I am innocent. I have no connection with anybody. I did whatsoever Shivananda asked. I am your servant. Please save me.'

Surprisingly, Suryaswami looked stressed. He put his hand softly on my head. Wiping my tears, he said, "Trust God. Everything will be alright. Do always as I say fortune will smile on you."

Within minutes, I was out of Pathankot jail wearing my saffron *kurta* and *pyjama* and sitting in an Ambassador car. It was the second time in my life that Guruji came to my rescue, when I was in dire straits.

"How long you have been here?" said Suryaswami.

Even though he knew, I answered:

'Three months, Guruji.'

"Do you have any connection with the extremists?"

'I swear Guruji; I do not know a single person'

"Did you know you can be liquidated any minute by the anti-terrorist squad?"

'No, Guruji'

"I have saved you today, my son. Do you understand?"

'Yes, Guruji, my life belongs to you now.' I said.

"No, no, I cannot keep you in the ashram. Instead you will be sent somewhere."

'Yes, yes... Guruji.'

"Do you know Gurinder's address?"

'I think, he is somebody working in the ashram garden.' I said hesitantly.

"Don't be oversmart. I'm talking about Bhawna's brother."

'Yes.... Guruji,' I said promptly.

"Great."

Then Suryaswami turned to talk to Shivananda. I thought destiny was smiling on me once again!

ॐ

To Be or Not To Be

It was afternoon. I was lucky to come back to the ashram, but not at rest. I felt lucky as I had never visited any place again in my life once I left it—whether it was my home town Sangariya, Vasai or even Haridwar. Memories of my past flashed in my mind. Of all, the worst image was that of Bhawna lying dead in the centre of Anand Ashram. With full force I diverted my attention from her and focussed on Suryaswami. Ok, he rescued me once to use me as a henchman in his hash-trade but why he rescued me now was a question! Obviously, I couldn't relax until I found the answer.

I took bath, had my lunch and was relaxing on my bed,

when Shivananda came and knocked at the door which was already open.

"Jogananda, come along to Guruji," he said.

I followed him to the basement of Kundali Jagran Hall and then into the personal room of Suryaswami. He was sitting in his royal chair relaxed, with Linda sitting beside the chair leaning over and listening to him very intently.

I went near and touched his feet, folded hands and said Namaskar to Linda. Guruji gestured me to sit down. Shivananda occupied a cushion seat on the floor. Looking at Linda, Suryaswami said in a very polite tone:

"Ma Leena (a new name given to Linda), Jogananda is a nice boy but is very unfortunate. His stars are not good for the time being. He was trapped by the police. God is merciful, through me He saved him. His case with the police is very complicated, although I have got him out temporarily. I wish he is helped and there you are to help him. Leena, I need your help in getting Jogananda out of this trouble. Even though I know that the charges are bogus, I cannot do more than this. This is a difficult time because of militancy. Take him with you to Denmark. I will make every arrangement for both of you. Just prepare his sponsor papers."

"I will do as you wish…Guruji," Linda said with folded hands.

"May God bless you, my child."

He wanted to discuss the matter with me, so she left the room. Shivananda moved closer to participate.

Suryaswami said, “Shiva go at once and check the level of water in the tank.”

Shiva walked away like a wet mouse.

Placing his arm around my right shoulder, he took me to his special room loaded with luxurious expensive accessories, electronic items including branded automated weapons. Looking straight into my eyes he spoke in a harsh tone, “Listen carefully, you have two options left for yourself—either die in an encounter with Punjab Police or enjoy your life in Denmark.”

‘I am ready.’ I touched his feet and said, ‘I swear, I’ll do whatever you say.’

“Finish Gurinder, shoot the fanatic asshole, before you fly to Denmark. He is raking up Bhawna’s case in the local media and ruining the fair name of the ashram. He is a screwball. Why you! I know you are friends. No foul play with me. Whatever you need, go to Shivananda and mind it, Linda should never know about it. Now go, you have only three days to carry this assignment otherwise…You understand very well.”

I was stunned. The mere thought of killing Gurinder filled me with guilt.

Shivananda supervised everything I needed. He got my papers and passport ready. First I was photographed and then Linda got some papers signed. This made me believe that something good was coming my way. Before killing Gurinder I had to kill my guilt.

Who sent me behind bars?

Who got me released and why?

In my room I thought about Suryaswami, how smart was he to exploit the bonding between me and Linda and then with Bhawna and Gurinder. I didn't think that Gurinder had done this much of damage to the ashram in the media. Gurinder was hot-tempered but not to that extent.

It would have been a great blunder to refuse the commands of Guruji. I had already seen that the police could keep me in a cell for months without any allegation...what Suryaswami could do if I dared refuse! There was no way out except to kill Gurinder.

I was angry with myself and with the whole world. Gurinder is not my 'friend' I thought to myself, but he is a true sufferer and a brother. My destiny and his were no different as far as our sufferings were concerned.

Out of all this depressing circumstance, there was a ray of hope in starting a new life in Denmark. I had read in school how beautiful Denmark was and that it was one of the happiest countries in the world. I thought about Linda, whether she was helping me or there was something else. Linda, now Ma Leena, didn't know anything about this terror plot. Suryaswami did one thing fine while declaring that the entire allegations were bogus in front of Linda and Shivananda. So she, I thought, was saving an innocent. Even the visuals of Shiva and Shakti were flashing in my mind. I remember, Linda inquired a lot from me about Bhawna. She once joked if I liked Bhawna. This might have been because of her split with Jesper. Suryaswami, with this idea in mind, was killing many birds with a single stone.

I will have to strangulate and suffocate to death my own

soul to kill Gurinder. But then Bhawna came before my eyes: her innocence, beauty, talent and her dream to live on, and her body lying in a pool of blood in the ashram and finally the scene at the crematorium. I couldn't think of killing Gurinder, a photocopy of Bhawna. I started crying and didn't know how long I cried.

At last I controlled my emotions. Suryaswami had made my passport with his connections in the police and the ministry of external affairs and naive Linda helped him for this genuine cause.

Uncanny Plan of Action

It was 2nd of March. Winter had mellowed down in the plains but not in the hills. I had a guilty conscience but was focussed on the job at hand. I left the ashram around 11 am in an ashram car with the driver-cum-handyman Jeeta. I had all the information of whereabouts of Gurinder. He had left his home-town and was presently residing with some friends in Singhpura Colony in the centre of Pathankot city.

Jeeta was a local man, speaking local 'Dogri' dialect mixed with sweet Punjabi. His job was to take me wherever I wanted and now he was driving down from the Himalayas to the plains. This time Chamba's serene beauty and air didn't feel refreshing but suffocating. Firstly, I doubted Jeeta. Maybe Suryaswami had sent him to keep an eye on me as he was working for the ashram for many years. He knew every detail of the ashramites including Bhawna and Linda.

I waited inside the car while he booked a room in Surya Lodge, situated in an isolated area of Pathankot, a highly populated city. I gave him a 500 rupee note and said:

'Ok, Jeeta...here is a 500 for you, relax and enjoy... till I am back,' I said and left him alone, walked along the road to the inside of Singhpura Colony. In about 15 minutes I found myself before house No 34; knocked at the door but nobody responded.

I knocked again, harder this time and called loudly, 'Guri, I'm Jogananda, open the door.'

"Sat Sri Akal, Pa-ji...wait...I'm coming," a voice was heard.

The door opened and before me was Gurinder. He hugged me, took me into his room with due respect. There was somebody else there, maybe his room-mate. He wished me, got up and walked away. He was Tony.

Without wasting a moment, Guri started abusing Suryaswami. "Pa-ji, I must take revenge on him. You know I left my home the day Bhawna was cremated. I have nothing to do with my parents. I'm sure he hypnotised my mother. My father, you know, has no balls. I must kill this bastard before I kill myself. I'm sorry, Pa-ji. Let me get you tea."

He went into the kitchen.

I was thinking to myself, Guri looked completely changed.

He was ready to kill or be killed. I needed to divert his mind from Suryaswami.

I called aloud, 'Guri, how about your studies? What do you plan further? Want to become doctor or engineer?'

He shouted, "I want to become a killer Pa-ji. Your Guruji hasn't left much time for him. I won't leave this lech and expose him through media."

'Guri, relax *yaar*. Ok, you must kill him. I am with you.'

He got two cups of tea with some snacks. Placing the tray on a stool, he said, "Pa-ji, I wanted to get a degree in journalism, but now nothing. I want only Suryaswami now."

'Forget him *yaar* for a moment; Let's go somewhere to eat or see a movie.'

I was trying to be comfortable and at ease, but Gurinder was not. When I first time met him in 'Rang Mahal' in Chamba, he was not volatile like this, rather he was very sweet and friendly.

I said, 'See, Gurinder, I have left the ashram, I am fed up with all this and now I want to start a new life. I'll be doing anything but not going back.'

He was happy to hear it. We had lunch together. I made him talk about other things except Bhawna, ashram and Suryaswami. After lunch he seemed relaxed and suggested we take a nap. Again we had tea at five in the evening. He was now ready to go out for a movie and dinner. My mind started calculating. It wasn't an easy task to finish him in the cinema hall, restaurant and not even in his room because his room-mate would be with him.

We hired an auto rickshaw. On the way we stopped for a while in front of Surya Lodge. I went inside and saw Jeeta enjoying drinks with his new friends. This really made me feel relaxed. In silent language I told him to continue with drinks and girls and I won't be coming back for night.

I tried but couldn't talk to Guri till we got down at Ritz cinema hall.

Ritz was showing Amitabh starrer '*Muqaddar Ka Sikandar*'. We purchased tickets and snacks and entered the hall. Gurinder enjoyed the film but I was giving final touches to my planning. On our way to Moti Mahal restaurant for dinner, to ease my tension I started humming a song from the film.

We reached Moti Mahal but found it overcrowded. I suggested going to Sanjha Chulha. There I ordered two tomato soups; Gurinder went to the washroom. Here was an opportunity to mix the poison into his soup. I couldn't because of a waiter not moving away from our table. I couldn't eat much. Two days were left. I was surprised when Guri asked me to stay for the night as his room-mate had gone to his native village in Amritsar. After dinner we didn't converse at all. Gurinder was in his own thoughts.

At night, when he was asleep, I took out my 0.32 mm silenced pistol from my pocket, stealthily got down from the bed. There was no gap between the bullet and his life. The muzzle of the pistol was nearly touching his heart. I was about to pull the trigger. The whole earth seemed to whirl, strange noises were heard in my head, my forefinger vibrated like an engine but showed no strength; my hair at the back of my head was wet. I didn't know who I was; I was almost losing my senses. I couldn't shoot him. As I turned, a small steel plate covering the jug fell off. The noise was enough for Guri to wake up.

Half-asleep, he muttered in confusion, "Who's there?" Then he saw me and asked, "What happened, Pa-ji?" At once I hid the pistol and calmly said, 'Nothing Guri, I wanted water.' He went back to sleep. I could not sleep the whole night. I had failed in both attempts.

I got up late next morning. Gurinder brought me a cup of tea along with a popular daily *Punjab Kesri*. The front page flashed the news that a tourist bus had rolled into Ranjit Sagar dam. Sixty-three dead. An idea flashed in my mind that this was the best chance to make this murder an accident, throwing him in the dam. It was my last chance for my salvation; a make or break situation. I finalised my plan.

I told Gurinder that I would be going to see Ranjeet Sagar Dam in the afternoon. Intuitively I knew he would go with me. He said he would give me company. At about 2 pm we hired an auto rickshaw. While taking NH-I we followed the Sujanpur Road. Travelling further 5 km we got down at Shahpur Kandi Fort, near the dam. Finally, we reached a lonely spot called 'Thein' named after the village on the edge of river Ravi on a high altitude area, hardly ever visited by anybody.

With nobody around, I decided to act. In an instant, with both my hands I tightly held him by his arms below the shoulders and said in full confidence, clenching my teeth and looking hard at him, 'Forgive me Guri, I am going to throw you into this river.'

He was shocked beyond all imagination. His eyes wide with fear. He simply said,

"Yogi…You too?"

I felt like Brutus killing Caesar, pointed revolver at the centre of his head and said, 'yes me…too'

"But you can't…I'm Bhawna's brother. Come on, shoot me."

'This is not a joke, Gurinder. I'm a killer.'

"What are you saying Pa-ji?"

'I am a killer; I am going to kill you right now. Jump else I will shoot you.'

"Pa-ji, what have I done?"

"Don't call me Pa-ji, you bloody fool."

He burst into tears. It was too much for me. I let go my hand of his arm and the pistol fell from my hand. I stood silent. He was crying; I was breathing loud, emotions overpowering my sense of reason. Wiping his tears softly, I shouted at him:

'Come on idiot, what made you think that you alone will kill Suryaswami. Don't you know his powers and connections. Don't you realise that you are a mere child before him. '

His situation overwhelmed me, bringing tears in my eyes. I told him the entire story why I was with him.

I held him again by his arms and said persuasively, 'Run away from here to any place, maybe Bombay or Delhi, otherwise you will be killed and if you don't run they will kill me or make my life a dreadful misery.'

"I am not a coward, I will not run; instead I will take revenge on him," he screamed.

'Relax, use your common-sense; you are too young, don't be rash. I promise I will be the first person to help you in taking your revenge. You don't know my story…my brother…I will tell you at the right time. Now listen, this is my order. Run away and change your name and identity; otherwise you will have to die like journalist Bharat Ram. Don't you understand? Get lost, I am telling you…, for God sake, get lost anywhere, and leave this place.'

I convinced Gurinder to leave the place forever detailing all the criminal activities of the ashram and the big nexus of police and politicians with Suryaswami. I made all arrangements. I gave him Rs 2,000. Chakki Bank Railway Station was 4 km from Pathankot, from where he could board the train to Bombay or Delhi. He opted for Delhi as he had some connections there.

Late evening, we were at Chakki Bank Railway Station and I made sure that Gurinder left Pathankot. We made a promise to each other that we would wait for the right moment to take on Suryaswami. Gurinder boarded Jammu Tawi Express in front of my eyes while I waved him off.

I came back to Surya Lodge where Jeeta was sleeping drunk in his room. I woke him up. We started our journey back to Chamba. Jeeta inquired about my task but I changed the topic to prostitutes. I was frightened as I did not know whether I had done it right or wrong but I had a perfect story for Suryaswami.

Reaching the ashram, I went straight to the basement where Suryaswami was about to start his 'Shiva Shakti' *kriyas* with young ladies.

Touching his feet, I said, 'Guruji, you will never see Gurinder in your life. I have thrown him in Ravi near the Thein village.'

"Jogananda, may God bless you. Get ready for your final liberation and flight to Europe."

I held his legs with gratitude. Suryaswami blessed me, stroking my head and said, "Your documents are ready. Go and ask Ma Leena."

Suryaswami again went to his class of advanced meditation to teach different postures of *Kama Sutra*.

I went straight to Linda's room. She was waiting for me with the documents. Seeing me, she smiled and gave me the passport. Usually, I was the dominating partner in our discussions with her, showing my language skills and of course the peculiar yogic skill of *Mayurasana*. But right now, I was a mute obedient pet following her orders.

Flight to Denmark

It was 15th of March and I was at Indira Gandhi International Airport waiting for Linda Christensen. Our flight was in the late evening. The scorching Indian summer had made its presence felt. Foreigners in half pants, some with T-shirts and some even without, but all of them with rucksacks on their backs were entering the airport, suggesting they had enjoyed the weather in India.

I even thought of running to Bombay or to Haridwar but no, I could be in trouble again. More so, if Gurinder was seen by Suryaswami or his men, he would certainly find me out of hell. The best thing was to fly with the wind.

I was waiting outside the terminal when Linda came up and stood before me. There were two other girls with her. They folded their hands in *Namaste*.

Linda pulled out a scarf and fixed it on my head, smiled and said, 'You look awesome baby.'

I liked the way she called me 'baby'. Then she got talking with them. I couldn't understand Danish, but from their expression and occasional laughter I could make out that they were happy and surely enjoyed their stay in India. In a group we went to the Russian Aerofloat counter and they issued our boarding passes. Linda had my passport and was doing all the formalities.

Linda gave me a book titled *Life in Scandinavia* and asked me to go through it while we were waiting for our flight to Moscow. Though I had no energy to read, I flicked some pages.

It was very difficult for me to relax, but I was trying my level best. I knew nothing about my future and was totally dependent on Ma Leena. Meanwhile, she slipped in a corner with her friend Maja.

Though I was pretending to read, I was focussed on Linda. I could make out that she was puffing a cigarette in the smoking zone. When she came back, she smelled of mint instead of tobacco. I laughed inside as she thought I was naïve.

Suddenly, I felt myself like an alien in my saffron sadhu outfit in this lounging area. Long hair, unshaven face and turban were so peculiar that many foreigners gave me strange looks, some even folded their hands and said *Namaste*.

I got rid of the exotic turban and sported the woollen cap in a stylish manner. I covered my saffron dress with a trendy jacket. Linda reacted immediately, "Jogananda, you look great, baby."

Now we were crossing the immigration check, one of the officers smiled at me while matching me with my passport photograph; Linda came forward and got it stamped and gave a bigger smile to the officer. We were approaching gate No 7B.

With childhood friends Nirmal Joseph, Sandeep Chaudhary and even Ali Murtaza, I dreamt about flying one day to a foreign land. Here I was entering in a big Russian plane along with Linda. Niels and Maja occupied seats on the right side, while me and Linda on the left. The plane was scheduled to take off at 3.15 early morning. The air hostess started the demonstration of safety belt and I got a little anxious. My anxiety doubled when she demonstrated about emergency landing, exit gates, parachutes, etc. Linda helped me in tightening the belt and whispered in my ear, "Jogananda, hum some *mantras*."

Forget about *mantra*, I was about to pee in my pants because of fear. I cleared my throat and started *Hanuman Chalisa*. Linda held my hand and whispered, "Slow... Jogananda...slow."

I lowered my sound to the minimum, Boeing took off with full velocity and my ears seemed to erupt. I was like an extraterrestrial in this plane where majority of the passengers were westerners and Indians were in western outfits. Linda was holding my hand with all the warmth. She didn't enquire anything; Why had I been in prison? What did Suryaswami want from me?

Early morning around six, we arrived in Moscow. We were waiting for our connecting flight to Copenhagen. Linda brought coffee for me and started to smoke. While sipping coffee, I glanced through a few pages about Scandinavia in general and Denmark in particular.

I had read in my school days that Denmark was the best milk-producing country in the world. Then I didn't care how a small country could make its people proud. More people were languishing in Indian jails than the total population of Denmark. My flight to Copenhagen was full of dreams, visualising a new country, new people, new climate and, of course, new culture. I recalled Bollywood films showing beautiful picturesque Europe.

We landed at Copenhagen at 10.30 in the morning. We came out and it was all white everywhere. It was snowing. Wow! Copenhagen looked spectacular. Weather was similar to early January in India.

Fellow travellers started complaining about snow, a long winter and, of course, recent climate changes. I had never seen this much of snow in my life. My childhood was spent in a desert. What a feeling! Man of sand now in the land of snow. What a renewal!

Linda hired a taxi for Vanløse, a suburb of Copenhagen. I sat beside the driver and Linda sat on the back seat. The city of Copenhagen looked great with clean roads, spectacular architecture and design. On the way we crossed many dazzling bridges over and under the beautiful sea-canals. There was no crowd, only a few people on the streets. Linda said something in Danish and the driver halted his cab in front of Seven-Eleven, a 24-hour open kiosk.

She purchased fruits, pizza slices, cans of beer, chocolates and a few packets of cigarettes. We headed towards a street called Herlufsholmsvej. She entered a big bungalow. Her's was a two-room apartment full of books, magazines and papers, lots of pens and a personal computer, typical of a journalist. She was living all alone, quite surprising for me, as I had never seen any female living alone in India. There was only a single bed large enough for two people to sleep together.

Throwing her bags down, she went straight to the bathroom. Surprisingly, she came out brushing her teeth and more surprisingly, she gave her own toothbrush to me, knowing I had no brush.

Back in the ashram in India we used *neem* for cleaning the teeth. In my happy days in Chamba, I remember, I lectured her on the medicinal values of *neem* for teeth and gum care. Colgate, Close-up and Pepsodent were only used by illiterate people, who did not know the value of ayurveda.

I was brushing my teeth in the washbasin when I saw my face in the mirror.

I thought to myself: 'Jogender, what the hell are you doing here man?'

I laughed a little at myself.

Linda took her bath and suggested that I also needed one.

She looked smashing, even the most beautiful heroines of Bollywood couldn't have matched this Scandinavian beauty. When she came out of the bathroom, she was wearing a white loose night suit, only the upper but lower was missing. She put on her lower in front of me. It was quite a cultural shock for me, but normal for her.

I immediately rushed into the bathroom and opened the knob of the shower in excitement. I screamed as burning hot water splashed on my face and later on my naked back.

'*Hey Bhagwan* (oh God),' I exclaimed.

"What happened, Yogananda?" she asked.

'Nothing, nothing.'

I adjusted the knob to correct the flow of hot and cold water. I was trying to create foam out of the soap when Linda opened the door.

"Here are your shorts and t-shirt."

She did not look at me, but I felt nervous.

In sky-blue T-shirt and brown half-pants, I looked entirely different. I used this type of uniform when I was in St. Mary's School.

Meanwhile, she laid the table with eatables. A candle was burning in the centre.

She poured red wine in glasses for her and me.

"*Scold,*" she said.

'What?'

Scold means 'cheers' in Danish.

"Cheers for your new life and, of course, escape from the police."

Hesitantly, I also said, '*Scold.*'

"I will be happier if you simply say Linda," she suggested.

'Ok, then call me Jogi instead of Jogananda,' I said.

"Ok...Yogi."

'Jogi.'

"Yogi."

'Jogi.'

"Yogi.'

"Jogananda, we pronounce 'Jogi' as 'Yogi' in Denmark."

I realized that Danes pronounce 'j' as 'y'. So, I finally became 'Yogi' in Copenhagen. It was a divine transformation.

I took the glass and in a second finished the glass full of wine like Bhoora used to drink in Ambedkar slums in Mumbai and said, 'Ok, I am Yogi.'

Linda started laughing at my speed but complimented me.

"Great, Yogananda, you are an expert."

She again filled my glass.

I realised my blunder when I saw Linda sipping the wine. I tried to copy her.

I was feeling very light, as if flying on wings. She looked like somebody from the seventh heaven and she started to roll a cigarette the same way as she had rolled in Mount View hotel back in Chamba. She burnt the weed and mixed it with tobacco like an experienced player.

We smoked and drank an hour-and-a-half while we shared our experiences in the ashram. While smoking, I recalled the images of Kali and Shiva. 'Charas' in India is used to awaken *Kundalini*. At first *chakra* it hits the sex centre. It was hitting both of us.

The natural urge took over both of us. I can't recall how it started or who started it first, but I found myself lying flat on my back while she was on top of me. I nestled my face into her bosom and closed my eyes. I was transported into the other world for a while. How long it lasted I cannot exactly remember, but the experience was so overwhelming that it made me crave for it again and again.

Linda was sheer magic. She taught me what making love could mean on earth. '*Kama Sutra*' and '*tantra*' seemed a failure in front of Linda.

She was like a nature deity, symbolising sexuality and fertility, like an earth goddess and I was rain quenching her thirst in those magic hours. It was the blessings of Lord Shiva or the effect of marijuana, I do not know.

Cannabis was showing its effect on raising a serpentine energy inside my system, extending from the brain to the base of the spine. It was an amazing, most fantastic experience of my life. I fell into sleep, so sound and deep as never before.

We slept on the bed meant for one person.

Next morning, Linda was sitting near her window and was reading a newspaper with a mug of coffee in her hand.

"*Namaste*, Yogi."

While avoiding eye contact, I pretended to remove something from my eyelid and said:

'*Namaste-ji*… Ma Leena, sorry sorry...Linda.'

Cycle–Tour Around Copenhagen

Next day, Linda was ready with two cycles to tour around Copenhagen. I was a bit reluctant as I hadn't cycled for many years but cycling is a skill you never forget in your life. I had cycled last when I was 12.

It was a cool, chilly and windy day as it had rained last night. The sun was playing hide and seek. As soon as the sun appeared, Linda yelled, Wow! But for me even the cloudy sky was fascinating. There were no signs of humidity even after the rains. When we got out, I saw altogether different lanes and traffic lights for cyclists. There were more cyclists on the road than cars, in contrast to India where the cycle is only driven by the poorest of the poor.

It was unbelievable to see the traffic lights at the famous City Hall Square. Cyclists were first to go as soon as the light turned green followed by cars and later by buses and heavy vehicles. It would have been reverse in India: first trucks, then cars and cyclists, forget the pedestrians.

After half-an-hour, we reached Tivoli Gardens, the world famous amusement park like Appu Ghar in Delhi. Danes and other white Europeans including their children looked so neat and clean, disciplined and happy, buying tickets at the counter in perfect order. In India, was a crowd sweating, elbowing, pushing, shouting or pick-pocketing. I really wished to stay here for the rest of my life.

Linda had specially prepared tuna fish for the day. She sandwiched the tuna fish with boiled potatoes in black bread. We had our breakfast in Tivoli Gardens and soon we were on the most famous 'Walking Street' of Copenhagen. It is a long 4-km street starting from City Hall, ends at the harbour, with every type of shopping mall and eating joints at every square. On both sides of the street, street performers were showing their spectacular skills. Primarily, they were guitarists, pianists, acrobats, magicians, clowns, buffoons, South American dancers and modern dancers. I remembred my Indian street performer Mastana and our first street performance at Haridwar. I wished I could perform here.

In the afternoon, we reached the harbour and the tourist spot called Nyhavn. Soon, we were in the motorboat, surprisingly, with our cycles. I came to know that cycles are allowed everywhere, in buses, trains and even in the metro train. There is a special space and stands for cycles. The boat journey was thrilling, spectacular, till we reached world famous 'Little Mermaid'.

Little Mermaid is a statue on the shore of the sea dedicated to Hans Christian Andersen, the great story teller of Denmark. I guessed even fairy-tale writers needed fun for creative writing. The wooden boats tied to the piers were the clearest reminder that Nyhavn was once the destination of sailors arriving on ships from the Baltic and beyond.

People were sipping beer and relishing the moment. Beautiful Danish girls were sipping beer and enjoying the sun at the sea-shore, lying on mattresses naked and half-naked, with their cycles parked beside them.

I felt like a chimpanzee allowed by destiny to have a view of heaven on earth.

I was almost lost when Linda said, "Yogi, would you like to see 'Free Town' today?"

'Free town! What do you mean? Better than this?'

"Yeah, of course, better than this. Christiania is a town of hippies, a town without government. This amazing place is a self-proclaimed autonomous neighbourhood of musicians, artists, intellectuals, social security recipients, pensioners, and immigrants."

We were cycling over the sea canal bridge connecting Copenhagen to Christiania when Linda stopped and asked me to look to the sides of the bridge. There were two specially designed buildings on either side. Opera Theatre gifted by the richest man of Denmark on our left side and Nordea Bank building on the right.

Magnificent, dazzling, alluring, the Opera Theatre stood in the centre of the sea, water all around. What an architectural design. Linda lighted a cigarette and blew spirals of smoke in the air. She looked great as her hair turned golden in the sunlight. What a country, man! Open and free.

Soon we were in Christiania walking on the most controversial street of the world, called Pusher Street, full of marijuana shops and hippies. Houses were built in an extremely creative, improvised style on the banks of canal and some even in the canal, like water boats.

The beauty of the town was enhanced by many folds of sea canals. I found Christiania a bit closer to my heart and roots as I could see some Buddhist flags on top of buildings, like Majnu Ka Teela in Delhi.

Linda said, "This is a crazy place developed in 1971 at a military base by hippies and artists." In fact, the green ramparts of Christiania appeared much more recreational and attractive to me than the well-maintained gardens of municipal Copenhagen. Another attraction for me personally were the people practising yoga in the park. Artists, musicians, painters were busy in their creative arts.

It was evening and time for us to go back to Vanløse. She stopped for a while to purchase some weeds. This street gave a spectacular ambience similar to little '*paan-beedi*' shops everywhere in India. There were dozens of shops with every kind of weed displayed in a dazzling style with multi-colour bulbs. The red-light areas of Mumbai, Bheendi Bazar, also has the same architecture and light design. I did not know who copied whom.

Linda purchased a hash-smoke, lighted and puffed. She didn't seem happy with the quality of weed from the vendor. I moved forward with total authority. Smelling and tasting a little weed with the tip of my tongue, I said, 'This is neither Kashmir nor the original Afghan'.

The pusher and his friends were amazed at my expertise.

"What's your name?"

Linda responded quickly to avoid any trouble.

"Yogi…Yogananda…my friend from India."

He picked up another small black piece from the stall, gave it to me, and said:

"I will give you two free smokes if you can identify what this is."

It was a challenge. Many people gathered to find whether I was right or wrong. I exchanged a look with Linda. It was slightly different from our Indian stuff but I had seen it too. It was greenish brown and a bit hard. It had no aroma. I tasted and found it was not spicy either.

Hesitantly, I said, 'African'. For a few seconds there was complete silence. He came close to me.

"Great, this is Moroccan," he exclaimed. "Hey Man… I am

Lars Rinnerup. He is Bent… Michael and he is Janik Møller, the Boss." Janik was sitting in a chair and was tuning a guitar.

After introducing all, Lars Rinnerup came to me, gave me a can of beer and said, '*Scold*'.

Janik, middle-aged boss, now got up from his chair, picked up another piece from the stall and gave it to me. He really seemed like a boss of this group.

"Hey man, can you tell what is this?" he asked.

It took me no time to recognise it, but deliberately I delayed my reaction.

The piece was black from outside and brown inside. It tasted spicy and sweetish.

'100 per cent Nepali Mandir Bells.' I said with authority.

"Waw! Great! Man, you are genius."

Janik high-fived first me and later Linda.

"Hey… you sweet Indian, you are fantastic," Janik appreciated me for my worth.

'Hey Janik, you forget about the name. I can even tell which stuff is good for heart, liver, meditation and for a good sex,' I said with a mischievous smile.

Everybody laughed.

Janik, the boss hugged me and then said, 'Namaste' folding his both hands. We were leaving. He invited me to meet him again. He said in a jovial mood, "*Farvel…* Linda, *farvel...*Yogi, you are always welcome if you need any help and, of course , free *chilm* (hash) in particular."

'*Chilm*' and '*Namaste*' were the other Indian words used

by Janik Moller which made me at ease and made me sure that this man had some strong Indian connections.

Night at Vanlose was almost a complete replication of the first night but with more advanced *kriyas*. As a good student, I was learning the art and trying to make Linda happy. I mimicked Mastana in love making. We had a mind-blowing time and, of course, mind-boggling sex.

Soon, I acquainted myself with the Danish black bread, Copenhagen cycles, Scandinavian salad, European beer and addictive hash. Destiny was again smiling on me.

Black and White

I was in love with Linda. She loved me no less. When she was out for few hours it seemed like days. Love is great, beyond boundaries and barriers of the world. We would remain silent looking deep into each other's eyes for hours. Tomorrow she was to join her job. I also needed a job to survive in this most expensive city of the world.

Linda brought *Copenhagen Post*, a leading English newspaper, and marked some vacancies. Though in every job, the pre-requisite was Danish language but she comforted me and said that in Copenhagen almost everybody speaks English and secondly for helper job, there was no need of fluent Danish. She asked me to contact all and try my luck.

I tried and tried but didn't get a single response. Confident of my human skills, I thought I could find a job easily, but it was difficult.

After two weeks, I decided to meet in person the agencies and owners of Indian restaurants. I took out my cycle and started exploring the wonderful city. Copenhagen had many Indisk restaurants. But to my great surprise, majority of them were owned by Pakistanis, known as Indians to avoid being called as fundamentalists or Talibans. Danes gave a damn about this Indian or Pakistani stuff, for them it was all the same; they loved the Tandoori Chicken.

Pakistanis were very generous and welcomed me with warmth in their typical Punjabi accent.

"*Sat Sri Akal,* Singh Saahib," one said.

Without wasting a single moment, I became Punjabi and responded in the same dialect.

For them Singh meant Sikh. They didn't know that Singhs are found everywhere in India. In majority of them, I noticed hatred for Hindus and love for Sikhs. They always offered free food but never a job. I made a list of Indian hotels, pizza houses and cafés and started visiting them one by one. I didn't get a job but made good friends.

This struggle made it clear that there were only slim chances of getting a job on legal papers. A job with black money was the only possibility. Immigrants called it *kala* meaning pay no taxes. Danes were very particular in paying taxes as they had a strong social security system based on taxes.

Frustrated, I was trying my level best to find any type of job. I made a connection with a kiosk owner who spoke Pashto-Urdu. Gul Mohammad, an Afghan in his late forties, was a nice man. He offered me a job when I showed him I could mimic like an Afghan.

My job was to fill the empty refrigerators with beer, milk and juice cans, in return for 150 DK per day. It was around 15 DKK/hour against the legal minimum of 100 DKK/hour. When I informed Linda, she became furious of this injustice and I had to leave the job at once.

I stopped working with Gul but he became my good friend. Gul told me everything about the '*kala*' and 'white' work. Surprisingly, he himself was jobless on paper and was drawing a big unemployment dole from the government. Simultaneously, he used to smuggle 'Coke' from Germany and distribute in Copenhagen. This kiosk was in the name of his brother-in law Rashid Malik. A smart act! He was not paying taxes at all. He looked very pitiable but was, in fact, a millionaire, had big land, farming, orchids back in his village, Haziriyaat-e-Hind in Kandahar, Afghanistan.

Eight weeks passed and I couldn't get a job that Linda would approve. Linda was adamant that I should get proper money and not be an under-paid worker. One day I got a lucky break. 'Pizza cum Shawarma' house was ready to hire me as a kitchen assistant on paper with a salary of 110 DKK/hour. Makhdoomi, an Arab, was running this shop.

Makhdoomi fired me within four hours. Though it was a simple job of chopping onions and cabbage, I couldn't satisfy egotistic, long-bearded fundamentalist Arab.

Frustrated, I tried everywhere. Three weeks later, Indian restaurant 'Shezaan,' run by a Pakistani, Mansoor ul Haq, hired me as waiter. It was on Istergade Street, full of red-light clubs, discos, striptease joints and pubs. At night on the street you could find tourists and locals wandering in search of prostitutes.

I found Istergade Street more interesting than my job. Beautiful girls of all colours from every continent of the world could be seen. It was a street of gangsters, pimps, prostitutes, burglars, gamblers, nightclub doormen, swindlers, and all the others for whom the red-light district was a natural environment to thrive but there were no fights at all.

After around two weeks, Mansoor also started the half-black and half-white salary routine. I had a little quarrel with him and subsequently left the job.

Danish language proficiency was the biggest barrier to find a decent job. Linda enrolled me at Norreport Danish Language school. I joined the school and started learning basics like *Hvorden har du det, Velkommen, Undskyld*, etc:

How are you, welcome and sorry.

I tried many jobs but none actually worked out. Honeymoon period was over and the frustration of making some money had started getting heavier. I keenly observed and copied Danes: how they talk, how they walk, how they eat and how they behave.

It was not easy to understand Danes. They were very straight and clear but very private. More than 70 per cent of the population was living all alone. After 16 years, the government encouraged the young ones to live alone. There was no concept of a joint family. Most of the Danes were either divorced or never married. Live-in relationships were quite popular. Even the gays and lesbians were living in this fashion. They were truthful but not emotional.

I got many offers to work as a driver. I thought of becoming a driver. But acquiring a driving license was a big hurdle. Driving exams were as tough as PMT/IIT exams in India.

I found Linda increasingly stressed. She was hassled because of her job or because of me I failed to understand. Meanwhile, she helped me in my documents including the all-important 'yellow-card' essential for my legal residence. One afternoon she came back from her office in a very bad mood. To calm her down I made a cup of coffee and an emergency joint. I decided to meet Janik Møller at Christiania.

Christiania–My Mini India

Struggle and adventure have always been an essential part of my life. I entered Christiania with 100 kroner in my back pocket, courtesy Linda. I was in search of Janik Møller and his hippie gang whom I had impressed in my first encounter.

I was wandering in search of destiny in this oasis of self-governance, collective spirit, and individual freedom that had lived with its own will, tolerating vices and soft drugs. It was one of the world's last remaining anarchist communes. Cars were banned and residents printed their own currency.

The walls of houses were decorated with flowers and paintings like it were in my home town, Sangaria.

Like in India, Christianites preferred vegetarian food as majority of them were converted Budhhists or Hindus. Christiania had three yellow dots on a red piece of cloth as their national flag. This community abused the European Union on a big billboard.

Presence of leash-less, stray dogs made me feel I was at a place close to my roots.

A St Bernard, a dog the size of a pony made its appearance from nowhere while I was crossing Sunshine Bakery. First, he inspected the whole area with a single look, like he owned the place. Then it came near me, howled wildly and started licking my hand with love and warmth. So, I got a canine welcome considered lucky in Indian mythology.

Like in India, there were many handicraft shops on both sides of the street, the way we have in the Himalayas but no brown-black Indians bargaining and hawkers hawking in a melodious sound and, of course, no Janik Møller. I stood before an Indian handicraft shop to enquire about Janik.

"*Namaste*, What do you want, Baba?" said an old woman.

Bettina, a 50-year old lady, owner of a little shop, was selling mystic Indian articles. Bettina became my immediate friend. She was financially contributing to an orphanage in Benaras, running this shop for the last 30 years. A regular visitor to India, she had adopted four orphan girls and was helping other less-priveleged kids. She said she purchased cheap handicraft articles from Paharganj market and sold at a good price in Christiania.

"*Chai chalegi*?" she asked.

Desperate to meet Janik Møller, I said impatiently, '*Phir kabhi*, I want to meet Janik Møller right now. Do you know him?'

"Come on, who doesn't? Oldest of the old hippies. Go straight and you will certainly find him on the street. But no permanent fixed place for him. Sorry, he is like that."

I went ahead and witnessed a wonderful graffiti: Live and let others live freely. There was a wonderful carousel-sized Buddhist stupa with a string of multi-colour flags like we have in Tibetan colony near ISBT, Delhi.

My mini-India! I gave a new name to this place, which was once the site of Danish naval barracks. Soon I reached the extreme right corner of the extremely popular and controversial street of Christiania called Pusher Street, where Janik was playing drums with a guitarist and sipping beer simultaneously.

I went close and started listening to the beautiful harmony. We exchanged a look and Janik immediately stopped playing, came close to me, hugged me warmly and yelled, "Wow, here comes a little genius."

He opened another beer and gave it to me. There were two other guys sitting with him. He gave me a stool to sit. Musicians again started playing. Forgetting my worries, I started enjoying the jazz orchestra. Everybody was relaxed and smiling.

Musicians finished their performance and Janik started delivering a long long speech like a soliloquy of a play. Janik used wonderful literary words and his accent was intoxicating. He was drunk or might be on a trip. He spoke mixed English and Danish. Only after a while I came to know that he was discoursing on stress-free living.

He smiled and again introduced me to all, "Meet my exotic friend Yogi."

Abruptly, he said, "Yogi, Hey man, you are from a great country. What the hell are you doing here? Go back from this hell."

I was shocked as I was expecting some job and here he was asking me to go back. When I finished my beer. Janik gestured and his assistant gave me another. I was not in any position to refuse. Janik started criticising his own government.

"Christiania is not a place. It is our religion, our way of living, and the result of a Cultural Revolution. We, the old hippies, came with this idea of free living. I was among the first who smoked *chillum* here."

He said, "Do you know about *chillum*?"

'Yeah… of course,' I said.

"Then you must be knowing about *tantra* also."

'Yeah I do, but not much'.

"Great! you are from a wonderful land which we used to call the dream-land of hippies. What brings you here, man… maybe your bad *karma*. I still remember my first journey to your motherland, India. Wao! What an adventurous journey! There were few phones at that time and it was next to impossible to call back from India. It was in 1970. You were not born then. I started my journey with my hippie friends from Copenhagen Central Station. What a journey! I still remember passing from the Khyber Pass in Afghanistan to Pakistan. It took us one month to reach India through East Berlin, Athens, Istanbul, Tehran, Kabul, Lahore and mystic Delhi. I love Delhi, a dreamland of hippies. I cannot forget that horse tonga which we hired at Ferozepur border, and that gigantic steam engine of the Indian Railways. Wonderful, warm, exotic people, ever smiling tea vendors, strange smells and the dust. What a country, man! What a journey!"

Soon he asked, "What you need, man? Afghan, Kashmir or Moroccan? Oh yes, you need charas."

'Boss, I need nothing but a job,' I said.

He sighed, gulped a full beer and said, "Do you speak Danish?"

'No,' I said, 'I am learning but I need some job that does not require speaking Danish. Secondly, the job should be on papers as Linda is not comfortable with black money.'

He took a long puff, placed the empty bottle of beer on the ground and said, "Tell me, how much you need, Yogi? You can borrow from me."

I was silent.

"Ok Yogi, you are welcome in our business, but you have to work and follow our system and discipline."

'Yes', I said.

He high-fived and said loudy:

"Great, now we have our original Indian vendor selling

Shiva's magic weed. Yogi can differentiate different varieties of weed, and that is all about our trade. Ok, you will work with Eric in a street shop, 150DKK/hour and incentives. If you need any thing else come to me straight."

"*Scold*," he said.

I imitated and said '*Scold*'.

So I got the job as an assistant in a small beautiful decorated marijuana shop owned by Janik and his freaky friends at famous Pusher Street of Christiania. Salary was far better than the normal jobs.

It was relaxed and happy. Even the timings were flexible. I was to deal with a variety of people, which I liked. I was lucky to be amongst the most intellectual, well-travelled artistes of different genres. All of them spoke English. They were well mannered. I felt life was going to be beautiful.

Happy Time in a Hippie State

It was the luckiest day of my life in the happiest country of the world. Life is never a straight line but an electrocardiogram. When I was mulling how to convince Linda about the Christiania job, I got more great news. I was appointed to distribute a free advertisement paper *Metro Express* at 100 DKK/hour on papers. I was interviewed three months back for this job by Jorgen Mortensen. In my heart, I thanked Surya Reddy, a south Indian IT student who introduced me to Jorgen. Surya was studying computer sciences in Copenhagen University and was working part-time with *Metro Express*. In paper distribution, there was no need of language skills so majority of expatriate students were doing these types of jobs. Only requirement for this job was a broad smile and the sense of timing to throw the paper to cyclists.

Being a theatre artiste, I had the skills in abundance for the job. I sported a red nose of a clown and used my body rhythm. I enjoyed my job of street distribution like a street performer. Initially, I was offered the job for two days in a week in front of Nørreport Station, but within a week I impressed my employer with my jovial mood and theatre skills. I was shifted to Tivoli amusement park traffic lights. Likewise, my job days were doubled from two days a week to four days.

Standing at traffic lights, I was able to engage in non-verbal dialogue with cyclists and pedestrians. Other guys lacked charisma. Within weeks I became the best distributor as there was cut-throat competition with another free advertisement newspaper *Urban Express*.

I purchased different types of wigs and typical South American hats from a secondhand market. I became so popular that cyclists missed me when I was on leave. Lotte, a beautiful Danish girl, working in Danske bank, got so impressed with me that she threw a little red packet at me while accepting the *Metro Express*. Though for many weeks we were smiling and waving at each other, but it was a big surprise. After distributing all the papers I opened the gift packet. It had a box of chocolates, a red rose on a piece of paper.

Hurriedly I opened the letter. It was a beautiful handwriting, written by a green sketch pen on brown paper with a picture of a red rose: 'You are amazing man…love you…we should meet.' Lotte Karlsson, Call me: 80404040, 89 Vesterbrogade Street, 4th.

Every day after finishing my job with *Metro Express* I used to rush to Christiania and in the same way smile, interact and perform in front of my marijuana shop. Both jobs had common philosophy: interaction and socialising, a trait I cherished most in my life. I became friends with vendors, musicians and artists of Christiania.

Many Danish business organisations used Christiania as a showplace for their foreign friends and guests. The purpose was to show something special that they could not find anywhere else in the world. Evening time was always spectacular, with around 40 well-decorated stalls selling different kinds of cannabis – the weed of Shiva. It was the happiest time in my life. Fun and money were abundant.

Linda lost her job but blissfully got pregnant. Linda was not upset losing her job. The Danish government provided double the normal salary to pregnant women. The government was encouraging its nationals to have more children. Muslim immigrants were exploiting this clause to the maximum. It was a lovely time dreaming about an exotic child. Linda was imagining that the future baby would inherit my curly hairs and features but her green-blue eyes and colour. It was her desire to become a mother. Children born here as 'brownish-white' were most confused. Born and brought up in western culture, they were under pressure to understand Asian culture and languages but they couldn't digest why their forefathers were so rigid and set in their ways. On the other hand, Asians were unable to digest that their children had turned gays and lesbians or freely had sex.

I became addicted to Christiania. Good money and free smoke made the situation cool and acceptable for Linda. It was really a very good money, even a small-time dealer used to make $1000 in a day in those happy days in this hippie town. I thanked Lord Shiva for His blessings and His magic weed of *ganja*. In the *Metro Express* job, I made friends with immigrants, students from Asia and in Christiania job mind-blowing hippies like Erick, Finn, Nils, Bettina and performers.

Finally, I left my newspaper job and joined Solvognen, an internationally acclaimed theatre group, who also staged many happenings in Copenhagen.

The protest songs of Christiania were creative and funtastic like *'I kan ikke slå os ihjel'* (You cannot kill us).

I believed in this *mantra* and started to integrate in this lovely country with these fantastic people of Scandinavia. I didn't love Denmark as much as I loved Danes, they were extra-ordinarily great crazy and hard-working people.

Finn Holbaek, an old hippy, managed to smuggle around 30 kg of hash from Nepal by hiding it in a set of *tablas*, a percussion instrument. Actually, when he was taking some *tabla* lessons from a Guru in Benaras, he found *tabla* very interesting not because of its sound but because of its structure. A black material is pasted in the centre of the skin to create a resonance and inside it is hollow. The colour of this material was similar to mashed weed or hash. Instead of learning, he made a special big *tabla* in Benaras and got it filled with Nepali Mandir Bells, a kind of Himalyan hash, and dared to smuggle it into Denmark while chanting *Hare Rama Hare Krishna*.

Finn didn't waste a single day. He collected a huge money and went straight to Thailand to find a beautiful girl for himself. Malee was the name of the girl, meaning flower in Thai language. Malee further flowered in Copenhagen and is now the proud mother of five lovely kids. There were many Thai girls married to middle-aged Danes. Adventure-loving Danes married them, got them Danish passports and finally divorced them. Now these girls were in their mid-thirties and were on dole. In addition, they were engaged in the sex business in massage centres.

Danish women were one step forward as they preferred muscular Africans instead of soft Asians for their adventures. End result of both enterprises was same. Danish women also would get bored with their blacks after some time. A lot of divorced and unemployed Africans can be seen around the happening streets of Istergade selling cocaine illegally. Only a few hard-working ones work as cleaners and dishwashers.

Surinder, an Indian from Vadodra and Titoo Pa-ji

from Chandigarh, owner of Deep Indian Restaurant, were now my new trusted friends. I employed Salim, an illegal immigrant who came on famous 'donkey visa'.

I renewed all my contacts back in India. Most important among them were Dr Sandeep Chaudhary, Nirmal Joseph and Ali Murtaza.

Dr Chaudhry was professor in a college, Ali Murtaza was the right-hand man of Telgi in Bombay who was involved in many illegal businesses like hawala. Nirmal Joseph finally had joined the government. Gurinder was settled in New Delhi. Guruji Suryaswami was now appearing on television.

Sandeep could not write a single page of Hindi without 20 grammatical errors, forget about English. With correspondence studies he managed to get a bachelor and then post-graduate degrees while he was busy with his real estate business. He passed NET (National Eligibility Test for lecturers) as somebody else appeared in the exam on his name who was already a lecturer of Hindi. He bribed authorities to get a PhD degree from a south Indian university.

His name was recommended by the chief minister. So every member of the selection committee signed, though they knew Sandeep could not teach Hindi even to a primary class. It was all because he belonged to a dominant caste of the region. He was now a big shot coloniser and was still operating from the office meant for teaching and research of Hindi language. He had more mobile sets than books in his library.

On the other hand, my slummer friend Ali Murtaza was a rich and responsible member of society and was involved in making false stamp papers, false travel documents and even passports. Anything was possible in a free country like India. Ali did one thing magnanimous and that was he married the same bar girl Zareena whom he dated when he was a teenager.

Three Stooges

What a feeling to be a father! I was blessed with a lovely son, whom we named Aryan, further suffixing it with 'Yog' and making it Aryan Yog, lifting his identity beyond boundaries. Linda loved to call him 'little Shiva'. Our baby was an exquisite, gorgeous fusion of East and West in appearance and intelligence as he luckily inherited the best of his mother and father.

Aryan was neither black nor white but brown in colour, curly hair, blue eyes, with broad shoulders and a mystic smile. Linda was a proud mother and never left him alone even for a second. Aryan brought good fortune for me. I was getting popular in Christiania because of my Danish accent, attitude and, of course, the unique talent of differentiating the varieties of weeds. As an expert, I was invited for the final verdict on the stuff when big deals got struck. I was paid for that and my fee would go up to 20,000 DKK, equivalent to Rs 1.5 lakh. With influx of money and popularity, my esteem was growing leaps and bounds.

Saleem, a Rajasthani illegal immigrant, joined me as an assistant in the shop owned by Janik Møller. He preferred working with me than being exploited by the Indo-Pakistani hoteliers. He then introduced me to another illegal immigrant, Raja, a Pakistani from Dera Ghazi Khan. We were in the same age group. Under my guidance, they started selling hash in Tingbjerg street for their livelihood. Tingbjerg was known for its reputation as being Copenhagen's second-largest market for cannabis after Christiania.

Later, we three made our own business group in Christiania itself. Muslim immigrant drug dealers used to operate round the clock. Norrebro, a locality in the centre of Copenhagen prominently inhabited by the Muslim immigrants, was also coming out as an alternative for hash demand. I met this fanatic Chacha Imam during this time. He was worried about Muslim rights and brought for me tasty home-made potato-*paranthas*. But his communal talk was not to my taste. He was always hyper and idiotic and didn't know exactly who I was. I would always get bored when he started discussing cruelties on immigrants. Instead I would sing and narrate stories mimicking

Bollywood actors. Salim and Raja would give me company.

Future of Christiania was not looking bright with the present rightwing government. I was contacted by an immigrant hash dealer of Cobra group for supply of 'gard' a kind of hash called 'dust'. This high potency hash made from dried marijuana was the purest form, without any additive chemicals, made primarily in Afghanistan and Kashmir. I helped him and his group Cobra to create new routes with my knowledge. Earlier, the smuggling route was through Casablanca.

Saliulla Bukhari, an Afghani national based at Kandahar, was the main supplier of Afghan hash including *gard* in the international market. I knew him since my days in the ashram. Hash smugglers openly used porous Indian border, bribing the army officials of both the countries. Doda in Indian Kashmir is the main centre for *gard* smuggling. Once Shivananda took me to a secret meeting where Saliulla Bukhari, officers of India and Pakistan and a few other unknown but influential smugglers were present at a place 1.5 km from the international border in Doda district itself. I finalised this deal between Cobras and Saliulla Bukhari with Chacha Imam as guarantor. This deal brought me for the first time 25,000 euro in one shot. Cobras got their delivery verified and I got my commission from both Cobras and Bukhari.

I became rich overnight. I purchased a two-room flat near Amagerbo facing the sea canal with a basement called Celler in Danish for our weekend parties and leisure time. Later, it was to become the office-cum-store for our group. Most of the time me, Raja and Saleem stayed in this apartment.

Linda, meanwhile, was getting upset with me and we often quarrelled without much reason. She purchased a new flat in Kingosgade in greater Copenhagen and sold the old one in Vanlose. Our relationship fell to the lowest low. My friends in Christiania convinced me not to worry because Scandinavian girls were like that. Being a typical Indian I couldn't forget the sweet memories. Gradually, I lapsed into loneliness and frustration.

To bust my anxiety I started to spend most of the nights in the streets with Danish funkies or playing my piano alone in the recently purchased Amagerbro flat. Same time, the new government decided to end illegal activities at Christiania, specifically the cannabis market and criminal activities. The politicians demanded the end of 'hard drug' sales, including cocaine and amphetamines. In fact, hippies were not selling the hard drugs like cocaine, which were governed by Hells-Angels and Bandidos. The decision angered old hippies like Nils and Post who had pioneered this noble idea of self-governance in this beautiful piece of land in Denmark.

Janik Møller said in anger, "Fuck this government. They are stifling our concept of freedom and killing a noble idea."

I suggested comically, 'instead of a ban, this stuff should be made mandatory for everyone on the earth. It feels so divine, and then play Sufiana music the whole day. It would bring peace and tranquility in society.'

"I love you, man, and your free spirit. You are right. Christiania is a land of Mahadev. These rascals don't understand the philosophy of Shiva. In your country, sadhus smoke so openly," Janik said while smoking a joint.

'I am not joking, Janik. According to a Hindu myth, long before the creation of the universe, the Gods had churned a cosmic mountain with a view to obtain nectar for eternal life peace and tranquility. It is said that marijuana plants germinated at all places where the nectar dropped or touched the earth,' I said in a philosophical mood.

Hippies liked my comments like the way they always had with thunder of applause and roaring of '*Har Har Mahadev*'.

The government decided to remove the marijuana market from Christiania. In response, we the cannabis sellers covered our hash shops in military camouflage nets as mark of protest in a creative and humorous way.

The police made more than 20 arrests and a large part of the organised dealer network of Pusher Street was eliminated. Many dealers started to move huge amounts of cannabis out into the city of Copenhagen and the rest of the country instead. Many new clubs made their appearance in the north-western part of the city, especially in Norrebro. Still, the Copenhagen pot market was strong and vibrant, with annual sales estimated at around $250 million, most of it going to criminal gangs.

There were huge protests against this government policy in and around Copenhagen. There was support from Sweden. Intellectuals were giving the reference of America in this context and were speculating that it will be a failed experiment.

A Christianite who had lived here since the 1970s, said: "It is our way of living they want to kill. These people who live here cannot live like other people in other parts of Denmark. We have another way of thinking now. We hippies are different and we can't adjust ourselves in any other pattern."

Suddenly, I was not feeling happy in this happiest country of the world. Though I was making good money but my personal life was in a mess. Negative energy and my bad *karma* started taking over. Breaking up with Linda was the main reason for my frustration.

I accepted another lucrative offer of the Cobra group. The situation was getting worse in Afghanistan. It was difficult to smuggle *gard*-hash as the Pakistan Army had launched a campaign in Waziristan where Saliulla Bukhari had his business. Even in these adverse political circumstances, I was making an all-out effort to crack a direct deal with Saliulla Bukhari. After the fall of the Taliban regime many members of the Taliban forces fled to the northern border region of Afghanistan and Pakistan, previously under the control of Pakistani army. Even in this war-like situation, the cultivation and smuggling of cannabis was in full swing.

Here in Christiania too there was a war-like situation, with the government trying again and again to have control over the hash business. Eventually, it led to a war between the two most powerful outlaw biker gangs of the world: Hell Angels and Bandidos. A 26-year old Christianite was killed and three other residents injured in a violent assault on Pusher Street.

Violence was rising. Nonetheless, Kurt Westergaard, the controversial cartoonist, rendered the caricature of Prophet Mohammed wearing a bomb as a turban. He was forced into hiding with his wife and moved by police from location to location after Danish police received credible death threats from Muslim extremist immigrants. Three Muslims (one Moroccan and two Tunisian) had already been caught in a conspiracy to kill the humourist. The re-publication of the cartoons was followed by youth riots in the immigrant neighbourhood across the country. Danish embassies in the Islamic countries were closed for weeks and protest marches held. Demonstrators in Damascus stormed Denmark's embassy in Syria and burned it to the ground after rumours that copies of Muslims' holy book, the *Koran*, were going to be burned in Copenhagen.

Copenhagen was burning. The downtown area of the Danish capital looked like a war zone. About 700 people were arrested, many of them below 18 years.

At the same time, frustrated Chacha was making his all-out personal effort to vent the anger of the Muslim community. Without any reason, he found in me the right man to execute his plans. He was provoking me now and again to stand up for the cause of the Muslims. Maybe the reason for considering me so pliant was my 'yes attitude'.

Instead of calming down the immigrants, the government was passing some stupid harsh legislation that would require all foreign workers to pass a Danish language test within six months, else lose their permanent residency permit.

I cracked the *gard* deal with Saliulla Bukhari in this worsening socio-political situation. I was able to deliver the best quality of *gard*-hash in Christiania. I got my 10 per cent commission in advance from the Cobra gang. Chacha again played as mediator and guarantor. Salim and Raja knew about this deal but they were not part of it. They were busy in their own shop. Chacha was sticking to me all the time. Initially, I thought he wanted to make thick and fast money, but I was wrong. He was a hard-core fanatic. He had some other weird plans in his mind.

With all my theatrical skills put to use, and knowing well Afghans' love for Bollywood films, I mimicked Amitabh Bachhan's voice and said on phone to Bukhari in Soorta, the barbar, style, '*Pathan ka bacchi, Kya hum Shehansha se baat kar sakte hain.*' I delivered my first dialogue.

"Who is it?" Amused Saliulla asked.

'*Ristey mein to hum tumahre bacche lagte hein, naam hai Yogi,*' I said in Amitabh Bachchan style.

He burst into laughter. Recalling our connection at Doda in India and our earlier deals, he agreed to an independent deal.

I got the money in installments from Cobras, which was supposed to go to Bukhari in three weeks by an illegal money transfer. Situation in Afghanistan was getting worse with every passing day. With the logistics and air support of the United States, the Pakistani Army captured and killed numerous

Al-Qaeda operatives such as Khalid Sheikh Mohammed, wanted for the killing of *Wall Street Journal* reporter Daniel Pearl. It was my worst time in Copenhagen.

According to the law of gangland, after three weeks, I was with a hawala agent at Norrebro, a Muslim immigrant-dominated suburb of Copenhagen, with Raja and Saleem. Surprisingly I could not make contact with Bukhari and even his assistant Khan. We heard that United States had carried out drone attacks on targets all over the tribal areas. Bukhari was living there. Usually he used to connect immediately after every delivery himself or through his agent. We tried two other hawala agents and an independent broker, but failed. We came back to our Amagerbro flat without delivering money through hawala. I had 30 million DKK left with me; with police dogs sniffing all the time. I wished I was free from all the responsibilities and obligations!

It was a bad time. Most civilised and respected Danish police started behaving like the Punjab Police. The chief of the police was isolating the protesters one by one without discrimination. The police were confused as they never had this type of situation in the past. Christiania was bleeding and inhabitants were weeping and abusing the police.

'*Absolut Nul Tolerance*' by Danish Politi was the headline in all the newspapers including *Politiken* published from Denmark. The police's adaptation of a zero tolerance with an unprecedented 700 arrests, including detention of hundreds of minors, was evident. Police's apparent joy in beating up unruly adolescents hardly led the way towards a greater mutual understanding. It was difficult to call a winner, but easy to identify the losers. Extradition of Turkish-born nationalised Danes further inflamed the crisis. Open riots broke out, which resulted in the smashing of windows of banks and of the offices of the other capitalist and multinational corporations.

I was concerned all around. Chacha Imam was being over-emotional and hanging on to me. I was trying my level best to avoid him and his religious group. I knew they were going to do something unexpected, making the most of the frustrating socio-political situation.

The youths in the immigrant neighbourhood engaged themselves in seven consecutive nights of rioting as there was re-publication of the Mohammed cartoons in other newspapers.

Even in India the US interfered in 1980 and forced a ban on this wonderful gift of the Lord Shiva though it was legally open since the days of the Indus Valley Civilisation. The result was sudden appearance of mafias and gangs in India.

Wonderful thing was that Naga Sadhus never gave a shit to this prohibition. To hell with the laws of the US or UN, these lovers of Lord Shiva listen only to their Lord and nobody else. Starting and ending their day with a puff, chanting '*Har Har Mahadev*'.

ॐ

Greatest Act of My Life

I was alone and there was none to share my worries. Linda stopped talking, though I was allowed to meet Aryan once a week. Chacha was stalking me. Surprisingly, I found my trusted friends Saleem and Raja too on his side. It was ridiculous to share my feelings with hippies or even with Janik Møller. Frustrated, I thought of telling everything to the Danish police, but it would be suicidal. I regretted my adventurous deal.

After three weeks I got a surprise call from a different phone number, the caller declaring himself to be Saliulla Bukhari. It was not a call from the number he used to call from. It was not even the voice of Bukhari, with whom I had talked many times, perfected dealings and received advance money.

The caller demanded the money but only knew the amount. He had all my contacts and personal information. I was sure he was not Saliulla Bukhari. A surprise call from Suryaswami further complicated the affair, as he had no role in this *gard*-hash deal, though he knew Bukhari.

Guruji Suryaswami said, "Jogananda send the money to Bukhari."

'But Guruji…'

"No buts and ifs; return his money by tomorrow through hawala."

'Ok, Guruji, *Pranam*.'

I put off the matter till next Saturday. A trap was laid for me on all four sides, from this caller, from Chacha Imam, from Danish Police and from Guruji Suryaswami. I doubted all. To confirm my doubt I went to Norrebro to meet Gul Afghani. Saliulla Bukhari and Gul Afghani belonged to the same village in Afghanistan. I came to know from Gul that the whole region of Panjway district of Kandahar was bombed by the US allied forces including their native village. It was claimed as the birthplace of the Talibans, located about 25 km south-west of Kandahar. The US forces further attacked the border districts of Maywand and Arghandab. Not a single soul was left in the whole region.

So who the hell was this new Bukhari? Someone somewhere was hatching a plan against me. The money couldn't be transferred to just anybody. It was also against the laws of the underworld. I was badly scared but I didn't want to make the matter worse; I would give the money to the original Bukhari and nobody else, whatever the consequences. I made up my mind that I would not allow anybody to take advantage of this situation.

The deal with the Black Cobras was fairly clear and over. Though Cobra gang knew that I had money but they had no right to interfere. I decided that this was my last deal and would never ever contact these fellows in future. These were going to be my last days in this trade and thereafter I would sever my connection with all these people. I was trying to relax but that was not to happen. There was violence all around on television, newspapers to the streets and my home. On one side, coalition forces were making war on two fronts—Afghanistan and Iraq and the Danish government on two cultural fronts in Copenhagen – the hippies in Christiania and the squatters in Youth-house. Of course, the people of Afghanistan suffered more by the illegal imperialist war than the 'hippies' and 'squatters' in Copenhagen.

Even during such a catastrophe the Chinese devised an innovative video game where an American soldier had to clear the hurdles by killing the Afghans and getting bonus points for killing the Iraqis. How sad! their market followed no rules of humanity.

In Denmark, the unemployment figures, crime rate and the education dropout rate was significantly higher among minority groups and were sometimes alleged to be indicative of discrimination on the basis of religion. However, it was difficult to separate religious differences from differences in language and ethnicity, and the latter might be equally important in explaining unequal outcomes in access to well-paying jobs and social advancement.

The integration of immigrant groups from Islamic countries was an important political and social topic of discussion. Government was more focussed on language tests rather than integration policy based on love and equality. I didn't know what to do with the money. If Bukhari was dead then who will get the money?

Might be Chacha knew about Bukhari or Guruji. Continuous monitoring frightened me. I felt they were spying on me, wherever I was. Though Salim and Raja were with me, I never forgot to carry my German pistol whenever I met these fanatics.

I got the ultimatum call to reach Brondby Muslim graveyard, otherwise there was a danger on my life and family. It was a warning and they said they know all about me, Linda and Aryan. I immediately doubted Salim, Raja and even Janik Moller. Except them no one knew about my private life.

I was under constant pressure of threats and persuasion. It was clear that I would not be spared if I didn't act as they wanted. I was more worried about Linda and Aryan than my own self.

They wanted me to kill Kurt Westergaard, the controversial cartoonist and humourist, else carry out a blast in the centre of Copenhagen. Why would I kill an artist? I am an artist too. I didn't know from where I got the courage to kill Chacha. Invoking Lord Shiva, my half-mad mother Bhagwanti, I shot that fanatic bastard Chacha right in the centre of his forehead. They underestimated me, thinking I was a comedian.

Thanks to Salim and Raja who helped me in my escape on that Saturday night. I was eating *paranthas* in the company of Sardar Harbhajan Singh at Brussels airport. My sincere thanks was also due to President Bush and his human-free Drones who inadvertently triggered this heinous act in making a super-rich from a street-performer. Maybe this was the biggest blunder or the most courageous act of my life.

While shooting Chacha I had Suryaswami on my mind. I decided to take revenge on Suryaswami.

I was in Delhi for over three months but nothing was happening. Gurinder kept changing the sim cards in his old mobiles. I was safe in his room and felt secure as no police was heard or seen searching me. Through Saleem, it was clear the Danish police cared little about the murder of Chacha Imam. After a long wait of 10 days, I finally got a call early morning from Suryaswami. It was Thursday. He instructed me to meet him in the ashram at Chamba and said once I was there he would manage everything as usual.

Though it was dangerous, I asked Gurinder to arrange my flight ticket for Hamburg on Sunday. Immediately I called Saleem in Copenhagen and Abdul in Hamburg that I was reaching him on Monday. He would drive me to Copenhagen.

I gave all the contact numbers of Sandeep, Nirmal and Ali Murtaza to Gurinder and fixed time for the 'desert' operation at 11 in the morning on Saturday. Rest of the plan was clear to Gurinder and Kamini. Dr Sandeep Chaudhary, the self-styled professor, was specially needed to give logistic support to Gurinder and Kamini.

Gurinder got me a Lufthansa ticket for Hamburg scheduled to fly at 4.45 am on Monday from Delhi. There was not much time left.

I got out of Delhi on Thursday and reached the Chamba ashram in the late evening. Well prepared and confident, I performed like a seasoned actor. Suryaswami welcomed me. I heard that Shivananda had separated from him, levelling serious allegations in public against him. Ma Nirmala had also deserted him.

I convinced him that he would have to come to my hometown, Sangaria, to take his share of money that was kept safe in the isolated village farm. With my experience of dramatics on stage and then dealing with so many varied situations in my life so far, I was able to convince Suryaswami. Half my battle was won.

I told him in plain words that I had to go back to Copenhagen the next night. I showed him the Lufthansa ticket for Hamburg. He would collect the money and go back to his Chamba ashram and I would fly to Hamburg.

Both of us agreed on the plan. We also agreed that it was Chacha Imam creating the nuisance or I would have returned the money then and there. Within I was smiling to see the lion walking into the trap. He didn't want anything except Rs 15 crore, to hell with negative developments in the ashram.

We set out to Sangaria, I was with him in his car, his security sadhus in two other cars escorting us, one before our car, the other trailing behind. Suryaswami had saved me from the Punjab Police butchers, so he was my saviour; He accepted me as his disciple, so he was my Guru; He raped and caused Bhawna to commit suicide, so he was a rapist; He got me trapped with the Punjab Police, so he was a conspirator; He killed journalist Bharat Ram, so he was a killer; He involved me in Bhawna's suicide case, he was a manupulator; He blackmailed me into killing Gurinder, he was a blackmailer; He wanted the unclaimed money, he was a cheat. Now he was sitting beside me, at the back seat of his Tata Safari. I wished I had my favourite German revolver and could shoot him there on the seat!

We were about to reach Sangaria in the morning when I suggested that our car lead so that I could show the way ahead. We passed by St. Mary's School, turned left and went straight half a kilometer to our farmhouse. It was a lonely place, with a tubewell and a large triangular room of brick and cement with a thatched roof for the labourers to store the hay and crop temporarily, and take rest sometimes. There were three four *kikar* trees of the desert around. It was peak summer, 11 in the morning. The villagers could not even imagine moving out of their houses at this time. We stopped our cars about 100 metres from the store room.

I made a gesture to Suryaswami to follow me to the room, while the sadhus were instructed by him to remain there and wait. We went into the room. There was a huge pitcher full of water kept on the sand on one side and stacks of hay on the other.

"Where is the money?" he said casually.

Clearly, destiny was on my side. I was full of confidence, my arms folded on my chest, my neck straight and up, and my eyes looking into his. 'Which money?' I questioned.

"What do you mean Jogananda, I am getting late," he was irritated.

I wanted to stretch him to his limits.

'You raped Bhawna and her mother?'

"Yes, I did."

'You killed Bharat Ram the journalist?'

"Yes, I killed him."

His pitch was rising. He lost his temper completely and shouted, "Who are you to ask me all this?"

'You and Shivananda got me trapped with the Punjab Police. Didn't you?

"Yes I did. You are a beggar and a bloody fucker. Get me the money or I will shoot you."

His eyes were red hot, his teeth chattering and suddenly there was a pistol in his hand pointing at my head. He shouted, "I want my money or you are killed."

'You can't do it.... Your time is over. My time starts now,'

I said with a grin.

He shot me in the leg.

Two gunshots were heard and Suryaswami fell dead before me.

Coming out from behind the forage in the room, Gurinder emerged with a gun in his hand. He emptied the remaining bullets into his back. He hugged me, crying madly. My eyes were wet. Kamini came out from the hiding with a camera man. He zoomed the camera on the dead body while she started reporting live:

"Here you can see the dead body of the smuggler, rapist and the killer Guru Suryaswami. He has just admitted that he killed journalist Bharat Ram and raped innocent Bhawna. This is Kamini with camera person Paresh reporting live for IBN7."

Sandeep Chaudhary and his men had taken complete control of the situation and the criminal sadhus in particular. Ali Murtaza, my slummer mate of Ambedkar Colony had specially come to help me from Mumbai. We didn't speak to each other, but I acknowledged his help with a smile.

I was bleeding in my leg and they took me to the hospital in the village. What a coincidence! Dr Meena at once took charge of my treatment. My father, Dr Om Parkash Sharma, was working in this hospital under Dr Meena when we were living in this village. I wasn't seriously injured as the bullet had only pierced my thigh muscle. However, Dr Meena admitted me for a day. Kamini with her bureau chief Neeraj Gupta, cameraman Paresh, Gurinder, Dr Sandeep Chaudhry, Nirmal

Joseph and Ali Murtaza all were present in the hospital.

I was taken to an operation theatre. They were about to give anaesthesia when Guri came with Kamini and said, "Pa-ji, you kept your word. My mission is over with Suryaswami's death. Pa-ji do you know who Kamini is?"

'Yes I do,' I said.

He smiled and said, "No, you don't. She is Kammo, whom we met once at Rang Mahal at Chamba. She is the only child of the brave journalist Bharat Ram and a friend of Bhawna."

She expressed her gratitude to me with tears in her eyes. At once, she wiped her tears, cleared her throat and started reporting live:

"Welcome again, this is Kamini Bharat Ram reporting live for IBN7. Jogender Dutt Sharma alias Yogi is battling for life in this poor hospital with hardly any modern surgical facilities. He is the man who exposed Suryaswami, a rapist, smuggler and killer and his hash-smuggling international nexus with Europe, Afghanistan and Pakistan."

Reporting over, she smiled at me. Guri and Kamini went out of the room. I had to stay in the hospital till the police came to record my statement. Waiting on the bed, I felt happy and fulfilled. No matter Guri didn't follow the plan in toto, maybe he was immature. I felt happier to see Gurinder and Kamini so much relieved.

I was alone in the hospital room and reflected on the turn of events in my life. Everybody wants happiness. But what they get is always a temporary satisfaction. So they speed up this race to have more and more rounds of the temporary pleasant feeling. That's how the money becomes more important than other things. The mind always goes circular. Seeking happiness through making somebody happy gets us out of this circular pattern of the mind, and one can have access to the everlasting happiness of peace of mind in life.

When I woke up, I was surrounded by police, journalists and a local politician. Gurinder had already confessed and surrendered. Police recorded my statement and Dr Meena's. While the police was taking me out hundreds of people were shouting outside the hospital.

The policemen made way for me through the crowd to a police van.

Kamini was still reporting outside this police van and local crowd was shouting:

'Jogi – Jogeshwar *–jindabad...jindabad- jindabad.*'

'*Dhongi Baba–Murdabad...Murdabad-Murdabad.*'

Policemen were forcing me into the van where Gurinder was already seated. When I got in, some TV journalists rushed towards me poking their microphones at my face.

One of them shot a question.

"When are you joining politics, Jogananda?"

Then another voice heard.

"Who raped Bhawna? Suryaswami or Shivananda?"

Before I answered the question, Guri pressed on my feet and indicated that I shouldn't speak. In the police van itself, we got the news that the Chamba ashram had been looted by the local folks after the live coverage of Suryaswami. All the ashramites including foreigners fled out of fear. After looting the most expensive things of the Anand Ashram, it was set on fire.

After about half-an-hour we reached the police headquarters and got another breaking-news that villagers from the adjoining area took everything with them including expensive electronic items and satellite phones. Guri and I were lodged in the jail. There was no sign of worry or regret in our mind. Rather Guri was quite excited. He was bursting to tell me something.

"Thanks Pa-ji for one and all. I love you… and now I want to tell you something very special."

'Even more special than what you did today?' I said.

"Yes, of course, Pa-ji… very special!"

'Then why are you wasting time?'

'Pa-ji… Bhawna was in love with you.'

I was stunned.

He went on... "Pa-ji, she told me about it back home. She couldn't tell you because of the pressure of the family, Suryaswami and mainly because of your safety in the ashram."

I was transfixed and couldn't see clearly what destiny expected of me now!

Tihar Jail–Delhi

Next morning we were remanded to 14 days judicial custody at Sri Ganga Nagar. The long tiring Indian judicial process was on. Gurinder said, "It can take seven to eight years for the final verdict going through session courts, etc." I said, 'I am ready for the worst'.

Sandeep Chaudhary, Nirmal Joseph and Ali Murtaza would come to meet us frequently. They were more worried than us and so they were thinking and devising ways to help us, fearing we might waste many years and lots of money fighting our case. I was neutral in the circumstances having reconciled myself with my fate. I wasn't excited to do anything particular in my life for now. But there was no chance for Gurinder to escape the gallows because he had already deposed before the magistrate.

Sandeep Chaudhry put his mind, money and labour, contacted people in Delhi and got our case moved to Tees Hazari courts in New Delhi. More ashrams were reported to have been looted across the country. Suryaswami's murder was clearly our personal revenge, but media made us popular at the national level. Therefore, it became easy for Sandeep and Ali Murtaza in the legal corridors to shift our case and fight it better. Instead of Sri Ganga Nagar now we were lodged in the largest prison of Asia, Tihar Jail.

Ali Murtaza hired the most prominent and expensive criminal lawyer Kapil L Antuley for us but I had lost all interest and was ready for any consequences. The days passed and we became part and parcel of this jail.

Tihar was full of some very special, notorious people from different sections of the society. Doctors, teachers, politicians and even sadhus were lodged here. Their stories were hard to digest even though our act was the most adventurous.

Each of them had such a criminal background that would outdo, outshade our murder case. We were criminals in the eyes of the law but heroes in the eyes of the public. In my school days I wanted to be a hero like Amitabh Bachchan and today in Tihar Jail, I was a public hero, even more real than a Bollywood hero.

The petty criminals were as miserable in the jail as they

were outside. In the real world, it was an irony that the real thieves and murderers were not getting life imprisonment but life achievement awards and citations from social organisations.

In Tihar Jail, Guri and I were considered as crusaders.

Guru Bhimananda, a 30-year old guru, was in our adjoining cell. This self-styled guru was illiterate, and started working as a low paid security guard in a massage-cum-prostitution centre in the heart of Delhi. He was caught in a sex scandal and was behind bars for three years. When he came out from the prison he as Guru Swami Bhimananda amassed a lot of wealth and constructed a 200-room capacity hospital and an English medium school in his home town and a big ashram in Delhi. Sadly the self-styled Guruji never left his lust for massage girls. Now he was again in Tihar.

Peer Gulam Fakir Shah, a highly respected and popular Muslim Guru of central India, was also our jailmate. He used to treat gynaecological diseases of women with black magic. While making fool of the local folks he used to do a fire trick and take the women inside his bedroom to make them pregnant.

Satya Baba was making fool of millions since more than 40 years. He even claimed that he would never die. Many videos proved his magic tricks of ash-balls, lingum and necklace, which even a simple magician would not appreciate. He was a multi-billionaire. Six teenagers were killed in his private room when they tried to expose him. Forget about any action, even their FIR had not been registered. When BBC showed a documentary of a European teenager who was victim of a sex scandal, the foreign minister blasted the journalist.

Most scandalous story of all appeared in newspapers and was later flashed in all news channels. A young married woman follower of a sect wrote a letter anonymously to Prime Minister, President and Chief Justice and a DGP claiming that the Baba of the sect had raped her more than 50 times. Almost every woman of the ashram was victim to this so-called guruji, she claimed. After the publication of this letter in a newspaper, the editor of the paper was murdered the same way Suryaswami had killed Kamini's father Bharat Ram. The CBI registered a case and, surprisingly, the guru got bail.

In Kerala, a Christian guru lured a 15-year old school girl to his bedroom. Instead of converting this poor Hindu girl to a Christian he converted her to an innocent mother. In the adjoining state called Tamil Nadu, it was really special when whole of India almost saw the live telecast of a romantic, hot, bed scene between a super star heroine of Tamil cinema and most respected spiritual guru of the South named 'Nityananda'.

Meanwhile, there was this mystic guru who was creating waves with his typical yogic exercises. No sex scandal, just breathing exercises (Pranayam) made him a household name. His growing popularity, wealth and his war against the corrupt did not go well with the contemporary gurus and government establishments and numerous cases were slapped against him.

All this and every new story about these gurus further confirmed that what we did was right. We never expected this much hype though.

Gurinder was always involved in jail activities while I preferred to stay all alone in my cell reading most of the time. Born in a Brahmin family, I, in fact, knew the value of a guru in one's life. Parkash uncle, my theatre guru, and Mastana the spiritual guru had taught me a few lessons. Guru is one who has knowledge, wisdom and authority and can guide others for enlightenment and self-realisation. The long wait helped me to spend time reading variety of contemporary and religious literature. Apart from *Bhagavad Gita* I read about some real gurus in the Hindu tradition. They were Adi Shankaracharya, Shri Ramakrishna and Shri Chaitanya Mahaprabhu. Other gurus who continued the yogic tradition into the 20th century were Swami Chinmayananda, Swami Vivekananda and AC Bhagtivedanta Swami Prabhupada.

Our trial case was maturing for judgement any day. We were in jail for the last four years. Sandeep Chaudhary and Ali Murtaza were in regular touch with us and our lawyer Kapil Antuley, keeping close track of the proceedings. They conveyed to us the probability of Gurinder being set free.

There was no apprehension about my release. I felt a bit worried but left it to the Almighty, praying for Gurinder's life and happiness. Suryaswami would have killed me if Guri hadn't shot him dead. Natural justice would have set him free; the law of land should be merciful to him was my sincere wish for Guri. I was happy to observe Gurinder and Kamini coming close to each other from the gifts that she would usually bring for him whenever she visited us in jail. Guri's life was now meant for Kamini, whom he didn't want to lose at any cost.

Honestly, I was praying for both of them and praying for a life ahead of me free from all personal worries, but dedicated to the cause of the poor, innocent and helpless.

Mercurial Antuley miraculously presented Gurinder's case as one of self-defence. I don't know how Ali Murtaza and Sandeep Chaudhary manipulated the whole proceedings, but the outcome was fantastic.

It was Monday, 15 April 9.30 morning, at Tees Hazari courts and the final verdict was announced in our favour. We were supposed to be out from Tihar Jail by 12 forever. Kamini knew about the outcome as she had brought new clothes for both of us on this special day. Sandeep and Ali looked happy as their efforts had borne fruit.

Guri looked happy in the new jeans and cotton shirt. Excited, he turned to me and beamed, "Pa-ji, nobody is looking more handsome than you in your blue faded jeans and white shirt."

Jail officer was escorting us through the corridors to the main office near the exit gate. We were happy, excited and jumping. Guri was laughing, clapping and congratulating me.

Now it was my turn. I went ahead. I signed the register and turned to go when I heard a voice:

'Good morning, Mr Redne Yog.... Welcome.'

I looked back and saw two Danish Police officers whom I hadn't seen in the first instance. Everything was clear to me in a flash. I knew my destiny.

'Hey officers...waiting for me. Great, hurry up,' I said confidently in Danish.

"Not here, Mr Jogender...meet you in Copenhagen," he said sarcastically.

'Fantastic, then book a nice airline...officer,' I replied sarcastically in Danish.

He stood up, handcuffed me and showed the arrest warrants he had got for me and said, 'British Airways.' Finn Jørgensen was his full name, the officer incharge of Denmark Police called 'Politi' in Danish. He was extremely polite and well behaved. I was normal, relaxed and smiling. Finn gave me a pen to sign the warrant. I did it in a second.

Sandeep Chaudhary, Nirmal Joseph, Ali, Gurinder and Kamini were waiting for me outside. They were beating a *dhol* out of sheer excitement and joy at my 'final' release. Chained and handcuffed, I had to struggle to walk out of the exit gate of the Tihar Jail with the Danish officers. There was a Danish embassy car parked near the exit gate waiting for me. Two more Danish police officers were standing beside it. As I expected, it created a scene. Gurinder rushed to me shouting, 'Pa-ji, what is this going on here...where are they taking you?' Danish officers were quite liberal and gave way to him. Sandeep and Murtaza also came close. Kamini looked out of sorts. She rushed up, held me by my arms and started crying. Guri followed her and looked mad with anger and confusion. "I'll not let it happen. I'll just call Antuley. How dare they handcuff you." He was drooling and lost his temper at Finn Jørgensen. I gestured to Ali to control him and take him away. It was too much for him. He hugged me tightly and started crying bitterly. My hands were not free. I wanted to comfort both Kamini and Gurinder but I couldn't do much. Affectionately, I shouted at both of them, "stop crying. They are officers from Denmark and doing their duty. I have to go with them to Copenhagen, but there was nothing to worry about me." Gurinder seemed to realise the situation and cooled down, although Kamini was still holding on to me and sobbing.

'Sorry Kamini, extremely sorry Guri, I won't be able to attend your marriage party next month.'

Controlling my emotions I said with an attitude, 'Excuse me. . . please...both of you.'

I walked fast to the embassy car and got into the car. Officers also got on to their seats. Guri and Kamini came close to car. Sandeep and Ali also joined them. I was getting restless and again said, 'Finn, let's go.' I took out my pocket '*Bhagavad Gita*' and started reading.

ॐ

Købehavn's Faengsler
(Copenhagen Jail)

We landed at Lufthavn the Copenhagen Airport at 2pm on 16th of April. It was dark as usual and snowing, even in summer. I was in a pensive and brooding mood. Heavy Danish force were deputed at the airport fearing demonstrations or attack on my life by the Islamic extremists. It was cold and I got an overcoat from Danish Politi. A specially designed Politi van loaded with ultra modern sophisticated weapons was waiting for me. Media had surrounded the area to capture the scene. But Politi had other ideas. I signed a few papers for immigration officers and they got me out from the airport through a less-known exit gate. Politi asked me to hide my face under the overcoat hat. I sat with Finn in the van and we were on our way to Vigerslev Alle Prison, in the heart of Copenhagen, with sirens screaming.

Within 15 minutes, we were in the prison complex. The main gate was open, yet the media failed to shoot me with their cameras. Finn Jørgensen escorted me to the front office of the jail and started conversing with Ole Molbaek, the main jail officer. He handed over all my documents to him.

After some initial investigations at the reception I was taken to a cross-shaped, panoptic four-storey building in Vigerslev Alle complex itself.

Now I was with Ole, a 45-year old prison administrator. He appeared nice. I looked around and found the jail not like an Indian jail but a kind of recreational art school, with better facilities than even a three-star hotel in old Delhi.

He asked me to sit on a sofa set and checked out my details on his computer. Prison employees interacted with me with a lot of curiosity and warmth. They included beautiful Pernille, kind Robert and generous Gert. Might be, they were excited to have a different type of mystic bearded creature in their premises.

I was lodged in the front house for two days and later transferred to an isolated cell.

Copenhagen Prison was the largest closed prison in Denmark. Their mission, vision and values were also highlighted in the writings on the walls and billboards like those of the Punjab Police.

Copenhagen Prison mission was to ensure that decisions

which the courts had taken were implemented according to applicable laws and regulations and to support and motivate the inmates to come out of their crime and depression.

I did not need to change myself because I was happy at what I had done in Copenhagen and in India. In the eyes of God, I believed I was not a criminal.

I was not in any mood to talk to anybody. Days passed.

Next week I was to be produced in the Danish courts. I had no mind to hire a lawyer. They might provide one, but I was sure I was not going to take their help. It was State vs Redne Yog. The public prosecutor would do everything possible to prove the charges of murder of Chacha Imam against me. I was prepared.

I was with myself, not talking to anyone or allowing anyone to talk to me, because I knew they would want to know about my personal life and about my involvement with Muslim extremists. I found it useless discussing all this with anybody in Copenhagen. I could share my feelings only with Guri, Kamini, Ali and Sandeep but they were not approachable. Here I could have shared it with my hippie friend Janik Møller or even Linda but it seemed next to impossible.

The jail authorities felt concerned when I declined all help including the lawyer. They were getting ready to call some clergyman, psychiatrist or a social worker to help me release my tension or maybe depression. Observing me closely, they decided to appoint an experienced social worker to attend to me. She was Bente Nielsen, 50, expert with depression patients and had an in-depth knowledge of Indian art and culture.

She came next morning. I wasn't pleased, but she was quite experienced and a loving lady. She tried to convince me into talking to her as a friend. She was not a doctor or anything, she said. She only wanted friends to be with me without any personal motive. Her age, tone, looks and behaviour and, of course, her smile made me smile too.

"I am sure," she asked, "You have some friends in Copenhagen. You should meet them. Don't you want to? You shouldn't keep to yourself only."

Finally, I told her, 'Ok, I want to meet Janik Møller – a Charistianite hippie and Øle Brekke, the comedian.'

"Alright," she said. "You will get to meet them. Don't worry. But don't please refuse to take a lawyer to speak for you in the court."

I didn't speak but I was convinced that we were friends now.

The court proceedings started. Unexpectedly many things related to my court proceedings directly or indirectly happened in and outside the jail. Øle Brekke brought some history books for me and Janik Møller a lovely gift of harmonium. Danish people are committed to the values of their life above personal consideration or social status. If there is anything happening wrong against the interest of the country, they would report the matter to the authorities, who don't lose time in taking action.

Bente Nielsen, my social worker, went into the depth of this murder case and concluded that it was not just a murder case but murder of the nationalistic feelings of the Danes at large. She wrote about the actual cause of this extremism and my apparent role in particular. Unknowingly, I had become a part of certain movement rising against Islamic terrorism in Denmark.

The local newspapers and one popular daily projected me as a crusader for humanity, fighting against Islamic terrorism. They said that Chacha Imam's murder was just a part of the circumstantial series of actions. Local journalists were hounding me for interviews but I didn't oblige. My case proceeding became the talk of the town through the print and later in the national electronic media. I was getting support from many corners, because of Bente Nielsen or maybe Janik Møller or even Øle Brekke.

Lars Nielsen, who founded the famous Hell Angels Motorcycle Gang and hash business in Christiania and was sentenced to four years in prison, was my prison mate. Niels Holck, a staunch supporter of Anand Marga, a Hindu missionary who dropped weapons in Odisha, was also in our jail. Akhtar Inzamam Abbas, a Danish national of Pakistani origin, who shot his sister Ghazala Rabeena Khan, two days after her marriage with an Afghan as an 'honour killing', was now my prison mate. Abbas was a staunch supporter of Chacha Imam and was present at American Plads.

Finally, the Danish Police arrested the man who mattered the most: Muhideen Mohammed Geelle. I heard that he had attacked Kurt Westergaard and nearly killed him. If he had done this act earlier I wouldn't have killed Chacha Imam. A Danish appeals court sentenced him to 10 years in prison for breaking into the home of Westergaard. The 30-year old entered

Westergaard's home on New Year's Day 2010 armed with an axe. Westergaard locked him inside. Police apprehended Geelle, shooting him in his leg.

The prosecution had requested Geelle serve 12 years in the prison before being deported and banned from ever returning to Denmark. This case had a direct correlation with my deportation case.

Annoying proceedings in the court were taking a comical turn. Ready for the worst punishment, I had no worries. Bente Nielsen made the case interesting. She kept writing detailed insights of the particular incident and the black history of Chacha Imam in local newspapers. Danish retired persons, media professionals and social workers stood behind me, as integration of Muslim immigrants was a national issue to debate in Scandinavia and Denmark in particular. Though I was not a native Dane but the support I was getting was more than a native Dane. We always had huge crowds witnessing the trial in the court. Even though the public prosecutor Andreas Jensen was supposed to slap the maximum punishment on me, yet he couldn't. He was confused because of the massive public support that I was getting.

I was tranquil most of the time. I got a little anxious only once when Bente came along with Aryan. He had the same inquisitive mind and questions. I was reminded of my childhood when Aryan asked me some unconventional but meaningful questions. He had his own destiny, but I felt happy to see in him further extension of my life.

Questioning and counter-questioning in my case became more interesting as Christiania got involved. I was slapped with many allegations along with the murder at American Plads. People know very well that in Christiania nobody pays taxes and they sell hash in the open markets so my answers brought laughter in the courtroom.

Public Prosecutor: Redne....So you had illegal weapon with you at American Plads?

'Sir, What are you saying? I think murder can't be done with a potato or a tomato.'

PP: Do you know just possession of hash can lead you to six months jail?

'Christianites have tons and tons of hash stored. Do you want to put all of them in jail? We don't have space to accommodate the whole country in Copenhagen jails. Secondly, we already have skilled labour problems. Then, why send 40 per cent more labourers to jail?'

PP: You worked in 'black' in Christiania?

'No, Christiania is popular for white work, they pay their taxes. Isn't it?' I said sarcastically.

Courtroom giggled again.

PP: Redne...Don't divert from murder case. You have nothing to do with what Christianites are doing. Whether they pay taxes or not is not your problem. You are a violent creature. Aren't you....do you accept?

'Every mammal on this planet is violent. We humans are on top of the food chain; under us are billions of subjected life forms, from bacteria and mould to insects and to fish. The higher up in the food chain you are, the more multiples of creatures have died to provide you food. Nature is violent, amoral, uncaring, deadly and dangerous. Even you are not an exception, having killed and eaten countless chickens so far.'

PP: You are a religious fundamentalist and you are trying to hide your personality.

'What is religion? I don't accept religion illuminated by religious preachers. People want religion to be an escape from the truth. Truth and honesty together is religion. The one who imbibes humanism is religious in the true sense. Most difficult is to be human. I am, of course, a fundamentalist, not religious but humanist.

PP: What a surprise! You believe in humanity and freedom?

'Of course I do. I am a human being. I believe in uniformity. What do you mean by religious freedom? It is nothing but a nuisance. Any religion that creates division and causes death is sinful and the biggest evil.

PP: You created a kind of 'spiritual terror' and disturbed the communal harmony of the country; didn't you?

'No I didn't, that I don't accept. I am a staunch supporter of communal harmony. In fact, I helped to maintain the harmony. Your government doesn't have a perfect policy for integration. I am pretty sure this vacuum in the world can only be filled up by intellectual nationalism and utmost humanism.

Again I got applause.

'Come on Mr Andreas Jensen, relax. I have been telling you

and everybody that I killed Chacha with 0.45 mm German pistol with my own hands at American Plads and I have no regrets at all. What else do you need!'

PP: Do you know the consequences of what you are suggesting? You will have to face deportation to India as a result.

I slipped at once into the mould of actor that I was by birth. I thundered, the way I thundered 'Othello' in St Mary's School.

'Deportation...What fun! Sheer wastage of time, money and energy. I am already deported in my life. Why send five officers to India to bring me here? Now deportation! Who will bear all these expenses, sir? Air fare, you know, is going up day by day.'

Everyone including public prosecutor Andreas Jensen laughed. The court decided to continue with the rest of the charges. The prosecutor tried to throw doubt on the authenticity of my reply until two of the audience, maybe they were social activists, hurled up some placards and posters showing their anger against Islamic terrorism. They were shouting slogans in my favour and against terrorism.

The judge then ruled that the case would be temporarily adjourned while the prosecution was still attempting to bring forward some additional witnesses against me who had already turned hostile in the incident of shooting of Chacha Imam at the Amerikan Plads.

ॐ

Shower of Divine Blessings
A Beautiful Ashram

Verdict of the case could be announced any day. More than anything else, the surprising element of my story was left untouched by the Danish as well as the Indian Police. Nobody cared to go into the depth of the case and never inquired about the millions of Danish Kroners that I had made in that infamous *gard*-hash deal. God knows why this question was never raised, though it was the root cause of all the troubles.

Finally, on 15 May, life imprisonment was awarded to me. Bente Nielsen, Janik Møller along with many other influential intellectuals of Denmark were furious at the judgement and were thinking of making appeal to the higher court for quashing the order. They decided to take the fight to the streets. The most popular paper *Politiken* published a headline on the front page —'Denmark sans Intellect' The other daily, *The Bellingske*, also flashed on the front page 'Denmark Goes Intellectually Bankrupt.' The judgement had no effect on me.

It is right to disclose everything to one and all.

Final Disclosure

I was thankful to President Bush for his drone attacks on Waziristan and Afghanistan. If he had not killed Saliulla Bukhari in that attack I would not have made millions in my lifetime. It was clearly the 'hand of God' which turned a street performer a millionaire.

I made sure this money went into safe hands and was utilised for the welfare of the needy, deserted and helpless people.

Construction of a multi-storey orphanage was in progress on Mumbai-Pune Highway in 2005 as soon as Ali Murtaza received the first installment of Rs 20 crore in Indian rupees through hawala. Now this beautiful ashram is built up and functioning smoothly. Ali Murtaza, Bhoora, Kamlesh and my other slummer childhood friends sincerely devoted their time and energy for this noble cause. Ashram cum orphanage was later named 'Samvedna'—empathy—specially for the underprivileged kids and orphans.

Samvedna is without any guru, unlike in the ashrams already exposed. The orphanage has its own website 'www.samvedna.org.in' and its activities with beautiful pictures of the tranquil ashram can be seen on Facebook.

Ali Murtaza, my real slummer friend, himself an orphan, now a big gun in Bombay, is managing the ashram with total dedication. This ashram is doing great educating orphans and making them self-reliant. Nobody knows who was behind this vision. How can I forget the role of President Bush in realisation of the dream of thousands of orphans.

Once I wrote suggesting in light mood to Ali that he should put a statue of President Bush in front of the main gate of the building of Samvedna. President Sir, You are remarkable!

Here in Copenhagen Jail, my life is not a battle any more. No fear of life and death, forget about deportation. This jail could be my home or any other place, hardly matters now.

India is believed to be a holy land of saints with a lot of spiritualism being propagated around the world. The fact remains that only a few saints actually deserve our love and respect, dedication and devotion. Their status rises above all criticism and they are akin to Jesus Christ. Gautam Buddha, Mahavir, Guru Nanak Dev and Sant Kabir are the perennial source of spiritual inspiration not only for India but for the whole world. Shockingly enough their followers are committing unjustifiable crime by creating different sects with different ideologies, attracting and attaching different castes and communities to their respective folds in the name of 'God'. Their followers made sects like 'Buddhism', 'Sikhism' and 'Jainism', etc. They kept preaching and writing against the practices of caste system and *karma-kand* theory but when they died their descendants and followers do almost the opposite; the whole idea fails.

Whole of my life I could not understand hatred. Racism is ancient and universal. Bombay experienced racism of 'whites' and 'blacks' in the last century. Now it is open war between Marathis and North Indian immigrants. Actually, racism is in your heart. Asians feel racism in Europe. In Christiania, it was Muslims vs non-Muslims. In our school, it was locals vs outsiders. In my town, my father suffered because of Dr Meena: it was Brahmin vs Sudras. Even in my home it was Gaur Brahmin vs Saraswat Brahmin. (My dad was Gaur Brahmin. My mother Bhagwanti and Parkash uncle were Saraswat Brahmins) Gaurs were considered better than Saraswats. While beating me, my dad used to abuse 'Sarsoots', meaning a variety of fools. In Copenhagen, people from main town always considered the 'Jutland' people as illiterate and second-class farmers.

The world would be vibrant if our attitude is positive. If the attitude is negative, the whole world would seem inimical and always conspiring against us.

Over these two years with my natural dedication and passion I have trained myself into a perfect Yogi and a kind of Sufi singer. I have trained most of the prisoners and others in *asanas* and *pranayams*. I play on the harmonium that Janik Møller had brought for me, and sing religious songs. The prisoners as well as the authorities find it uplifting for their spirits and request me to do it in the common hall so that everybody comes and find peace. I agreed.

It was Sunday morning, almost all the prisoners and many officials of the jail had assembled in the hall. They were already instructed to cover their heads with their kerchiefs while attending and participating in the *kirtan*. I was seated on an improvised kind of platform facing them, playing on harmonium and singing a verse from *Holy Gurbani* based on Indian classical Raaga Bhairavi.

"*Koi bole Ram Ram,*
Koi Khudaye,
Koi seva gussaian,
Koi Allahe."

I noticed Linda, Aryan and public prosecuter Andreas singing with their eyes closed. I also noticed that I had no feelings or desire left for them or anything else. I wondered if I had become '*shunya*', a great void connected to the limitless.

It's more than five years since I was first lodged in Tihar Jail. My mission, that was actually not mine, but an assignment from God, was accomplished.

ॐ

Epilogue

In early 2012, Copenhagen became the first city in the world to fully legalise the public use of marijuana. The drug can now be purchased through a network of state-run shops and cafes. It was already being sold at the cafes in Christiania until 2004. In India, this drug was sort of legalised since the Indus Valley Civilisation.